Danny's Luck.
Julie's Fortune

DEREK MARLOWE

To order additional copies of this book, contact:
Bookwhip
1-855-339-3589
www.bookwhip.com

Contents

Part 1
Danny's Luck

Part 2

Julie's Fortune

CHAPTER 1

Danny

Danny was lying on his bed gently massaging his privates as he contemplated the future. He found that it helped to relax him and take away the feeling of urgently wanting things to happen in his life. Danny was sixteen years old. An 'outdoor' lad with dark hair and solid, sunburned features. He lived in a North Yorkshire village with his parents John and Marion Ross. As it was in the 1960s, he was at a stage in his life when many things were still out of his reach. A world of adventure and sex was beckoning him but he did not yet fully understand its implications.

Danny had only recently 'packed in' his early morning milk round, where every day, come hail or shine, he delivered milk bottles twixt doorstep and milk van at a jogging speed governed by the milk van driver's inconsiderate accelerator foot. He was covering many a mile around the village every day nonstop except for when they reached the long straight drive of the Manors estate when he was able to sit for a rest on the cab floor and the nursemaid chatted while holding the Manors four-year-old daughter.

He had finally realised that he was being exploited for just a few measly shillings per week.

Each day his school lessons had always been secondary in his thoughts, but now with more time to listen and learn, he found a secret attraction to the vulnerable Miss Herald, his History teacher. Miss Herald was not one of those confident mature women teachers who could handle a class of rowdy pupils. She was young and attractive but apprehensive and the class knew that it was 'Miss' and not 'Mrs' Herald. Danny thought that he understood her difficulties. She had so much to deal with in keeping one step ahead of the class she was teaching. She had to follow the history agenda, making it as interesting as possible, as well as watch for the unruly pupils at the back of the class. She had little time to think about her attire and posture.

Danny really wished that she would not sit on the teacher's platform with her knees slightly apart, not aware that her fashionable short skirt was occasionally riding up a little more.

Brian Bullivant had noticed it first, and purposely moved to the front row. With a nod and a wink to those near him he would keep dropping his ruler, looking up at the teacher's legs as he slowly bent down to pick it up and then mouthing" Pink knickers" to the class.

Danny was not comfortable watching this. He didn't care for Bullivant much, but he would have liked to have had a look himself anyway. He kept his views to himself but he really fancied Miss Herald and would have tried to protect her when her vulnerability showed to the class. Some of the class guessed Danny's secret and the aggressive Bullivant. was one who taunted him about it.

"Scared of having a look, Ross?"

Growing up, Danny had been encouraged by his father, John Ross, to face up to any troubling challenges rather than turn his back on them, so making things harder for himself in the future. And so he was quick to respond to Brian-'Bully'- Bullivant.

Some bullying went on at school. The teachers tried to prevent it but they were not around all of the time, and even then, a common sight was of Bullivant waiting outside the school gates for a target of his oppression.

Danny was not looking for confrontation, but was cornered into defending himself against 'Bully' who had picked him out to ridicule about their history teacher. It was a decisive moment in the development of Danny's character. Until now he had tended to take the easy way out when faced with a choice of actions. But now he had a feeling of growing up and fitness, as well as confidence, as his future beckoned. 'Bully' was a youth who constantly acted like he almost had to live up to the nickname the class had given him. Danny quickly weighed up the implications of standing up to him. He decided that it was better to stand up and face him now rather than be cornered after school, and his dislike of Bullivant's compromising of Miss Herald drove him forward.

Bully was out to show his mates and the girls of the same year his domination and mastery of the personality that Danny appeared to represent. The fisticuffs started when Bullivant grabbed Danny by the collar. The only fighting Danny had done was a kind of play-fighting with his Dad, who wanted to show him how to look after himself. But he had filled out a lot recently, and he had remembered some of his dad's tips- to keep dodging and moving, and in particular how to throw someone bigger and heavier than himself to the floor by grabbing his arm, getting his own shoulder under his opponents armpit, and then bending and quickly pulling down, so levering him to the floor.

The sparring and exchange of punches became clinching and grappling. Although on the end of some heavy punches, Danny was doing enough to let Bully know that there would be no submission from him, and Bully stepped back slightly to reassess his opponent before rushing forward again. Danny was waiting for this and just as the form master was appearing to put a stop to the fight, Danny employed his 'move', using the impetus to lever and throw Bully flat on his back on the floor. Danny followed up with a perfect right hook to the face and a cry of "That's for Miss Herald!" The fight was brought to an end, but not before Danny had shown the screaming schoolyard crowd that when aroused, he was certainly not the one who others should to try to take advantage of. Bully's bloody nose was there for all to see. Danny's feeling for Miss Herald was also there to see.

There were more girls in his form than boys, and they in particular were relishing the goings on. "Did you see the fight in the yard at break-time. Danny Ross won. He gave Bully Bullivant a bloody nose. You should have seen it!."

Afterwards, there were a few girls who quietly or openly fancied Danny as a new 'desire' amidst their emotional priorities. They liked the fact that he could stand up for himself, but wasn't a thug – quite the opposite – he had a gentle way with him and was good-looking with his soft brown eyes and cropped dark hair. One girl especially - Jennifer Holmes - was one who now seemed to be trying to encourage his company. Whether she just wanted some limelight, or really was keen on him, he could not tell. Jennifer had been excited by the schoolyard 'punch up' and was in admiration of the boy who had stood up to Bully's aggression. Danny started to respond to her looks and her company, and a feeling of pleasure arose from just being close to her. She also was ready for a learning relationship with some boy, taking a lead from her girlfriends' priorities where boys were concerned. The two sought each other out now and found it easy to talk together. Companionship of a member of the opposite sex was a new experience for Danny. In Jennifer he had got himself a tall, good-looking, slim girl who was developing naturally into a lovely, desirable female.

His physical and mental development was beginning to make him curious about the opposite sex, replacing a previous indifference to their presence. Talking together as friends and just holding hands seemed natural to them both, and they always looked forward to each other's company.

On the day of the sixth-form educational outing to the Dales Countryside Museum, Danny and Jennifer were with the party taken by minibus with Miss Herald in charge. The project was to gather evidence and information and submit a report on one of the museums subjects. Pupils were given two hours to roam the museum and grounds with notepad and pen. Danny and Jennifer soon sneaked off on their own, full of elation and a sense of adventure at getting away from the crowd. It was the chance to get to know one another, and a little close familiarity; not much thought to collecting material for their project!

In their infatuation they forgot the passage of time until suddenly they realised that they were late for the bus. With Jennifer looking a bit 'hot and bothered' they rushed back, unable to conceal that they had been together, and just as Miss Herald was setting out to search for them.

Of course, the rest of the pupils cheered when they appeared, and many ribald comments and jokes were made to embarrass them both. Miss Herald's comments that they were likely to submit duplicated reports was near the truth. It appeared to Danny that the young teacher's favourable disposition to him since the fight had changed to one hinting at annoyance and jealousy now. Did he really have a chance to get closer to her?

The warmth of Miss Herald's feelings, Danny would always wonder about, but never be sure.

Danny had gone up in the girls' pecking order, but his understanding of the complexity of females and their priorities and passions was minimal. The girls were always exchanging views and rumours about their experiences and relationships with various boys.

His embarrassment was in not really understanding his own emotions, and what the opposite sex could mean for him.

Nevertheless, nature's instincts were being aroused. Jennifer had initiated their first kiss and he found it pleasant and stimulating, but it left him uncertain of his own feelings. In his mind, and hers, was a suggestive hint of loving, sexual thoughts, and the stimulation they brought. Sexual matters were often in Danny's thoughts - but in the

1960's they were not often discussed at home. Books on the subject were rare and 'blue movies' were just becoming secretly available if you were lucky enough to have a little television set. The mystery of it all still prevailed for the pair of them. The body and mind of the opposite sex were on offer with Jennifer stimulating him as his first love and conquest.

End of term was approaching and holidays, careers and finances were a priority. Danny's interest in animals and the countryside pointed him to Agricultural College rather than a University, but he had no real career path in mind. During previous school holidays he had made a little money doing gardening with a friend of his father. He had worked on the gardens of a certain Mrs Charlotte Ramsden when earning a bit of holiday pocket money. But could he go there again?

CHAPTER 2

Charlotte, Jason and Shaun

C harlotte Ramsden was bored. Her best efforts were at present being required to just get through another day without letting depression take a grip, and holding back the hand that wanted to open another bottle of Vodka, but instead force herself into another workout on her absent son's treadmill and cycle trainer. With the passage of time her marriage had become somewhat tedious staying at home with not enough going on to easily fill her time.

She was lying face-up naked to the waist on her bed carefully feeling her ample breasts, flattened in sunny-side-up mode, her fingers searching for any signs of small hard lumps amidst the soft tissue. In the past the presence of such signs had been dealt with by a doctor with the thankful follow-up analysis report of 'Benign'.

Charlotte was thirty-six years old. At five-foot and eight-inches she was, for her age, blessed with a full, mature and athletic figure, with good calves, and because of her fitness routine, tight muscular thighs.

She could also look back at experiencing most of the common phases of life's progress. She had grown up with the hobbies of hockey and horses; the heartbreak of unrequited love in her late teens; seeing her girlfriends married off, and concerns about ever finding the love of her life. She had also got to know Jason Ramsden, who although three years younger than her, was to be her sexual partner and future husband.

Getting married, wholeheartedly giving of her love and her body to the man who expressed his love in return to her, but sometimes in a way that seemed to be prioritised only by his sexual demands. "Just a man's way" her mother would say in quick dismissal if she tried to air a worry she had about their relationship, and how Jason's moods seemed to be governed by sexual satisfaction.

The announcement of her pregnancy after only eight months of married life was welcomed by all, including Jason. A genuine excitement and anticipation of their baby's arrival was tempered for Charlotte by Jason's insatiable sexual demands and his lack of understanding of her. Sometimes she was uncomfortable when Jason experimented with different types of foreplay and new ways of reaching his fulfilment. Fulfilment that, he would tell her, was being practised and found to be good for his various mates and their partners.

It was all sexual experience for Charlotte, but Jason's selfishness and lack of consideration for her needs was always at the back of her mind and sometimes caused her passive responses to him. The hard work and the routine required in bringing up their son Shaun were quickly adopted, with Charlotte dependent, but never one hundred per cent happy with Jason's contribution. His job as an area salesman provided many opportunities to socialise on his own if 'the wife' was too tired or preferred a restful evening just taking care of Shaun.

The years had rolled by for all the family. Shaun developed through childhood then adolescence, always showing traits in his personality of both his parents' characters. On qualifying for university, Shaun's second choice of Nottingham University was accepted. A somewhat emotional Mother immediately missed his presence around the house. Home life, with just Jason again for company, led to some occasional friction between them.

"You need to get out and find more interests" Jason would say, but he did very little to help her to take up new activities or hobbies. A new man in my life would be nice, she often thought.

News arrived that Jason's job was in jeopardy, and a move to a Midlands sales area was the only alternative offered. The need to move house got a lukewarm assent from the couple, but little effort from either to implement the plan. Uncertainty about Shaun's future plans was often used as an excuse to avoid committing themselves to a move to the Midlands, and a continuing future together as a married couple.

Jason complained about the travelling. He often had overnight stays in hotels, and as his sales bonuses grew a Midlands apartment was deemed necessary. Jason was not nicknamed 'Ram' for nothing; he made the most of his extra freedom playing the field of available women in the Midlands area. His discretion hid his carryings on, but Charlotte's intuitions were strengthened by the aromas on him from other women, and the tell-tale marks and stains evident when the chore of dealing with his dirty washing was done.

Nowadays Jason's absence, and that of her son Shaun, gave Charlotte some freedom, but most of the time it was boredom, or the vodka bottle, or the fitness equipment that got her through the day; The bottle was winning, often followed by pleasuring herself. She had at least the freedom of the house to do so, but she knew that she was in need of some new activities, danger and excitements in her life … possibly of a sexual nature. But who with? She was not enjoying sex with her selfish husband. In fact, she had started to prefer the marital bed to herself in the absence of someone who could satisfy the desires within.

CHAPTER 3

Marion and John

Danny's father, John Ross was diagnosed with bowel cancer. He was a quiet, good-living man, comfortable in his own company or with Danny, but not an easy man to talk to as a father should be. He didn't know how to talk to a growing son about to discover the intimacies of the 'facts of life'.

Living in a small Yorkshire hamlet, John's primary interest was in racing and breeding pigeons. On his allotment he had erected a coup, and a little annexe with space for one old lounge chair where he would sit for hours, either grooming his prize winners or anxiously awaiting their return home from a local event. Mating and breeding lines were registered as keenly as in breeding racehorses. Young birds bred from cocks with championship winning records were relatively valuable to members of the Breeding and Racing Pigeon Society. Unbeknown to his wife Marion, John occasionally liked a 'flutter' on the horses and would send his son to the Bookies with a two shilling piece wrapped in a paper slip. On his way Danny would read the slip to see which horses his dad had backed and next day find the results and very, very occasionally collect his dads' winnings. This went without Marion's knowledge and saved them from her lectures about how hard up the family were.

Danny started spending more time with his dad when, with the illness, came a recognition that time was urgent and short-lived. John and Danny became closer than they had ever been before, and horse racing form was discretely discussed. It was a bit easier for Danny to discuss some of the facts of life with his dad, instead of following the classroom tittle-tattle. But John was not a good talker, unless breeding habits could be discussed openly in terms of the goings on of the mating pigeons: the preparation of the hens and the virility of the cocks; the dates of the covering; the speed at which the cocks - with flying wings and feathers - subdue the hen into what nature intended, and afterwards strut about as the preening ensued.

John did ask his son if, when the time came, he would continue with pigeon racing - at least until the young birds of excellent breeding had matured. Alternatively, he could find a new owner from a list of John's sporting colleagues who would give them a good home.

When John died Danny was devastated, although he knew it was coming. The sadness and the mourning by Danny's mother were overwhelming. She could not to be comforted and her pain seemed undiminishing with time. Danny's grief was supressed within by the need to support his mother through all that had to be dealt with. However, Marion was also a clear-thinking, practical woman who gradually with the passage of time recognised her future economic needs, as well as that of male company for when Danny grew up and spread his wings to pastures new.

Eventually Norman appeared on the scene, whether by 'introduction pairing', or amateur match-makers in the village one never knew. The introductions were soon followed by an invitation to tea, and the obvious 'This is my son Danny'. There were days out for Marion, and then nights in.

Danny hated Norman and reproached his mother. He was just the opposite to his father – he was a continuous talker – an 'expert' in every subject raised. But in Danny's eyes he was a bit of a useless pansy compared with his father and his mates.

When Norman gradually wheedled his way into Marion's bed, Danny was so enraged that he left home for a few nights and stayed with various mates. But economic practicalities prevailed. His mother said she wanted Norman to stay and that was that.

Anger was being fuelled by curiosity when Danny realised what was going on in the next bedroom. He could hear the squeaking of the bed springs and started listening with a glass tumbler against the dividing wall.

Norman's gasping and groaning noises, and his voicing of his excitement at climax, was in contrast to Marion's silence - except the occasional whispering of 'Shhh, keep it quiet' to Norman. Danny was very bitter when he imagined his mother lying in reluctant submission to Norman's demands. He knew that there was no love there and his mother was acquiescing to his demands for practical and economic reasons. But there was nothing he could do about it and life went on. He swore that he would work hard to get himself in a position where *he* could look after his mother's financial welfare.

CHAPTER 4

Jennifer

"Jennifer has this boyfriend called Danny. They have been sweethearts since they were sixteen"—that's how grown-ups talked about them. Over some eighteen months Danny and Jenny had spent a lot of time together. They went as a couple to parties, socials and the likes, even to all-night sleepover parties. Jennifer talked a lot with her friends about their relationship as if they were intimate. She was really just comfortable with having a boyfriend, so conforming to the trend set by the others. The fact was that she was anxious about what was to come in their relationship if Danny got his way. Despite much kissing and innocent cuddling, Danny's persistent efforts to get Jenny to open up to him were always stalled by her finding some diversion when things were warming up. Danny enjoyed Jennifer's company. She was the first girl he had got to know and now believed he loved. But he desired her and gradually, as months passed, that desire became desperation and utter frustration. He had read the sex books being passed round the classroom and his natural feelings had been aroused.

At long last his roaming hands were not grasped with the words 'Please don't, Danny, not here', or 'Not now'. He was allowed by a somewhat nervous Jenny to put his hand under her bra. His tentative fingers found wondrously soft, silky, tender skin, with pert nipples, and her breasts moved with a gentle, bouncy movement when cupped in his hand. He thought it wonderful. The door to feelings of tenderness he had never known had been opened. 'They're fantastic' he'd whispered. He went home with love in his heart for Jenny. She also was enthralled by his touch and him saying that she was perfectly made. She felt good that she could be an attraction to the opposite sex. Her prologue to sexual intimacy, but was she really ready?

However, the glimpse of what all this business was about after the initial thrilling pleasure had worn off had made Danny ever keener to go for more of what he heard from his mates. But Jennifer was still scared by her mother's warnings, she was plagued by shyness and embarrassment, of worrying what people might hear, frightened of the catastrophe of pregnancy.

Fear of losing Danny, was also something Jennifer was worried about. So, she did not voice her concerns when she called at Danny's home and found that with his mother and Norman away, Danny did not want to let their opportunity pass by this time.

The usual cuddling and fondling were this time expected to lead to the upstairs bedroom. In his own mind Danny had thought through what he wanted: not much foreplay, and he was soon ready anyway, a condom handy in his shirt pocket. His mates had inferred that all their girlfriends were now used to carrying a condom in their handbag to ensure their own protection, and they knew what to do with it.

On the bed - his trousers off, her skirt up out of the way, his manhood fully erect. She was aroused somewhat, knew of condoms from her mates, and had let her hand dwell briefly on him when Danny had moved it to his bulging front. She had seen the pictures of men's privates in the explicit books the girls passed round and giggled over. But this was the real thing. She panicked when she realised that he was seeking fulfilment this time. The use of the condom was hindering the job now. He snatched it off and forcibly pressed himself upon her with urgent intent. She knew she was supposed to show something now, some pleasure, but was shocked, embarrassed and afraid, and Danny's weight thrust upon her was too much. She eventually pushed him away and wriggled away from under him. His forced withdrawal caused embarrassment for them both. Jennifer was visibly upset as she straightened her clothes.

It had been a complete disaster! Both parties were hurt; not sure of what had actually occurred. It was a first time to keep quiet about rather than cherish!

Danny, still partially naked, moved to the bathroom, but had the presence of mind to stay in there to give Jennifer some time for composure. He sheepishly emerged eventually, just in time to see Jennifer on her way out down the stairs and heading for the door. Danny was dismayed. He now realised that they were both just not ready for it.

A miserable Danny kept himself away from his school's end-of-term timetable. His father's betting legacy and the pigeons were his only company for a few days. When he did eventually surface, he was met by one of his classmates.

"I reckon you and Jenny have finished," the lad said.

"Have you two had a bust-up? She says she hates the sight of you!" said another.

"Yeah. Well it was going nowhere anyway. I'm going working for Steve on his gardening round."

Danny was moving on.

CHAPTER 5

Charlotte and Danny

Husband Jason, to his credit, did see that Charlotte could manage financially while he was working away. But on his visits home he showed no interest in the jobs that needed doing around the house and the garden. It was the pub for him, late nights with his mates, plenty to drink and then a stagger home to see what mood Charlotte was in.

But money was tight, he said, and Charlotte worried about the future financial implications of their deteriorating relationship.

As a child and as a woman she had always been comfortable financially. As she grew, she'd owned a well-bred horse at the local stables. After marriage, with Jason driving a company car for his sales job, a second family car was shared with her son Shaun after he passed his driving test. With her son living away at university, the car was hers, but its age and lack of routine maintenance was beginning to show. Similarly, the facade of the house needed maintenance, the garden too, and hence a weekly two hours from Steve's 'Down to Earth Garden Maintenance and Landscaping' business was organised. They attended to the lawns and borders, the pruning and weeding, and the like.

During the spring and summer, Steve's gardening business ended up with more customers than he could deal with alone, and so a part-time temporary role for Danny was the arrangement, paid in cash in his pocket -undeclared by them both.

Danny had no transport other than a bike, although he'd had a few driving lessons in the local driving instructor's Ford Cortina and had booked a test.

Steve had three customers in the same avenue. He introduced Danny to each of these, showing him what lawns and borders needed doing, and the equipment he needed to supplement what the house owners already had for him to use. Steve worked with Danny on each of the householder's gardens, weeding, mowing and tidying the borders, but the next week Danny would be on his own.

"Here's a number to ring me if they have any jobs that are extra to the normal maintenance," Steve said. And of Charlotte – "Don't go sniffing round her! She's too owd for thee any road."

When Danny called at Charlotte's she was exercising on her trainer in sweater and shorts, and she hastily put on a robe to answer the door to Danny's appraisal.

"Yes?" she asked."

"I'm here to do your garden".,

Oh. Pleased to see you again. I always make Steve a cup of coffee while he's here, so give me a knock when you're done. You can have a drink then and I'll pay you."

An hour later, with the work done, he knocked to collect the payment; his cup of coffee was waiting for him. Charlotte sat in the porch with him with her own drink, which was strongly laced with vodka. 'Call me Charlie' she'd said after he had called her Mrs Ramsden. They got on well together and chatted about the cars condition, the gardens, and gradually about bits of their lives and circumstances. When she asked about Danny's hobbies, and he said 'breeding and racing pigeons', she, in pursuing the conversation - which she was enjoying - wanted to know more. She talked about her involvement in and enjoyment of horses, and they found similarities in the breeding lines and progeny from the results of mating well-bred hens or mares with championship-winning cocks or stallions.

When she asked about Danny's girlfriends he blushed and shook his head. This aroused Charlotte's curiosity, but was not pursued by her. She sensed his frustrations about women and sex. She moved the conversation on, asked about him going to agricultural college, the future it held away from home, and even mentioned her own loneliness and frustration with her son Shaun being at university. She could not help but think about Danny's physicality.

One week on, when she had gone out and left his money under the doormat, he felt real disappointment at not seeing her. He had rushed to finish the earlier chores and had begun to look forward to the hint of seduction she brought into their conversations; in fact, he really fancied this fit, mature woman, but imagined that she was only for his dreams.

It was pouring down with rain at the next visit. Danny was absolutely soaked, despite an old waterproof jacket. He came into the porch for his coffee and sat down on the bench. His hair was ringing wet. Charlotte laughed when she said, 'You look like a drowned rat!' She took a big towel from the rail, lent over him, and started rubbing his hair with it. And then she stopped, realising in her mind that she was treating him as she would her son Shaun when he was about 12 years old! More importantly, she realised that in bending over him and drying his hair, her inner thighs were rubbing gently against the wet knees of his jeans. She laughed loudly when she saw that Danny was a bit self-conscious, as she stood back and threw the towel straight into his face.

Danny reacted to her joking gesture instinctively, without thought, by jumping up and grabbing her around her waist in mock retaliation. They were both instantly aware of one another and the feeling of the closeness of their bodies. Danny's first reaction was to pull away quickly. He may have dreamed of holding her, but now he was afraid of it. But Charlie held him to her and they now looked at one another face-to-face. Danny was in unchartered territory, but not Charlie. She had become frustrated by Jason's absences from home, and his enjoying himself or showing a selfishness and lack of consideration when with her. But now she was pleased by the thought of helping Danny's initiation. Danny's lusty flush of adolescence would be a new, eager experience, with nothing taken for granted. For her it was either back-off time, or the time for her to help him through his frustrations and into the unknown sexual pleasures which some experience would open up for him.

She didn't say anything except a quiet, "It's okay, Danny," before she kissed him. With the feel of her warm body through his wet shirt he began to respond, and then they both knew where this was going to end.

It was going to be standing up against the kitchen wall, because moving to another, more comfortable spot was not in Danny's thoughts and Charlie was afraid that he might not see it through if she gave him time to think!

There was not much working up to it. He had no belt to his jeans, and they dropped to the floor on her undoing the single button and unzipping him. Her simple wrap-over skirt similarly fell away on the undoing of one button. Revealed was a short, silken underskirt - the feel of which sent Danny's heart racing as his hands lifted it up. The French knickers he pulled aside, no time for their removal. She had seen the massive bulge in his underpants and pulled them down, cupped his balls briefly in her hand, and ran her fingers gently along the length of his erection. There was no time for more!

Danny's now uninhibited urgency was likened in this woman's mind to the sweating, quivering frenzy of a young stallion brought out at the stud farm to cover the thoroughbred mare, teased and held ready. This was a sight she vividly recalled as a young girl when she had crept from the car to see what she was not supposed to witness. Now she was the receptive mare and there was to be no time for foreplay. His first thrust was quite brutal. She still had her high-heeled shoes on, and her height helped ease his second more gentle penetration, but now they were stronger, deeper and with quickly increasing rapidity. "Take it slowly, Danny," she tried to whisper, but to no avail. He was quickly reaching climax with a groan and gasp of ecstasy. Although she herself was thrilled and excited with his size and his action, she was far from her climax. But foremost was her consideration for Danny. That the loss of his virginity was to him, a glorious sensation, also that it was not now followed by him having recriminations about it.

She hugged him tightly, noticing the muscles forming under his young, firm skin, and kissed him and whispered, "That was wonderful," then waited for him to recover and for his pleasure to register. She could see a boy whose frustrations had just been removed and who was now beginning to relax in a sense of achievement.

When both parties gradually calmed, she said to him, "Now you must not worry about consequences. I am on the pill. You know about that don't you? This must be kept secret between us, because if you go bragging, then both of us will regret it. I will not tell a soul, and you must not either. This should be the beginning and the end of it for us both, a one-off Danny, do you understand?"

Danny suddenly panicked as they redressed. Had anyone seen anything? What if Steve had been to collect his machinery? He was anxious, but her words were sinking in now and they reassured him somewhat. He wanted away now and indicated that he must leave, and as unobtrusively as possible. It was getting dark now anyway, and as she saw him away on his bike she said, "Now don't worry."

She felt exhausted, but thrilled with the danger of her actions. She decided to run a bath and have a good soak to relax. After this she could enjoy a little fun of her own.

CHAPTER 6

Norman

Things at home were not good for Danny. The comfortable family relationship with his parents had been natural and good as he grew through adolescence. Allowances were made when he was in an awkward mood, but there was a line drawn whereby his dad would first talk kindly to him, but then get tough if necessary, to make his point.

With Norman's encroachment, the atmosphere had changed drastically. Norman was careful at first to not upset things but he was starting to take his position for granted and change things to suit himself.

Money was tight for Danny and his mother, and Norman's salary and contributions were really needed. He made the most of any parting with his money. He provided a new, bigger television, and he brought this up as a reminder whenever he wanted to draw attention to his being head of the house. From Danny's perspective after the bust-up - when he realised that Norman was in his father's bed - he often kept quiet when his hate was surfacing, Norman did not see or realise that the youngster was growing up and beefing up, or that after the events of about two weeks ago, he had found a new confidence in himself.

Norman was spouting off as usual. He was constantly telling Marion and her son what they should be doing to run and keep the household (as he wanted it).

"You should have got off your backside and cooked me something decent, not come up with a pizza," he roared at Marion. "And Danny, when are you going to get a proper job or bugger off to that college?" Two sensitive digs, which on top of the continual hail of his criticisms, Marion could not take. She dabbed away her tears with her handkerchief as she went into the back kitchen. Having seen this, Norman closed in on Danny who was sitting in the old rocking chair. He cuffed Danny from behind – as people did in those days to a naughty boy. "And you sort yourself out and quick," he yelled.

The built-up resentment for this little dictator finally burst out. Now that his mother had left the room, Danny was out of his chair like a rocket and straight at Norman's throat. His hands gripped the scrawny neck, shook it, and then gripped at the collar. He lifted Norman off his feet by the neck, and butted his forehead against Norman's nose.

He then literally threw him into the chair with a crash. "If you ever shout at my mother like that again, or touch me or her like that, I'll break your bloody neck in three pieces. Understand? *Your place here is last and I'll make sure you know it.*"

Marion returned to the room, instantly aware that something had gone on, but no one spoke. The new Danny was beginning to surface; Norman just kept quiet and dabbed at his bloody nose!

CHAPTER 7

Charlotte's Day

Danny and Charlotte could not avoid each other as the gardening visit came around again. They both were a bit nervous about how the other would have taken on board what had happened. For both it had been tremendous. Wrong maybe, but no doubt about it - an exciting new experience!

Again Danny, having got the mower and machinery that Steve dropped off for him, did the other gardens first, leaving Charlie's until the last. He did not knock, or see her anywhere around, but got straight on with the work. When it was finished, he thought about just clearing off home. But he usually collected the money, and so he went to the door and saw the usual two cups of hot coffee on the little table. He called, "Hello!" and sat down on the bench. Maybe Charlie was making him wait, as though she was busy at other things. Maybe she was nervous to see him now.

She appeared wearing her exercise suit, but well-groomed and, to Danny, looking absolutely desirable. She seemed to keep her distance. "I wasn't sure whether you had finished with the garden jobs to get ready for going to college," she said.

"Can't afford to. I need all the money I can earn," was the reply.

The ice was broken. After that it was 'Well, how are you?' and 'Oh, I'm all right, I've just baked some scones. Will you try one?' and Danny replying, 'Yes, alright then'.

Then silence again as they drank their coffees. They were both sitting with their own thoughts (and unable to express them), when Steve drove up to the front gate and came down the drive to the back door.

"Thar' on a cushy job here aren't tha," he said to Danny. "Don't let him get his feet under t'table, Mrs Ramsden!" Little did he know that Danny had got a lot further than his feet under t'table'.

"Come round tonight, Danny. I need to talk to you," Charlie whispered as he was leaving. She thought that he was still worrying about the consequences of what had happened, and she thought that he might soon go off to college, and she wanted him.

"I must be off," Danny said, with the tiniest of nods to Charlie, and left the two alone. He hurried home. Now he was beginning to wonder what she wanted to say to him.

That evening he knocked lightly on the front door, glancing over his shoulder in the fading light to check that no one was watching. Charlie answered immediately and invited him in. He thought she looked ravishing, and that it was little wonder that he fancied her and was seduced by the soft fullness of her figure and lovely face, complimented by her smiling eyes and sensual voice.

"Are you alright? Do you want a drink?" She didn't wait for him to answer, and instead poured him a full glass of red wine. "Sit on the couch so that you can put your glass there," she added.

He did as she bade him without saying anything, just wondering what was to come.

She sat on the other end of the couch, smiled, and raised her glass to him. They clinked. " All the best for the future," they said and then they sat quietly. For a time, they enjoyed the warmth of the fire, both gradually relaxing in the other's company.

"When are you going to college, Danny? I wanted to be sure that you had no worries or regrets about what happened. I am okay about it, you know, as long as it is kept between you and me. I wanted to help you down the way, to give you a first-time experience without anxieties, mishaps or embarrassments. No misgivings if you ever look back at your first time, eh? You were good, Danny, I enjoyed it, so no recriminations okay?"

With these words in his ear, Danny began to relax. The warmth of the fire, the comfort of the couch, the effects of the wine were all lifting his mood … also the nearness of Charlie and the smell of her perfume.

He now found his voice. "It was great, Mrs … Charlie," he said. "I was happy with the experience and ever grateful for what we - you - went along with and the way you were. I will never forget it, or that day, and I'll never forget you -whatever my future brings me."

Without thinking he leaned over and kissed her and again felt a stirring in his groin. It was what she was waiting for as she responded by prolonging the kiss and holding him close. She could show him something about kissing and fondling as well, she realised. They were drawn together as naturally as the opposite poles of two magnets.

They slid from the couch onto the soft fireside rug, and their hands beginning to softly wander a little, now controlled, with no haste, only pleasurable feelings.

Danny now remembered her words from before: 'Slowly, Danny'. The feel of her ample and firm breasts through her blouse and soft bra enthralled him. And the strength of his bulging groin made Charlie realise what she was missing with Jason's absence. She sat up a little and unclipped her bra strap so that it fell away for him to see what she prized and knew were assets for her. Both his hands grasped her and she pushed his face to her cleavage to nuzzle her. He remembered the feel of Jennifer's soft, velvet skin and pert nipples, but here he found full, firm breasts, soft, but somehow representing Charlie's strength, fitness and maturity. He caressed them with his lips This time the pleasure from the foreplay was recognised and enjoyed by teacher and pupil. Charlotte was finding feelings of both comfort and pleasurable anticipation from the touch of this young man's hands, and also a need for more. A lot more!

She slowly unzipped him to reveal all. She cupped and fondled him, and again found him rock-hard. She was anxious to seek the ecstasy she had not experienced for quite a long time, so she slipped off her knickers and straddled him, her breasts in his face. Danny was certainly taking it slowly this time. Now wanting to feel where he was going down there, his fingers stroked gently up her inner thighs. He had the most mind-boggling, amazing, rapturous surprise in that she had removed all pubic hair and created smooth, moist lips, waxy, and opening to his hesitant feel. It was a memorable first-time experience in touching a woman in this way.

She could wait no longer and 'took control'. The movement of her body on top of him controlled the speed and depth of the thrusts and rhythm. Both of them were ecstatic, she now moaning with uninhibited cries.

Danny reached his climax with a gasp and tried then to slow things down. Charlie was having none of the slowing down - she was in absolute, total control of him, the weight and force of her body continuing the rhythm. She was completely and wonderfully carried away by the fulfilling of her needs. Finally, she got there with a shriek. Danny was just beginning to feel some discomfort, and to feel that perhaps he was being used and unable to assert any control himself. She eventually released his manhood and collapsed alongside him, now slowing things down to absorb the pleasure and satisfaction. She hugged and held him, and whispered to him, "That was the best experience I have ever had. You're marvellous." They now lay quietly together, hands making discoveries by stroking firm buttocks, feeling again hardening nipples and lithesome waists.

Then, when she said, "We're roughing it on the rug here! I've a comfy bed upstairs," she broke the trance they were in.

Danny, with the trauma that he felt when Norman made it into his father's bed said, "No, that's Jason' s bed." That broke the spell, with them eventually recovering their scattered clothes.

More normal and appropriate relations were resumed with a cup of tea, and he moved things on by telling her about his successful enrolment for the Agricultural College, and the dates when he was due to start the course.

She was clearly upset that this time was due, and with Danny's enthusiasm for it, and she made no effort to conceal it. Sobbing, she said, "Danny, I can't manage to live without you now. After tonight's marvellous experience, I need you to be mine. If it was the same for you, and I think it was, you can't just leave me and go away. At least come again before you go to college."

Danny was beginning to realise and learn that despite it being a first-time-great for him – as with most men in sexual encounters - it was both a sexual and very emotional state for women. He remembered the exhilaration, but also Charlotte's insatiable need for him and the potential hazards of this, and thought of the complications to his future life that the relationship might bring. What Danny had learned would change his future.

He had to move on. It was a decisive moment in Danny's development with his agricultural course on the horizon. He recognised it as such, and regretfully bid Charlotte a loving goodbye … and no promises.

CHAPTER 8

Agricultural College

Danny arrived at the campus in Nottingham to a hive of activity. Tomorrow was first day of term. He was again a raw scholar, with prospectus and timetable in hand, and wondering just what he had to do.

The college did not have its own halls of residence, and many of the prospective students had anticipated acceptance on the course by pre-arranging rented rooms in an apartment block, where the upper floors had become almost completely student-based. Danny had been busy arranging his mother's welfare, and for one of his dad's old mates to take over the keep of his pigeons. Lack of planning for college and lack of good finances had left him with a problem. He found himself in the entrance to the apartment block being told that no rooms were left for rent.

He happened by chance (or it may have been by her doing), to meet a female student on his course. She was very small, barely up to his chest, pretty, but thin and underdeveloped. She was a hive of activity, never still, with nervous energy. She was never quiet, but always hustling and bustling, and had no inhibitions about talking to anyone or everyone.

"I'm Maureen Bannister. Which room have you got? Who are you in with?" she asked Danny.

"I'm too late. But I can't afford the rent anyway," Danny replied.

Maureen had got a room and assumed that she would find another girl to share with her, but had not been successful - perhaps because of her uninhibited chatter and first impressions. "What are you going to do?" she asked.

"I'll have to look for a bed and breakfast somewhere close."

"Look, I know that mixed sexes sharing is not the done thing normally, but there are two separate bedrooms and a lock on the bathroom door. I'll be paying for the flat anyway. I don't mind if you join me. You can put a lock on your bedroom door if you think I might molest you! If you can't afford a share of the rent all the time, don't worry, my allowances will stand it. I should tell you that I was a nurse for two years on a men's ward, so I've seen most things and wouldn't be phased by your presence, and neither should you be on my account."

Maureen stopped for breath and Danny just said "Okay."

And so, it was that Danny shared a flat with Maureen; an unlikely pairing for flatmates, but solved their problems, provided company, and perhaps in Maureen's mind, some notoriety! Her nursing experience had enabled her to be familiar with the male anatomy. In fact, her nursing duties included assisting in washing, bathing and showering seriously injured and disabled young men. She had to be immune to their ribald comments and remember her strictly medical role. One young soldier of a normally sincere and quiet disposition, with hands and arms swathed in bandages, had pleaded with her in the privacy of the washroom, to dwell longer in washing his groin. He wanted reassurance that his reproductive tackle was still in working order after his injuries and subsequent sexual deprivation. She did satisfy his anxiety, although she knew that it was an employment risk if it became known. She could not of course tell him of the effect that the action was having on her, despite her nurse's training. She was so close to intimacy but Oh so far from fulfilment! However, when the soldier asked if Nurse Bannister could be the one to again assist him in washing, suspicions were aroused, and it did in fact tip the scales in Maureen deciding on a career change into Agricultural College and veterinary ambitions.

At the first few classes it became clear that among the students there was a clique of five farmers' daughters, typically rich, brash and sexually experienced. They were familiar with most aspects of farming and animal husbandry, and experienced with the range of animals. They made snide jokes among themselves, and at some of the other students who might be embarrassed by breeding methods and the like. Maureen was never afraid to chip in with her frank opinions. She was able to speak with the eloquence of the aristocracy on most subjects, but could change her accent and the coarseness of her words if needed to fight her corner in an argument with 'The Five'. She had been nicknamed 'Little Mo', and then later, 'Little Moo'.

Living in the apartment, Danny tried to maintain some privacy and respect Maureen's habits: first in the bathroom in the morning; avoid breaking wind, etc. Maureen, however, with her nursing experiences, was so uninhibited and unashamed about another's presence that at first Danny was slightly uncomfortable when she would, for instance, wander into the kitchen where he was cooking as if she did not know she was wearing just her bra and knickers. She showed not a scrap of embarrassment in openly talking about sexual matters. But he was not really physically attracted to her underdeveloped femininity. They gradually became just good mates, but with a lot of familiarity between them. They helped one another in various ways: she with his tuition timetables and his homework for the course; he with some protection and support when required outside classes. She could certainly hold her own with the group drinking sessions at weekends, though, and was quick to order and pay for another round at the bar.

After one heavy drinking session, including the temptation of a drag on a spliff, Danny staggered back to the flat in a stupor, leaning on Little Mo, and collapsed onto his bed out to the world to sleep it off. Towards morning when he finally awoke for the bathroom, he found Little Mo snuggled close to him on his bed both covered over with a blanket, her hand resting casually in her sleep on his privates. He slid away to the toilet, but on his return, she had not moved at all from her deep sleep. He had no alternative but to again share the bed with her until it was time to get up.

She was just like a loyal pet dog to him sometimes. He hadn't had real sexual feelings for her, but just wondered at her actions when he was completely flaked out.

"What happened last night?" he said, when she (for once) was not chattering away. "Were you pissed as well?"

"Yes, but not as bad as you, but I was still groggy." After a pause she continued, "I was freezing Danny. The heating was off. My bed felt cold and damp. I felt so much safer and warmer lying next to you and holding you. I'm sorry."

"It's okay, Mo," he replied, and smiled.

Gradually the Saturday night booze-up - which Mo was mostly financing from her parents' allowance was unaffordable for Danny. It usually resulted in him accepting Mo sliding into bed beside him, now just in bra and knickers, and he having usually managed to kick his trousers off. She would sometimes very gently rest her hand on him when he slept ... blind-drunk and without any sexual inclination. They were becoming bed mates but without sex. However, she was enthralled by his physicality and the familiar effect of the touch of her hands.

One evening Mo rushed into the flat in a panic. "Danny, can you get a lock and fix it to my bedroom door before weekend?"

"That's a good one! I've never gone into your room. I can't say the same for you with me, though!"

"I know, but my father and mother are coming to see me. They think we are in separate apartments and only sharing the kitchen."

He managed to buy a sliding bar and fix it to the inside of her bedroom door. He planned to keep out of the way when her parents were due. He went to watch the college football team, but when he returned, he found Maureen's mother patiently waiting for his return. " We just wanted to meet you," she said. "Maureen mentions you when she phones home. Having seen the accommodation here, they are not what we expected. I must ask you to be sure to respect Maureen's situation and privacy and not take advantage of her."

"Of course, Mrs Banister, I would always do that. You don't need to worry."

Maureen was behind her room door giggling!

The class of agricultural students were chattering loudly while waiting for the lecture to begin.

"Morning, Moo, is the platonic relationship still platonic?" The farmers' girls of their class could not abide knowing that she was rooming with Danny. "I would have had the pants off him by now. If you haven't seen him in the raw coming out of your bathroom then his modesty must mean he hasn't got much to show off!"

It was a trick remark and Mo fell for it. She was thinking that Danny would not want to be branded as 'small' by these girls. " That's not true" she said.

"So he's well-hung then? You should know, you being a nurse."

She nodded her head. Then she immediately regretted it. She was thinking that more publicity would result. But maybe also jealousy, and the jealousy could be hers if Danny was attracted to one of them.

At this particular time the tutorials were dealing with animal husbandry and Breeding Soundness Examinations (BSEs), and the clique of farm girls were having a field-day with jokes, supposed innocent questions to the lecturer, and snide remarks for the class to hear. Many of the jokes were hinting at comparisons of animals and human breeding techniques, their reproductive organs; and Danny's anatomy.

"We're practicing doing BSEs in flat 22 tonight, Danny, if you would like to come and be tested," shouted out Jill, a big, blond girl with oversized breasts.

Danny was getting smarter and his quick reply brought about a cheer from the rest of the class.

"Okay Jill, I'll come at milking time. Will I need a bucket and stool?

Danny and Mo were getting on fine. They had a good understanding of pulling together in tackling everyday living, with routines and jobs to be done. Maureen always wanted to talk about the lectures and any preps and revisions to be done, and this helped Danny to keep focused and up-to-date with the course work. This had brought about a feeling of close friendship and respect, but not in a sensual way. Mo, however, was fanatical about losing her virginity. Apart from what she thought other people saw in her, she felt that not having this experience was holding her back in some way. For fulfilment she figured she needed a partner. She had love for Danny, but knew that this was only returned by companionship and she was a little jealous about his interest in other girls at the college.

One Saturday after a good night out at the pub, lying together in Danny's bed just talking, she suddenly said to him, "Danny, would you have sex with me?"

"What did you say?"

I would love you to be the partner for my first ever sexual experience. I don't mean just now, but I want you to. I'm not expecting you to start loving me, but I can't start living a full life while I'm still treated like a little virgin. I promise you that there would be no repercussions, but I have to know what it's like. And how it changes a woman."

Danny was a bit shocked and hesitated. He did have a lot of feeling for her but had never envisaged sex with her. On reflecting, perhaps when his thoughts went in the right direction, he may be able to rise to the occasion in consideration of her desperate needs.

"It might spoil what we have in a platonic friendship. Should you not save yourself. And what about your mother's lecture?" he asked, concerned.

"My mother won't be the one who's getting it," she said loudly, breaking into a laugh to ease the tension, and it was left at that.

However, Mo was adamant that this was what she wanted. She brought a bottle of wine home one night, dressed in her slinkiest outfit, and after their meal she asked Danny if this could be the night.

She kissed him in a longing sort of way - which was new to Danny - and snuggled her body close to him. The silkiness of her dress and her manner did make his thoughts gear-up differently, and he did begin to respond.

"Here, use this, its lubricated," Mo said. Practical Maureen had a condom and everything prepared. "Come through to my room in a minute." You're probably too heavy for me, so I'll be on top". She clearly was in charge." Is the condom on properly?"

"Come on, I know what you've got and I am ready for it."

She had her knickers off, the room was in darkness, and there was a pile of pillows on the bed. She climbed aboard of him. No timidity, no embarrassment, but just her nursing experience and veterinary education, as she rode him. "Go on Danny, Go on! "she urged.

Maureen had done a lot of preparing for this occasion. And was so very familiar with the event that Danny wondered whether it really was her first time. Her previous nursing career made him think about this.

As they lay together gasping for breath, she now suddenly seemed to be crying, and he was concerned. He tried to comfort her. However, it was tears of joy and excitement that he heard. "Thank you, Danny, thank you. Now I feel like a whole woman. It's allowed me to be free! What a wonderful experience. I was 'in sync' with you! I've been waiting for so long."

Danny was not sure what he felt, but had some guilt and concern about what he had agreed to. It was like with Charlie. 'Nobody must know about this! They wouldn't understand'. When you start saying this, is it because you have done something you should not have done? With Maureen close to him, they fell into a relaxed asleep on the single bed.

Maureen was the first to wake, feeling very happy. The old saying that 'Sex relieves tension, but love creates tension', seemed for her to be coming true.

CHAPTER 9

The Farm

It was the end of term. Danny and Maureen both had some plans made for them. Mo's mother and father had booked a holiday in France, expecting that Mo would be excited to go with them. They were surprised at her reluctance, but insisted. "You can't stay at home on your own. What would you do?"

"Who knows what I might get up to!" she replied. She had started thinking with more maturity and confidence than before and perhaps she should go to France, and maybe she could shake off her parents and go looking for a passionate Frenchman.

Danny called at home to see his mother and also to see how his pigeons were progressing, but he had also applied for a vocational job as a herdsman on a large dairy farm. It was owned by the Wallace family, reported to be rich landowners in the Yorkshire Wolds. He was surprised to have been offered a temporary job with immediate start just on the strength of his CV, and without having to attend an interview. The money would be useful as he had joined a fitness club near the college; his expenditure was rising and his funds dropping - despite Mo's generosity.

He arrived to meet Mr Wallace, who briefly and casually outlined what the farming tasks were and the schedules to be met.

He found the work to be exacting, and had to keep his wits about him. His responsibilities were considerable in seeing to a herd of some forty cows; where they grazed; what time they were brought in for milking; what feed and supplements they were fed. These were really jobs that the manager should be organising, but he quickly realised that the more work and responsibilities he took on, the less Mr Wallace did, and he had to continue doing. As for making all these things happen, there was only Danny, Martha, who was the Milkmaid, and two farm labourers called Matt and Liam. Liam could at least drive the old Fordson tractor and was a willing worker, but Matt was patently slow-thinking. The two labourers had been working on the farm for a long time and had adopted a certain daily routine. Any required changes to these routines and they tended to panic and do things wrong for sure.

To try to improve speed and efficiency of the work, Danny had taken over the farms quad bike - normally used by Mr Wallace to get around more quickly and ensure that all the essential jobs were completed.

One afternoon Danny opened up an inner stable door - which had been blocked off for some time - but which allowed a shorter and quicker route from the feed store to the cattle in their feeding stalls. He loaded Matt up with two sacks of cow-cakes on the sack truck and sent him off on the new route to the cattle stalls. He collapsed in a heap of laughter when a little later he saw Matt coming back … but by the old, longer route. He had not had the nous to change his habit and use the new quicker route for the return!

At this moment, when he was bent double with laughter, Mrs Wallace appeared in the barn doorway. She was smartly dressed in what Danny called 'City clothes': well-fitting short jacket, tight skirt (showing the contour of her thighs) and high heels, dark auburn hair very neat in a glossy bob. Hardly suited for farm work. For Danny she gave the impression of a sleek and beautiful racehorse at the peak of condition. She looked at what was going on with some disdain before saying, "Danny, can I have a word with you in the house?"

He wondered what this was all about. Mr Wallace had been the one to tell him what to do and occasionally check on whether everything had been done to order, but it had all been a bit haphazard. He had barely been introduced to the lady of the house, and now he was embarrassed by the contrast between her immaculate appearance and his own condition with clothes and boots which were covered in mud and cow muck.

Danny needed the job to make some money, so he did not have much choice when he realised that he was being exploited in terms of what he had to do and the pay he was receiving. Mr Wallace always complained about his bad back when the need to lend a hand was apparent, and his usual excuse was that he was required elsewhere. What a way to run a business - which could have been worth a fortune if it had been run properly.

A very cool and dominating Mrs Wallace was waiting when he knocked at the kitchen door.

"Come inside to the kitchen, but take your muddy boots off first. We need to talk." Her attitude left him expecting a reprimand for something, perhaps for the joking with Matt.

However, it was a sort of business-like, employer and employee, interview: Are you settled in at the lodge accommodation? Have you now got a grasp of the work schedules required? Where are you grazing the cattle tomorrow? When are you planning to move them to the high meadow? Has the water supply been restored in readiness? Are you able to ensure that Liam and Matt know exactly what's required of them on a daily basis? Is the milk girl getting up on time for the morning milking? Has the feed stock been delivered today yet?

It was a good thing that Danny had taken on the job in a serious and professional way. It was certainly more onerous and demanding than he had expected. Finally, after answering her continual questions, with each answer being almost interrupted by her next question, he finally managed to get a word in. "Mrs Wallace, I came here as a temporary herdsman on eighty quid a week, plus board. You really need to have a farm manager to see to a lot of these things."

What she said next surprised him. "I am hoping that perhaps I have found one in you. I am taking over responsibility for overseeing the farming operations. Mr Wallace has had to go to France. He has some problems over there. You could be farm manager. I need to see you each day to assess the progress made and confirm the next day's plan. I am increasing your hourly rate and you will be further rewarded if you measure up. However, I am not as easy-going as Mr Wallace. Many things are requiring attention and I expect you to follow my planning schedules promptly and without question. And don't think that I don't know what I am doing."

Danny realised that there had been no mention of the temporary nature of the job he had taken on. She appeared to be very bossy and demanding, almost arrogant and dictatorial in her superior new role. A right Mrs High and Mighty! But beautiful with it! He couldn't help but be captivated and mesmerised by her flashing crystal-blue eyes and trim figure. Impulsive he may be, but that evening he wrote a letter to the college informing them that he would not be able to attend the start of the new term; he had a temporary job and a secret ambition!

CHAPTER **10**

Mrs Wallace

"**D**anny, come to the kitchen after milking has finished. We need to plan tomorrow's work."

After a full day's hard labour, he did not relish the thought of another interrogation from Mrs Wallace. But he made his way over and took his boots off at the door. There were no pleasantries. She demanded that he report on the day's activities. She said nothing in appreciation, just made a few notes. Danny found her sergeant major's manner annoying. When she opened her mouth, it was always with an abrupt order - which she expected him to carry out implicitly, without question. She showed only a business- like manner.

However, despite her manner, he could not help but admire her attractiveness and sexuality. Tall and severe, but under the expensive business suit, he could see a very fit, trim figure: tight buttocks, lovely calves, and shapely ankles in her high-heeled shoes. He was gazing at her flashing dark eyes . What her inner thoughts were, he could not tell. She met his stare and their eyes met and lingered until it was Danny who looked aside.

After a few days of this routine, and conscious of his working clothes and dirty appearance, he asked if, before the meetings he could perhaps go to his lodge and change, and get a quick drink before reporting on the day's progress and receiving another batch of instructions for the next day.

"No, I need you here early. Bring some clean clothes to the barn in the morning so that you can change here for our meeting. You'll get a drink from the kitchen."

This was the procedure for future evenings, and he found her waiting for him with a mug of tea on the table and a load of questions and instructions. She had also suggested that he might shower and change into his clean clothes, before his work report, while emphasising that she would not want to be kept waiting.

So, a drink, and then off to the shower room. It was very posh - fully-tiled, with a double shower unit and central heating. Certainly better than the little tin bath and lukewarm water at his lodgings every night!

With the routine established and the climate between them less cool, as had become the usual way, he ran the shower at 'Hot', soaped off and took a moment to enjoy the luxury. He stood, eyes closed under the spray, thinking about the enigmatic Mrs Wallace. He was just about to turn around when he experienced a strange tingling sensation in his shoulders. He was then amazed to feel the touch of a body in the shower with him. He jumped with wonder, shock and unbelievable surprise when he heard a voice: "I decided to join you." The words, spoken quietly, were those of Mrs Wallace. He was stunned to the core and did not know what to do.

"Don't turn around," she instructed, rubbing his back and shoulders with shower lotion. He longed to turn around, but she was massaging his back … and then another order: "Keep still where you are." Lower and gradually lower down his spine and then ever so slowly round to his front she moved her hands, and when some pleasurable response was beginning to show, he just heard her say quietly, "Oh my." And then she stopped, as if she remembered to keep to her dictatorial manner. "Now turn around," she ordered. Completely mesmerised, Danny did as she bade him; she simultaneously turned her back to him. She reached for his hands and pulled them to her breasts, then poured shower gel over them. The invitation was quite clear to Danny. This time it was an instruction that he was beginning to enjoy carrying out. He relaxed and started to fondle her pleasurably. He massaged her back and breasts with wonder and excitement. She was naked except for a pair of frilly knickers – now, of course, completely wet through. She stopped his hands after a little while, when he started to wander, suddenly switching the shower to full-blast and 'Cold'. She let the ice-cold water wash over them, watched for Danny's reaction, laughed and then strode clear of the cubicle, turning for a quick, unbelieving glance at Danny's form. She then grabbed a towel from the rail and ran from the bathroom into her bedroom, slamming the door behind her.

Mary had been secretly captivated by Danny's masculinity. She had had limited opportunities to love someone and the disappointments of her married life were making her able to ignore any implications.

It took Danny some time to comprehend what had happened, and he just stood a while to settle down before drying off and dressing. What could he expect next? If she was still using him, it had suddenly become worthwhile! Now she was nowhere to be seen, and he wondered about her sergeant major character now. He eventually, sheepishly, went through to the kitchen. She was already sat at the table, sophistication itself, and ready to address farm business as though this additional part of the routine was the norm. Danny thought, have I been dreaming? She finally spoke: "That probably should not have happened. Now, I require your report on the decreasing milk yields. Tomorrow we have to sort out the dry cows from the milkers." It really was as though nothing had happened. Completely speechless and confused, he noted her orders for the following day. He had to admit that she had a complete knowledge of what was needed in management of the farm. But where was the missing Mr Wallace? What of the mystery of his wife? Did Danny really feature?

In the evening he wrote to the Agricultural College resigning from his training course. He also phoned Little Mo. He expected her to be distraught at his news, but she was full of life, talking non -stop as was her way.

"I'm sorry that you're not coming back yet. I still remember what we did together. It's changed my life. I met a boy in France when I was on holiday. His name is Jules and we're getting on famously together. He's coming to study in England and if you're not coming back, he will be able to come and stay in the apartment with me sometimes. So every cloud has a silver lining. I miss you, Danny, but I can't wait to get more of Jules."

Danny knew what she meant by that!

CHAPTER 11

Poachers

Seven young heifers were kept in a big barn at the farm. Straw bales fenced off an area from the rest of the barn. The heifers were just being weaned off milk onto hay and grass. When feeding them with milk supplement, Matt realised and reported that one was missing - but this had happened before - a mystery never solved in Mr Wallace's time. Matt checked the height of the bales and asked if a door had been left open. If somebody had stolen one it would not have been easy - being ready for sale for veal, they were frisky and lively and getting so strong that handling them was not easy, but there was undoubtedly another one missing. The suspicion was of a visit by cattle poachers.

Mrs Wallace's instruction was to get a local electrician and security specialist to set up a trip security alarm. It was costly, but she realised that the financial loss after the effort of breeding and rearing was becoming unbearable.

In the evening she came out to check progress with Danny. They were sitting on the bales of hay wanting to test how well the alarm would work, but both were, probably, thinking that they had nothing better to do or better company to keep.

"Are we expecting it to go off tonight, just because we have installed it?" Danny asked. "Let's give it a test!"

Mary smiled. She was becoming a little less aloof. After sharing the contents of a hip flask that Danny had brought to ward off the cold night, Danny was becoming bold enough to risk a little familiarity. The shower incident was not forgotten, even though not repeated, and he was waiting to see her reaction to his closeness. She seemed fairly comfortable now in his company, and after some questioning into Danny's life story - which Danny joked about - she relaxed somewhat and started to tell him a little of her own life circumstances. Hesitantly at first, but gradually, faced with a good listener, she began to open her heart to his sympathy.

Her mother and father were of a rich landowning family, owners of a country house and farm. She was brought up on the farm learning all the requisite farming knowledge. Her father was a keen horseman but had sustained severe spinal injuries when competing in the historic Kiplingcotes

Derby, the annual cross-country horse race; and soon after, her mother was diagnosed with breast cancer. In next to no time she found herself the sole heiress of a country house and farm she could not manage alone; a grieving and desperate young lady.

Many suitors wanted her for the estate, her money, or her hand. She was, of course, desperate for marriage, for love, and for physical assistance with running the estate successfully, so avoiding the need to sell the house and farm she loved.

Alex Wallace, naturally a Scotsman with a name like that, and supposedly a man of means, appeared on her horizon. Several years older than Mary, he courted her – after a fashion – and with a haste to marry. Once they were married, he claimed that they needed to sell the country house, but she insisted that they kept the farm and surrounding land that were the place of her childhood joys. She gradually found that he was not the man she needed either as a partner to run the business, or, she hinted, to love her. She had wanted a marital relationship and a family life. She needed a strong and dominating character, able to make tough decisions and follow them through. Alex was obsessed with money and not very interested in hard work, or in the management of the farm, and they argued regularly. After two difficult years, he said he was now off to France where he had business contacts. She had been left with a mammoth task and she inferred to Danny that she'd decided that the best way to cover her vulnerability in dealing with the staff was to take the no-nonsense, demanding, arrogant line she did. She found that it was successful in getting essential jobs done without questions, and she liked the effect it had. It gave the impression that she was an unapproachable, aloof, domineering character, though. Danny was beginning to understand her a little better., but he could not yet see that under the surface Mary was desperate for love, and a real partner to share the strife of making a success of her farm and her life.

About a week later, quite late at night, the intruder alarm went off with loud rings. They were not ready to react, and by the time they had got together and arrived at the barn it was too late: another heifer was missing and the poachers were gone. Mrs Wallace reported the theft to the police. The only clue unearthed was a white van seen speeding through the village crossroads. The use of sedative darts fired by pistol or rifle by the thieves was the only conclusion they could reach, and that perhaps the alarm was not sensitive enough, not giving them enough time to react. But exactly how they should react had not been planned.

Life and the farming tasks had to go on. The mystery remained of how the poachers had again got away with stealing a strong, lively, valuable heifer, and Danny could tell that it was worrying Mrs Wallace. She seemed quite depressed and subdued, and the vitality she always showed was missing - in fact she looked weary and dejected.

Danny arrived as usual for the evening progress report, knocked on the door and found that she was 'not inclined to talk or listen tonight' – there was no mug of tea either.

Her vulnerability brought out a genuine desire in him to comfort her. It led to Danny taking the initiative by staying longer than usual, and trying to cheer her up. He would never have dared to make a tentative suggestion in a joking manner before as he headed for the shower, but he was gaining in confidence.

"Why don't you join me in the shower again? Relax and don't worry ..." he said quietly.

His memories of the shower incident had been uppermost in his mind for all of the many weeks since it happened, and with it was an obsession to repeat the feel of her hands on him and his on her soft contours. She just shrugged, pulled a face, and waved him away into the shower room. He was instantly sorry for opening his mouth. All he could say was 'Sorry', as he left her.

He was ready for a good hot shower; he needed to relieve the tension and his embarrassment. He had just soaped off and was soaking under the warm spray, eyes again closed, when he was suddenly exhilarated by the realisation of her presence.

Her memories were of the previous shower incident and she had quietly sidled up to him without a word, and was standing in the shower - completely naked this time - with a forlorn 'Do what you will with me look' …

He just put his arms around her and gently held her to him under the hot, relaxing shower. She seemed to be completely exhausted and so he pulled down the shower seat, sat her down on it, and started massaging her shoulders and neck to try to relax her. He was stood, his naked front close to her chin, with hot water showering down on to them both. She seemed oblivious and comfortable with this, just sitting there looking at him, but made no other response; she seemed unhappy, almost traumatised.

Danny's main thoughts had been of concern and a desire to help to allay her depression, but now in this situation he could not prevent his thoughts turning to her naked beauty. To start anything further in the shower room would be tantamount to taking advantage of her, but his sexual thoughts were beginning to be revealed in front of her gaze. He switched off the shower, grabbed a large bath towel, wrapped it round her and lifted her wet and limp body in his arms and carried her to her bedroom. He laid her down on the bed, and then grabbed another bath towel and quickly dried himself and put his pants on for modesty's sake. Wrapped in the towel she hardly moved, but her eyes met his, and he knew by her expression that she wanted his comforting presence close to her, at the very least.

He hesitated, looked around the room, and then realised that this was her bedroom alone, and not shared by Mr Wallace. This thought made him feel less guilty and more comfortable, and he joined her on the bed. He kissed and hugged her, and now in a more relaxed mood, her response gradually changed from tentative to positive and longing. Foreplay was not frenzied, but was such that they were both relishing the pleasure and excitement and the discovery of hands on the contours of the body and the enjoyment to be had from this prolonged discovery mode. With the bath robe removed and Mary's body on top of him, breasts to his lips, he finally rolled her over. She was ready and took him with a contented murmur, and he paused to feel the 'wonderful within' sensation before he slowly increased the tempo. The timing was such that they reached a mutual climax with hearts beating rapidly. They gradually wound down, and then rested, before falling into a deep, contented sleep in the feeling of each other's closeness.

It was the middle of the night when they awoke with a start. They realised that the noise they could hear was the intruder alarm from the barn. It took them both a little time to collect their thoughts, realise what had happened, and then know that the noise could only mean trouble.

Now Danny was quickly on his feet and into shirt and trousers. He rushed out of the door towards the barn. Mary was not too far behind in just her dressing gown, having grabbed the old double-barrelled cartridge rifle normally used for scaring off foxes and the like.

In the same instance, across the yard, the door to Liam's lodge swung open and Liam rushed out still fastening his trouser belt, followed by milkmaid Martha in a similar state of dressing. Both the couple's secret liaisons were forgotten as they all ran forward at once.

They all saw the white Ford pickup parked near the barn and two men - having been disturbed by the alarm signal - deciding to leave the heifer they were dragging out and beat a hasty retreat. With Danny coming forward, now a little more carefully, one of the two raised a rifle and pointed it at him. He heard the snap of the silencer and ducked down to hear the 'swoosh' of a dart passing close to him. This was immediately followed by a loud bang from close behind him, followed quickly by another: Mary had fired the shotgun in the general direction of the poachers, but he was in as much danger from the rear as from the front. It was like a war had been declared. "Don't shoot Mary!" he shouted, as he rushed to the side to get the quad bike out.

The race was on. The thieves, scared by the return shots, rushed to get in the pickup and get it started; Danny rushed to board the quad bike. He raced across the field towards the entrance gate to the farm - his thoughts were not for his safety but only to slam it shut before the pickup could reach it and be away on the road. The pickup was roaring in about fifty yards away when Danny slammed the gate closed. The driver braked a little at first, but then put his foot full down on the accelerator. At about fifty miles per hour, the front of the pickup hit the gate full on. The vehicle came to a stop, its front end bashed in, and the wooden gate splintered into pieces. The passenger had hit the windscreen with a thud, but the driver had been braced for the impact. For a brief moment the poacher and Danny eyed each other, and each saw determination in the face of the other in this confrontation. However, the poacher had got the clear message that the farm now had a man who would not jib at defending his corner. He quickly reversed about fifteen yards and charged the gate again, like a bulldozer, this time battering through, and accelerated away down the road.

Danny's heart was thumping madly as he drove the quad bike slowly back to the farm to the waiting Mary, Liam and Martha. No one dared mention the obvious about the whereabouts of both couples when the alarm sounded.

Mary said, "I am going to ring the police," and headed to her kitchen with Danny following. The other two scarpered back to Liam's lodge. Danny wondered if they would carry on where they had left off. For him the wondrous intimacy with Mary had passed, and he retired directly to his own pad to reflect on the outcome and implications of following nature's instincts.

Early in the morning, Danny went out to get the work of the farm moving. The herd of cows had to be brought in for milking, then he had to clear the remains of the broken gate to allow the marketing board wagon in to collect the milk. When he eventually went back to Mary's kitchen, breakfast was waiting for him - eggs, bacon, fried bread, tomatoes and mushrooms, the full Monty - and a much happier lady.

He had heard it said that the following morning's reaction to the night's events in the bedroom revealed a woman's views on the matter, and a full breakfast on the table was a mark of complete satisfaction!

But where was Mr Wallace.? Danny did not know, but he could guess at some of the consequences if he found out about last night's liaisons.

CHAPTER 12

Mr Wallace

The full Monty breakfasts were beginning to become a feature. Not every day, because the graft on the farm and the planning, management, accounts and the like left Danny and Mary both tired out of an evening, but the hard work and good planning was reaping excellent financial results and money in the bank. It was a good partnership with equal contribution. Discussions about the running of the farm were often followed by exchange of ideas and ambitious plans about its future.

The plans being discussed were for automated milking equipment, developing a thoroughbred herd, which cows to sell, and which to cover for improving future milk yields. Then there were the benefits of artificial insemination and the future of Marco, their mixed-breed bull, whose previous appetite for servicing the herd was perhaps not insatiable after all. In the past these topics might have been difficult, but now everything was open and relaxed. On the occasional day off a discreet 'tête-à-tête' would lead to them spending the night together, with early breakfast to follow. Mary was becoming more and more adventurous, as though she was learning from the Karma Sutra of sexual positions. She was a woman starved of the sexual bliss that normally comes from marital copulation. Ten years older than Danny, she wanted to show him the suppleness of her body, the strength of her upper thighs and the ecstasy of variety. Their happiness with the relationship was clearly conveyed to each other. Danny was learning that his love for Mary was becoming real in every way, not just a sexual attraction. The shower room was still a favourite for them; Mary admitted that it was her desire for intimate comfort and affection in the shower room that had made her drop her high-handed manner and seek the excitement and positive response from him. They now seemed to have a mutual desire to give pleasure to each other. It was an ideal partnership in work and in play. Discretion within the small farm community was maintained by an unspoken pact with Liam and Martha about their relationships.

Danny really enjoyed the evenings in the kitchen together discussing the farm's progress and making plans for its future. He was completely involved, and his ideas and suggestions on the farm's conservation policies brought them closer together. Future plans were ambitious, but as Mary pointed out - were only for when they could be afforded.

After a particularly hard day, Danny opened the kitchen door as usual, expecting his mug of tea to be waiting for him, followed by a relaxing evening … instead, sat in the chair by the fire (usually used by Danny to warm his limbs), was the imposing figure of Mr Alex Wallace!

"What do you want?" he said to Danny, in a brusque manner.

"I am here to update Mrs Wallace on today's farm work and sort out tomorrow's workload," replied Danny, who was taken aback by events and needed time to think.

"Come back later, she's busy," said Mr Wallace, rising and trying to shut the door in his face.

Danny stood his ground for a moment saying, "I didn't know that you were back." He glanced at Mary, who although looking somewhat harassed, gestured an 'It's okay' to him.

All sorts of thoughts were passing through his mind as he crossed the yard. Had someone spilled the beans regarding his liaisons with Mary? This was her absent husband, but still her husband nevertheless! If Alex was back for good, where did Danny stand with his job? How would Mary react now? And what of the progress that their joint efforts had made towards the efficiency and profitability of the farm - for which Danny deserved his credit? Had all the graft he had put in been for nothing? What of his liaisons with someone else's wife? Was he just being used? Should he have requested a contract of employment? Should he have avoided the temptations that his time with Mary had provoked? Were the good times at an end?

He decided to go back and face them. And then other thoughts prevailed. They were married, after all, and it may appear that he was the intruder; the opportunist while the husband was away.

Outside the kitchen door he could now hear raised voices; they were both shouting in anger. From the snatches he could hear, some of the argument was about money, but the gist of what he heard suggested that Mr Wallace had left more or less without warning after arguments about his inability to run the farm, and also to perform between the sheets. He had returned now after many months away, without prior communication.

"You think you can clear off without a word, leave me in the mire as far as the farm goes? It was running at a loss because of your incompetence, and now you come back making demands. You never cared about the farm, gave me no sexual consideration, and only bothered about my money. Then you come back expecting things to be as though nothing has happened! Well there's neither love nor money for you here"! Mary was in full flow, verbally lashing out at him.

Then it was his turn. " What about marital rights? Ever heard of them? If you are not prepared to try again then you can start thinking about a divorce. I will put in an application and don't forget my share of assets on a fifty/fifty basis. I could ruin you!"

With Mary seeming to be holding her own in the argument, Danny thought better than to barge in and went back to his hut. He was confident that Mary could 'handle' him. However he was now sufficiently aware that there were going to be changes in the situation, and there was a possible danger that he might be implicated in a divorce case ... and goodness knows what else.

CHAPTER 13

Mary, Danny and Alex

The following morning, after a sleepless night, Danny checked and found that Mr Wallace's car was still there.

His mind was in turmoil. Was Mary wise enough to keep her mouth shut about their activities? What was this about 'marital rights'? He had barely heard of them. What had happened overnight?

He tried to concentrate on the farm work, but one eye was constantly on the kitchen door - which eventually opened. Mr Wallace headed for his car, slammed the door and drove off, after looking pointedly in Danny's direction. He waited around and then looked in the kitchen, but there was no sign of Mary. She did not show her face all day.

He did not know what to expect when he went for the usual briefing. She motioned him in. He saw that at least his mug of tea was on the table, but Mary was looking somewhat distressed.

"Are you alright? What's happening? Is he coming back?" Danny blurted out.

"Sit down, Danny, we need to talk."

Despite Alex staying overnight, Mary had listened to his suggestions, his propositions to start again, his advances and the like - and had rejected all of them. Next came his threats about the part of the money accessible to him, and then the threat to apply for a divorce based on her rejections and their separation - with a valuation and division of family property and assets on a fifty/fifty basis required. In his anger he did not yet seem to be sure that he might have an adultery case to pursue.

On her rejections he had said, "What's wrong with you? You know that you can't run the farm. It needs selling while there is something to sell!" She had replied by saying that she was managing things successfully with help from Danny and the other work people. He was taken aback by this and on leaving said, "You've not heard the last of me or of this matter."

"What can you do?" Danny now asked her.

"It's got to be 'we', not just me. We've got to make plans to save our livelihoods. It's all about the money he can get his hands on. Anything else is finished."

She explained as best she could that the money received from the sale of the country home had been put in a joint account with access for both of them. A lot had been squandered away by Alex and used to keep the loss-making farm from going under because of his mismanagement.

The farm, the land, and its assets were in Mary's name, but the money in the bank account was now being added to by the farm's current trading profit. Alex could draw cheques up to ten thousand pounds on his signature alone from this account, and the account summary showed that he had done so in the past. Mary guessed that this was again his intention.

"We need to watch out for his selfish scheming and lies. I will go to the bank straight away, then to a friend of my fathers who will advise us. You can drive me there in the Land Rover, drop me off, then go straight to the Fordson dealer and buy that second-hand tractor … and buy another quad Bike for us to use on the farm. I will give you a signed blank cheque. Fill in the amount and then tell the Fordson dealer to present it to my branch of the bank. We have got to reduce the size of the account on legitimate farm business before Alex can start his shenanigans, and stop him drawing cheques for himself and at ten thousand pounds at a time."

Danny dropped Mary off at the bank and was just revving away down the main street when he spotted Alex

Wallace walking in the direction of the bank. He had to delay him somehow!

He stopped the car right in front of Alex and rushed towards him. "Mr Wallace, can I talk to you? I want to know what's going on with the farm. Are you coming back to run it now?"

Alex didn't answer any of his questions; he wanted to be away to the bank. He had, however, noticed that Danny was using the old Land Rover. "Mind your own business. Just what do you think you're doing? You were employed as a temporary herdsman, that's what you should be doing, and you want to be buggering off back to college. Mrs Wallace had no right to give you other jobs. Just keep out of anything else that's going on. When I come back you will be out on your arse and the farm will be up for sale anyway. Now get out of my way."

But Danny needed to delay him further in the hope that Mary could finish her business in the bank. "Now hold on a minute Mr Wallace, we need to sort this out," he replied. "The farm is doing alright, and I need a permanent job. Just a minute, don't be rushing off. I need that job, so don't leave me in limbo."

Danny was blocking his way, and by now Alex was beginning to realise that he was being delayed purposely and he pushed hard at Danny. But Danny grabbed his coat lapels to restrain him. After a bit of pushing and pulling

Danny finally let go, and with a few foul words Alex set off at a pace towards the bank - just in time to see Mary exiting the door in the distance.

As Alex walked away Danny noticed a small leather card holder on the pavement. It had been dropped unknowingly by Alex in the tussle. It contained a business card for a company in France owned by 'Alexander Wallace, Chief Executive', and named, 'Your Gold, Fine Metals and Jewels Recovery'. The other card was a bank card for a bank in Lille, France. He smiled to himself as he put the card holder in his pocket; his immediate job was to spend some of the money in the farm account with the blank cheque signed by Mary. He made his way to the dealer.

The Fordson tractor they had looked at previously, while nowhere near new, was in far better nick than their old one. The dealer thought that fortune was shining upon him with the quick sale, and ready money as well, for both a tractor and a quad bike. It suited him to take the cheque straight in, as instructed, and present it in person to the bank manager - who now knew the position of the farm account and was doing the paperwork implementing Mary's instructions about other signees and opening a new account for the farm's funds.

Mary had said that they should arrange to meet at the street café - upstairs where it was quieter. Danny was there first. He heard someone climbing the steps quite slowly, unlike Mary's normal brisk walk. She looked worn out by all she had done, and Danny felt likewise. She sat down and he was almost passed out in anguish as he heard her words: "Danny, I think I'm pregnant."

"What did you say?!"

She repeated the same six words.

"How can you be? Whose is it?"

"Danny, you know how babies are made. And I certainly haven't been artificially inseminated! It's yours!"

CHAPTER 14

French Experience

A traumatised Danny helped Mary down the café stairs as if she might be eight months gone.

Mary was annoyed. "Get a move on - I'm not an invalid. I only said that I might be pregnant. It's not bloody paralysis!"

The shock, the reality, the anxiety and the fear that overcame him at the sudden news, was gradually receding, to be replaced by the exciting thought that Mary would be carrying his child! A father to be! What a new and wonderful feeling!

When they arrived back to the farm, Danny told Mary about the confrontation with Alex and then about finding the business card and wallet. Mary summed up the situation. Alex was likely to apply for a divorce on the grounds of a two-year separation, she explained. In this sort of case the divorce court would have to award a share of the assets, starting from a fifty-fifty split, and considering the contributory actions of both parties, award a smaller split to the more guilty party. Mary thought she just might counter-claim on the grounds of desertion.

With Mary's possible pregnancy, if admitted, Alex could use voluntary adultery as the grounds for divorce; the share out would then be In Alex's favour. Things appeared to be stacking up against them, and in favour of Alex.

However, inside the wallet that Alex had dropped was the bank card for the bank in Lille, France, and also the business card with Alex's company details.

"He has bought a business in France, making him money that he has never told me about," Mary said. "He must have drawn money from the farm account pretending it was to keep the farm going. This might provide a weapon for us to use. We have got to find out about this. Danny, you are going to have to go to France. You'll need to organise a passport straight away."

"I'd be completely lost on my own," Danny said, completely aghast. He had never been abroad before.

"You will have to take Liam with you. I'll get Matt to ask Poofter to help him with the farm work while you're gone."

"Poofter's not much good for grafting!"

"He might be gay, but he can think straight, and watch that Matt doesn't do anything stupid."

Two weeks later, with a date apparently being set for the divorce hearing, the plan was ready for action.

Danny and Liam took a long drive to Hull for the overnight ferry to Rotterdam, and would then have another long drive, 'on the wrong side of the road' to Lille in France. The conversation along the way made for familiarity and some exchange of confidences, but Danny was careful how he answered some of Liam's questions about his relationship with Mary.

On the Ferry, relaxing with their third beer, Liam opened up then Danny asked about Martha. "I've had to move back into my own shack - except for weekends," he said. "She was wearing me out. She's a nymphomaniac. We would have it off and then in next to no time she was back for more. I would fall asleep and then wake up with her squeezing the cheeks of my arse, ready again. I was knackered! Then she sulked!

Danny had to admit he was a little bemused by this confession.

The ferry's bunk beds were comfortable - if you were drunk - then the noise of the ship docking, people shouting in a strange language and cars starting up would bring you to your senses. Which is exactly what happened, but by then they realised they had no time for breakfast and had to move their vehicle.

Armed with a road map and Liam's reminders about the 'right side of the road' and to 'look left' at roundabouts, they managed to clear Zeebrugge and get onto quieter countryside lanes. Danny was able to relax once he had settled into driving on the right-hand side of the road. He was able to appreciate the arboreal greenery of casual France, the open fields, the hedgerows in straight lines, the lack of heavy traffic, and the views uninterrupted by buildings. When the signposts for Lille started to appear, he quickly remembered why they were doing this. They arrived in Lille around lunchtime, went in for a cafe au lait, and asked in broken French (from their little book from the ferry) where the firm 'Your Gold' was and the whereabouts of the Banque de Français. The owner replied in perfect English that the bank was but 200 metres away, and he looked in his directory for the whereabouts and telephone number of 'Your Gold'.

"Get another coffee and some food," Danny said to Liam. "This guy might be good enough to help two good customers." He didn't know how lucky he was in thinking this.

In between ordering more food and drink, they persuaded the proprietor to ring the firm as a prospective client with good quantities of gold jewellery to trade in. Sure enough, Alex Wallace was the man who answered.

"You have Gold and Jewellery to sell?" His Scotch accent was unmistakable, "I have good cash prices for melt-downs and fifty per cent off retail profit on selling items of jewellery.."

When asked about surety, Alex, in his ignorance of what was going on, referred the client to the local Banque de Français in Lille!

The cafe proprietor's wife was also able throw more light on the 'Your Gold' company. She had met the lady who she thought was the proprietor's wife: a middle-aged, attractive lady who looked after things while her 'husband', a man with a Scotch accent, was away.

With this confirmation and proof of this revelation, their purpose was quickly achieved and they couldn't get on the road back to the ferry fast enough to convey the news to Mary.

"En voiture, en voiture!" shouted Liam, to show that he had learned some of the French language.

They did stop once on the way back for Matt's sake. He had asked them if they could get 'some of those letters from France' that he had heard people talking about in the local pub. La Pharmacie was the stopping place for the French Letters … especially gift-wrapped for Matt.

CHAPTER **15**

The Outcome

Mary, accompanied by Danny this time, was ready for another face-off with Mr Alex Wallace. They would find it difficult to conceal their adultery, as the results of it were becoming noticeable with Mary and their secret was likely to be revealed. Alex would feel usurped and be furious, obviously, but would think that his divorce settlement plans were favourably reinforced.

"We'll let him mouth-off for a time, and then when the time is right, we'll hit him with our knowing all about what he's been up to in France, his absence from running the farm, his neglect of me, his French mistress, his business in jewellery, and the evidence of drawing cash from our account for use in France!" Mary said.

They had to wait some time before he showed up again. He eventually arrived, full of scheming confidence that he could get what he wanted by verbal abuse and aggression. He had not bargained for the presence of Danny, who managed to keep his cool and not land one on him. The settlement by the judge against Mary could ruin her, he said, and the farm would have to be sold to pay his major share of the assets.

And then it was Mary's turn. She hit him with what they now knew of all his scheming and activities in France, his bank drawings and their use for wrong-doings abroad, and his neglect of the farm and his duties. Then there was the threat of complete ruination of his case, and the maximum publicity at home and abroad by Mary, which would damage his name.

He was completely taken aback. He tried to bluster his way out, and then to seek a settlement to protect his assets abroad. He finally left with his tail between his legs, Danny marching him to the car he had come in, pointing out to him that they knew he had bought it with Mary's money!

They later heard that his application for divorce had been withdrawn, and therefore all that remained was an uncontested application by Mary for divorce on the grounds of his desertion. What a load off their minds!

"We'll soon be able to get married!" shouted Danny. It had never been mentioned before.

"Hold on a moment," Mary said, "I'm carrying your child and you haven't asked me properly yet! Down on your knees if you want me to be your wife."

The daily grind of the work on the farm had to go on. There were cows to be milked early morning and evening, the dairy had to have the full pails of milk ready for collection, there were heifers to feed, cattle markets and slaughterhouses to visit, and land, fixtures and fittings to be maintained, and much more.

But they were a happy team of people working together. Danny had learned a lot in short time. He knew how to respect and value all the staff, and to acknowledge their different capabilities. To help each one of them know that their job was important, no matter how mundane, routine or repetitive it was, was so vital for morale. Likewise, away from working hours, Liam and Martha seemed to have worked something out, and even Matt had been 'taken in hand' by a widow from the bakery in the village. They repeatedly reminded Matt to take those French letters with him! Poofter? Well Danny really didn't know what to make of him, but he certainly had a brain in his head. What else he had; he did not know!

Mary and Danny were happy and contented. Early nights were about care and loving consideration for each other, bodies and minds being shared to achieve a successful, satisfying outcome. They loved falling asleep and waking up contented in one another's arms. Plans for the farm programme were usually discussed while still comfortable in bed, and they still had the occasional full-Monty breakfasts on quieter mornings.

Mary had been to see her solicitor with the farm's year-end draft accounts. Her pregnancy was now clearly noticeable, and she often placed Danny's hand on her abdomen as part of his bonding with their baby.

One day Danny was repairing some fencing where the cattle had gone walkabout down to the bottom fields. Not wanting to walk all the way down track and meadow, Mary decided to take the old tractor to go and see him. She really wanted to tell him how good her solicitor friend had said they were doing financially - and the accounts were proving it.

All the thoughts and plans for what they could do when they could afford it were racing through her mind, and now it was also about what they could do as a family. There would be more automation in the dairy and in the cow sheds, there would be extra finance by selling off the bottom field with permission to build about five houses, and a smaller herd - saving both time and money that would enable them to spend time watching their child growing up.

Mary could see Danny over on the other side of the field from where she had driven down the track. She left the track and travelled across the sloping terrain, her speed reflecting her excitement and impatience to give him the good news. The old tractor was not as stable as the newer one, and suddenly the front wheels hit a massive rock at speed. The steering wheel was jerked out of Mary's hands, and with the tractor out of control on a steep camber, it toppled over onto its side, tipping and trapping Mary beneath it. Her rib cage was smashed completely; she did not have a chance.

Danny heard her yell, and watched in horror as the tractor started to tip, and then started running to the overturned tractor.

"OH MY GOD, OH NO, PLEASE, NO!" he screamed.

He managed to drag her from under the heavy mudguard, but he knew straight away that she was dead.

What could he do? He took the rifle he had with him, loaded it and fired both barrels in the air, reloaded it and fired both barrels again. It was the emergency signal and what he had told Liam to do to attract attention for assistance in any emergency. He was just hoping that Liam would hear it and respond. He cradled Mary's head in his arms and waited. He was dizzy with shock. He would not leave her and was desperate about the baby she was carrying in her womb.

Liam had in fact heard the shots, and grabbed the quad bike and raced to the scene. He could see from a distance what the terrible situation was.

Danny shouted to him. "Don't come nearer, Liam, get back! Ring 999. Ambulance and police!" He held Mary and knew that everything Mary meant to him was gone, and gone forever. From now forward it would be only memories. He broke down and cried, and clung to her head, and held the face he had loved. He wrapped her in his jacket, feeling that her body was going cold.

The ambulance finally arrived, and they ran with a stretcher and emergency equipment across the field from their ambulance on the track. Danny told them about her pregnancy. They listened to him, examined her, and shook their heads.

CHAPTER 16

Danny and the Future

The funeral, with its condolences from shocked distant relatives, friends, and village neighbours, turned out to be a traumatic business. The villagers attended the service in force, saddened and emotional about the tragedy, but wanting to know among themselves what would happen to the farm. Details of the inquest made the press, and the health and safety executives were seeking information. Danny's mother, who had attended and then stayed with Danny, was a comfort to him, because she knew his ways. At the right time she tried in her practical way to ask what was to be done about the house and the farm and the complexities to be faced.

A distraught and heartbroken Danny could not speak to anyone without breaking down and in this situation could not face the farm work. Liam, Matt and Martha soldiered on out of necessity, despite their own grief. They wondered if Danny would ever be free of the memory of Mary, and also what the future held for them now.

Danny wandered about the house. He constantly recalled his times with Mary: the way that the serious planning talks at the kitchen table had cemented them together; the shower room pleasures they had shared; the bedtimes when he would make a 'chair' with his knees for her to lie in, protected by his arm around her waist; waking together with a kiss and a cuddle, and then facing challenges of the day ahead. He now fully realised that his loving relationship with Mary in every respect, sexual or otherwise, was the ultimate, the definitive, because it was always about what they could give to one another as loving partners, and not what they could receive. But had it been right in the eyes of others? He had no misgivings when he recalled the way that Mary would bring variety and adventure into their sexual encounters. It might have been the surprise at finding her completely naked body awaiting him as he slid between the sheets, or one which was waiting to playfully resist the slow removal of her 'protective' underwear until she had him naked first. They both knew that the other's body was a masterpiece for their indulgence. The gentle and slow fondling for the satisfaction of the other that could be changed by either partner into a rough and urgent progression, before slowing things down again to relish the utopian moments along the way to them becoming as one, the differing rhythms that either one would indicate was right for their mood and desire, as each one's body became the property of the other. All such pleasures in Danny's life had now gone with the death of his beloved Mary. His dreams were all shattered.

Where was Alex now? Gone for good he hoped.

Danny could see no way out of his deep and desperate sadness. He tried to apply his mind to the farmwork but his recollections frequently made him grief stricken again.

Finally, his mother's comforting and persistent questioning helped him to start looking forward again. She tried to impress on him that there were many things to do going forward. So far, he had avoided a visit to Mary's solicitor and friend, but now he thought that he was ready to face up and talk things through. The look of diplomacy on the solicitor's face suggested that he had serious matters to reveal.

Danny was shocked to learn that Mary, only a few weeks before her death, had made a new Will and Testament - leaving all her possessions to Danny! He eventually absorbed the meaning of this. The full responsibility for the farm would now be his, but it would be a task to be done without her.

It was almost as if she feared something would happen, although Danny believed it was her pregnancy and their being unable to marry that had prompted her secret action. New, real plans were again needed, and he could address that now. He gradually, with much thought and time, compiled the following Action List:

Sell a large plot of the farm land, with building permission for housing.

Reduce the size of the herd. Make it all thoroughbred, reducing and automating the work.

Allow the positioning of telephone and television reception pylons on the farm land. And receive good rentals.

Pay for Liam and Martha's lodges to be knocked through into one good dwelling to keep them happy.

Take on a new Agricultural College graduate. Train him to manage the farming, but also eventually to act as consultant and locum to other farmers to enable them to get a break from farming's twenty-four hour, seven days a week grind.

Socialise more. Involve himself more in the county farming community.

Return home more often and ensure that his mother and her home were financially secure.

Plant a cedar tree beside the farm wall in memory of Mary. He would scatter Mary's ashes amidst the roots on planting it. It would always be Mary's Cedar.

Danny started a regular ritual to this sacred place - which made him imagine an aura of presence and feeling that the past and Mary were closer than imagined. She would give him the strength and energy to tackle the plans! She must have wanted a child with Danny to miss taking her contraception. He recalled that during the difficult times Mary had said to him - 'If the farm goes under you must move on, forget me, and find a good woman more your own age'. He knew she meant it, but doing it was going to be difficult with his memories.

CHAPTER **17**

Learning Liaisons

After several months of action some of the plans were beginning to take shape. Danny referred to his list again with some satisfaction, but he was not really happy. The truth was that he was becoming a solitary, lonely man. He began to wonder what he was doing all this for. He was pleased that Liam and Martha were happy and excited with the progress on the house, and the changes to the herd, and the graduate farm manager seemed to be settling in, but he still couldn't visit the cedar tree where Mary's ashes were scattered, without breaking down.

His socialising with the county set was less successful than he had hoped, because without a partner he was left out of some of the events unless he agreed to go with young women that he did not know, or that he found to be immature and inexperienced. However, one day, he was introduced to a young lady who rode with the local hunt. Her name was Julie, and with her shiny, almost black ponytail and big brown eyes, was quite beautiful. She apparently came from a 'well-to-do' family who had protected her from the outside world and its temptations, leaving her inexperienced and virginal in every sense of the word. Danny was attracted to her, but guessed that his background and lineage wouldn't nearly be pure enough, and he really was in no mood for complications from her immaturity.

He decided to spend a few days with his mother. Norman had moved out and he felt much happier knowing he wouldn't have to see him. On the journey there he could not resist a diversion to just drive past Charlotte Ramsden's address and the place of his initiation. He was sad to see a 'Sold' sign on the property, and the gardens overgrown and neglected. A young couple were on the driveway, just leaving the house.

Danny stopped and spoke to them. "I see the house is sold. Do you know anything of the previous owners?"

The young man replied that he thought that there had been a marriage break-up, and that the lady who had initiated the sale was moving abroad. Danny reminisced with some sadness. He had special memories of his affair with Charlotte at this house and learning what sex was all about. He often thought about her, and in his mind, he could vividly remember the details of that first experience. Her firm breasts and cleavage through the white silk blouse, her thighs through the tight, silken skirt, and her husky voice when she spoke quietly to him. Did she know how much she was enticing him? Memories!

On his arrival at his mother's she informed him that a letter had been delivered, marked for his attention. She also had a cutting from the local newspaper that she had saved for him. The headline said 'Celebrity Girl Comes Back to her Roots', and read: 'Jennifer Holmes, the beautiful, raunchy and outspoken celebrity newscaster for Southern Television, is moving back to the north in a career change to work as the chief advertising and fund-raising executive for the Marketing Research Council'. She was quoted as saying that the combination of 'high living, late nights and early morning news-casting had become such that it was no longer a pleasure but a hard grind'. She was 'in need of a less public and controversial lifestyle'. Jennifer had recently bought Moorland View, the five-bedroomed former barn conversion on the outskirts of the Yorkshire village.

Danny would hardly have recognised her from the photo; she had matured into a shapely, immaculately dressed woman. His heart missed a beat as he recalled the happy days they had together, the nervous fondling that went on behind the school bike shed and then the embarrassing, naive, sexual disaster that had ended it all. He had often wondered how her future had worked out.

Danny was in the process of opening the envelope as he read the newspaper cutting, but was diverted to the letter when he saw with great surprise that it was from the very same Jennifer Holmes.

It said:

> 'Dear Danny, hope you don't mind me contacting you after such a long time. I have now heard about the unfortunate accident that has taken your partner away from you. I am so sorry. It must have been terrible for you and must be taking some getting over.
>
> I am making some changes in my lifestyle - for the better I hope - and since returning to the north I have been hearing about the things you are achieving. Frankly, Danny, having burnt my boats down south, I am missing the company of a genuine man for many of the social events and fundraisers I go to. I need an escort, mainly to discourage men's attention, but perhaps for more. (I am afraid that my media reputation has followed me north!)
>
> If you would like to meet up again, to look to the future rather than to the past, please give me a ring.

Yours sincerely,

Jennifer Holmes

PS I know how to deal with a condom now! Pity I didn't know about the pill.

PPS I have bought Moorland View. Please give me a ring if you're interested. My telephone number is on the letterhead.'

Danny did not tell his mother the details of the letter, and she knew him better than to ask. He tucked it away in his pocket. A few days later, at a moment when his loneliness was getting to him, he gave Jennifer's number a ring. A woman's voice answered and explained Jennifer was not available, but she had been instructed that if Danny rang, to make a date for them to meet, perhaps one evening, at the Bistro restaurant just out of the village.

A date was fixed, the day arrived. He scrubbed-up for the occasion, and put his 'socialising suit' on and a spotless white shirt (washed and ironed by his mother!). He arrived slightly early at the restaurant and the waiter showed him to his table.

The atmosphere was quite lively and noisy, but suddenly went quiet as many noticed the astonishingly beautiful lady entering the room and waited to see who the lucky man was that she was meeting. Her blonde hair was swept back from her face in an immaculate style, and her blue eyes and make-up accentuated an expression that declared beauty and utmost confidence. She wore a figure-hugging dress that revealed her perfect figure and legs to match. Danny stood up to greet her. The high-heeled shoes she was wearing made her as tall as he was. She strode across to him and before everyone's gaze put her arms around him and said, "Oh! Danny." She hugged him and kissed him in a long passionate embrace, her arms around his neck, her lips open to his. In contrast to Danny, Jennifer was revelling in the attention she was getting from the other diners. She was a woman who just knew she was strikingly attractive, with celebrity status to-boot.

They finally sat down and quickly ordered the meal. She knew exactly what she wanted. And then she said, "It's been such a long time, tell me everything you have done since I last saw you! Or perhaps not quite everything!"

The conversation was as easy as it was in their school days of the past, when they were really just teenagers, except that Danny had difficulty keeping his eyes away from the cleavage between two ample breasts, he thought, she's put on weight in the right places!

Jennifer was coming back to the north, leaving the 'Big City' where more liberal attitudes to casual sex were accepted in the life styles.

The Bistro food was first-class and confirmed Jennifer's taste and familiarity with dining out. The wine in particular went down very well, with the second bottle ordered by Jennifer, and Danny trying to keep up. Any inhibitions were lost and replaced by little jokes and suggestions that maybe they had similarities in their present situations - in that they were both now going short of intimate company and what could go with it.

"Would you like to have coffee at my place? I'll show you around the house and tell you what my plans are for modernising it. We had better leave our cars here and get a taxi," Jennifer suggested.

She was clearly inviting sensual familiarity by sitting so close to him in the back seat of the taxi. They were soon familiar without caring what the driver could see. They then tumbled out of the cab laughing, and Danny threw some paper money the driver's way.

They literally fell in through the front door and as soon as it was closed, they both had the same thing in mind. The race was on! His jacket was thrown on the hallway floor, his shirt on the seventh stair. Then her shoes in the hall, her expensive dress ripped off by the top step. Kissing and tumbling into a bedroom at her guidance, he was unzipped and the trousers expertly removed, and they fell onto the bed both panting and desperate for fulfilment. "Whoa, Danny, we don't want any heart attacks!" Jennifer laughed. " Slow down a bit and enjoy!" They tried to do that, but their passions were the governing factor. Danny couldn't help thinking that what he had wanted so badly with Jennifer in their youthful past was now being put before him on a plate! He treated her quite brutally, but she clearly enjoyed that and held him as long as she could. They eventually fell apart, both gasping and exhausted, and held each other for a time, before quickly falling asleep and dreaming in a satisfied and drunken contentment.

Jennifer was not beside him when he awoke. She was nowhere to be seen. He went gingerly in search of his clothes. His pants were near the bed where they had been stripped from him, so he followed the route towards the front door in his pants alone, expecting to collect items of clothing one at a time on the way, but found them neatly folded in the hallway. He grabbed them and beat a hasty retreat back upstairs, partly because he got a feeling that someone was watching. Decent and dressed he then returned to ground floor to be met by a smiling Jennifer, wine glass already in hand.

"Good morning, lover, are you hungry after your exertions?" she smiled.

Unfortunately, this reminded him of the morning breakfasts after the night before in the farm kitchen with Mary and he was saddened. He felt a sort of tingling in his shoulders and some intuition, almost guiding him. He declined all but coffee and toast, and quickly said that he needed to collect his car and get back to the farm.

Jennifer would only let him go after a long and tempting kiss saying, "Can't you stay? I don't want you to go. We could have something going for us."

On the drive back he wondered if everything was okay at the farm, but he need not have worried. He found that everything was running smoothly, with Liam and Martha just finishing in the milking sheds and locum John cooling and paling the milk in time for collection.

Danny relaxed and began thinking about the wonders and availability of Jennifer, and how it may be possible for him to have the best of both worlds. The finances were very good. The downsizing of the farm's activities and with staff in place, meant that he was not needed all the time. He also thought about joining the local hunt crowd and even having the pleasure of educating Julie, who cut a good figure on her hunter. "What a good life," he said to himself.

After a few days with the staff, going over the progress being made with the future plans at the farm, he was ready for another touch of Jennifer's lifestyle. It seemed to him that when he contacted Jennifer that she couldn't wait for him to drive over. In fact, she was just desperate for more of his company.

This time, after a busy day on the farm, he drove straight to Moorland View, rang the bell, and was met by an attractive, dark-skinned young lady he had not seen before - not bad looking with clearly the body of a fitness fanatic. "You're Danny," she said. "Come in. I'm Samantha. Jennifer is in the lounge." She did not lead him there but returned to the breakfast room.

He wandered through and found Jennifer sprawling on a massive corner couch, watching TV in casual wear, whisky glass in hand, looking very relaxed - if not slightly tipsy. She poured Danny a full glass and herself another.

"Hi, Jennifer," he said. "Who's Samantha?"

"Oh, you've met. She's my companion and general assistant. She'll do anything: secretary, housekeeper, fundraiser, sympathiser, friend, drinking partner. Some think we might be lesbians, but don't you worry, she's all woman! Don't hang back, come, get on the couch, I've been waiting for you. Let's relax and play around a bit." She snuggled to him and he could feel the heat of her body.

The TV was soon forgotten. As they talked her hands were alternating between the whisky glass and his thighs. She was unconcerned when Samantha came in, poured herself a glass, and sat close to them on the couch. The girls chatted away and included him in the conversation. Jennifer took his hand to her breast, unconcerned by Samantha's presence, but Danny felt slightly uncomfortable. He took another good swig from his whisky glass to try to keep up with the uninhibited company.

After a while Jennifer was obviously 'wanting more action'. She pulled at Danny and said, "Let's go to the bedroom." Danny looked at Samantha to see her reaction to all this. What he saw was a lovely face, and dark skin reflecting a picture of perfect health. She was wearing a tight 'Zip Suit ' of fine material which fitted her like a second skin showing through the perfect contours of her body. No supporting bra necessary, hard nipples protruding through the suit. He guessed that running his hand and the zip down her front would reveal a near naked and perfect body that he could not wait to see, touch and fondle.

Jennifer saw his stare, looked at Samantha and back to Danny and asked, "Can you handle a threesome? Have you ever tried it? If you're up for it, I'll promise you it'll be out of this world."

Danny was feeling hot in anticipation of another new experience … and the alcohol was affecting his thinking so that the anticipation of the foreplay with two women were in his mind. He took another good swig from his glass.

"Close the curtains and put the light out; it's exciting playing in the dark," Jennifer purred.

The girls were quick off the mark, with Samantha more or less undressing Jennifer-presumably for him, as they moved onto the massive king-sized bed - which was big enough for even the three of them to lose one another in. Danny, down to his pants, joined them. It was like a lively game, and they chattered away and frolicked around, the aim being the removal of under garments and the girls competed for getting their hands on him. He soon realised that if he did not get into the action it would be like a girl's gang-bang, so he joined in and dominated the 'affray'. Samantha seemed to be holding back a little, but perhaps because that was what she was used to in her relationship with Jennifer. Danny managed to do what he had become desperate to do; and that was to slide that Zip slowly down and all the way until her physical fitness, dark skin and even darker nipples brought pleasure and added variety to the occasion for him. She also dictated a slower pace to the sex games' thus prolonging the pleasures for them all. Hands and lips were everywhere, and Danny was almost consumed by the two of them. Samantha showed the body flexibility of a contortionist. She was eventually receptive to Danny's best efforts, and when he did make it with Samantha, he found her an insatiable woman with powerful thighs, who gave him an experience to be remembered. With Jennifer feeling a bit neglected he did finally take a minor role to let him recover, while the two women maintained their familiar momentum towards relaxation together.

Finally they all fell apart and no one spoke for a while. Danny realised that the effects of the drink - which had carried him along to physical frenzy - was wearing off, and his addled brains started working again. He felt an aura of guilt and had uneasy feelings about what he had just been part of. The tingling sensation in his shoulders brought his beloved Mary to his mind again, and he just wanted away as soon as possible. Jennifer and Samantha were still recovering together as he collected his clothes in a bundle. They've finished with me, he thought to himself, perhaps Jennifer has this need to live the life of an outrageous celebrity and will always be in the news for good or bad reasons. Samantha was 'dangerously 'too good to be true'.

On reflection he concluded that Sex and temporary physical passion - alcohol assisted - came a poor second to that resulting from the experience and true pleasure he had found when making love to Mary. Their relationship had been a sexual wonder because they had worked together to make it so - in learning each other's feelings. He guessed that Mary would not have approved, if she had known of his mode. He wondered about the tingling in his shoulders. Was it a message? Was this a message from his beloved? Something was making him uneasy.

The two women would want him back for more when they were ready, no doubt, but was it for him? He wondered what Mary would think. And feeling a little guilty, thought, probably not. He should heed the strange feeling.

CHAPTER 18

The Sextet

H e heard nothing from Jennifer for some weeks, and then, just as he was beginning to forget the experiences, the postman delivered a written invitation to an evening meal for six people at a five-star country hotel - with rooms booked for overnight stay in the name of a 'Mr Ben Forset'.

The county town's auction rooms were owned by Ben Forset and his wife Helen, a prominent couple in the town. Those who knew them well were aware that their comfortable financial status made them want to live life to the full, with expansive and progressive views about staying young - which was not easy when involved in a dull profession amidst customers of older generations and small-minded wheelers and dealers. Their search for excitement or fulfilment had to come from something outside of business hours - from night clubs, casino rooms and expensive meals out.

Ben was a good talker - as would be expected from an auctioneer - but Helen was clearly looking for something more than just talk. She was a big, good-looking woman of thirty-nine years, with a full figure that she had kept in good shape. But for now, she had a pleasant amount of meat on the bone, a nice rounded bottom, and full breasts - that showed no signs of sagging - and a toned stomach and waist due to visits to massage and beauty parlours. All this effort though had left her clearly bored with the routine that Ben could offer. Ben too quietly fancied a bit of new young stuff, and if he could handle the sexual experience it would answer the questions in his mind.

They had money to spend and were keen to join Jennifer, Samantha, and her dark-skinned male partner, Akir, at the Casino, have a meal out and then enjoy drinks and overnight stay at the hotel. Danny was persuaded to make up the sextet. He succumbed to the temptation although guessing that he again might be 'playing the field' for pleasure. He realised that he had become starved of company in his daily work.

A good evening was had by all. They had plenty of food and strong drinks, with story-telling, jokes and the like. In Ben's mind was the idea that he might suggest a recently practiced game of partner swapping, which he did. The ladies expressed surprise, but Danny felt that this had been planned beforehand, and not just by Ben. It was Ben who really fancied bedding Jennifer or Samantha, while Helen's desire for the new experience of a younger man's prowess would also be fulfilled; by him!

By now Danny was in an impulsive alcohol-influenced mood, easy with anything a woman could offer, and couldn't care whether the draw was fixed so that Helen could get what she wanted. So the plan was Jennifer and Akir, Ben and Samantha, and Helen and Danny. Their overnight cases were brought in, and with more ribald remarks about being careful, each couple retired to their rooms with a bottle of vodka to lubricate the exchanges.

Helen had been on a very friendly and talkative high all night, and when Danny hinted that she did not have to go through with it, she did not conceal that she thought she had made a good draw and was up for it with no pretences. The Vodka bottle was cracked open, and with glass in hand, she revealed that Ben was in a rut - work being his main pleasure - and that he just turned to her when he very occasionally wanted sexual gratification for himself. "So let's get started, if you're up for it!" she said, standing in the middle of the room with arms and glass raised and legs slightly apart. "I want you to undress me, Danny, slowly and carefully, with you enjoying it as much as I will standing before you. Remember, this is going to be the best sex I have had since before I got married. I've been secretly told how good you are. We are going to be really good together"

With the lights dimmed, Danny started doing what she wanted. He removed her silk blouse and then her bra as she stood still, with eyes closed in enjoyment of this, and the knowledge that her breasts were still proud and showing a natural uplift. She pressed them against him now, her lips seeking his as she encouraged the removal of her skirt and underslip. She started to unfasten his belt and zip to drop his trousers.

This was as far as she got in the undressing stakes. Danny had taken over now. He would be in control of proceedings. With both hands on her firm and rounded buttocks he pushed her back to the bedroom wall. She felt his arousal and he felt her pushing against him and knew that she was the' eager beaver'. She became almost hysterical very quickly and nearly out of her mind with the feel of the deep, deep movement within her. He just gave her what she wanted - the lasting and best experience she had ever had. He felt her climax and continued afterwards until he thought that her legs might be collapsing under her in the ecstasy she was loudly voicing. He immediately lifted her up and lowered her on the bed, expecting that she would want time to recover, but was surprised when she rolled onto him, her mind in wonderland at the experience, and prepared for more!

She had changed in next to no time from a confident woman just wanting some fun and variety, to a mind-boggling female almost in disbelief about the experience she had just had. She'd had no idea who she really was until now, and would never be the same partner again. She was already seeking to relive the most satisfying sexual moments of her life, and Danny was required to prove that she was not dreaming.

In the next bedroom to them Samantha and Ben could not avoid hearing Helen's ecstatic outbursts and the solid banging against the partition wall. They lay in bed after their encounter, which was treated understandingly by Samantha, whose consideration was the pleasure she could give to her partner for the night despite the distractions.

Of the sextet Samantha was embarrassed, Ben annoyed, Jennifer relaxed, Akir thrilled and proud, Danny pleasantly moved, and Helen very very moved -- and now reflecting on her whole life in the light of what she had just experienced.

Danny, however, was not very pleased with the implications of the night. He again recalled his loss of the loving relationship he had experienced with Mary, and if he was ever to find it again with someone, this screwing around had to stop. The experiences from these encounters certainly added to Danny's education. The advent of the contraceptive pill seemed to have changed the modern woman's role in love-making from passive to proactive. From 'Should I let him?' to 'I'll make sure I have him'. If he thought that his education was complete though, he was wrong - he still had to learn that men's attraction to women would always accompany them. To the grave, and maybe beyond.

Only Ben and Helen made the breakfast room; the others left a variety of messages excusing themselves. The two were quiet, reflecting on whether they had done the right thing to agree to their secret, selfish sexual desires being met outside of their marriage. They both knew that after last night, through the 80's life was about to change for both of them. The past ways of living were the past. The future was going to be different, because they were different. But just how different was the unknown factor.

And what of Danny's future?

An emotionally battered Danny sought to work on the farm to rest his mind and body. His mother sensed that he was in some turmoil when she called to see him. She talked to him about her own experiences: the loss of her husband and Danny's father; how she came to terms with just the memories of him; how every day as you grow older your memories become part of your living time more and more. She recalled both pleasures and heartaches. Out of all the memories she had, she said, the memories of the good times of their marriage were the ones that still made her happiest, and Danny's memories of good times with Mary should be recalled with happiness too, and never be forgotten, illicit as they may have been to begin wit.

CHAPTER 19

Julie's arrival on the scene

No more trips over the county border for Danny. His response to invitations was that he was too busy. He did accept a couple of invites from the Hunting crowd. The first was a social evening where he again was part of a group which included Julie - who he found to be a picture of beauty and refinement, but rather awkward, shy and reserved … and she seemed to be keeping her distance from him. She appeared to be consumed with horse riding, training and breeding. She had a lot to learn about the lifestyle that he experienced or, about maturing, and much patience would be needed. Danny realised he would have to buy a horse to be part of the hunt crowd; and perhaps see more of Julie!

The fox hunt saw Julie riding a fine mare of some fifteen-hands, appropriately named High and Mighty. She cut a fine figure herself in her well-tailored red jacket and jodhpurs. Danny was just a spectator with the usual glass of sherry when the hunt returned, flushed with the thrill of the chase. Julie intended to dismount. She was sitting side-saddle, and as he was near, she started sliding down from the horse towards him. Danny put out his arms to catch her and she landed high in them and slid gradually down his front. His arms travelled the length of her body until she was on her feet – and was feeling embarrassed at the close contact. He had instinctively prolonged the tight physical contact, as any man would do with a woman he fancied, but he was surprised and excited about the surge of interest in this innocent, and as yet, untouchable girl. The bud of adolescence was moving towards full bloom. Her rueful half smiles and widened eyes conveyed to him what she was thinking and aroused anticipation that there might be something between them. And then it dawned on him. This was the grown-up version of the little girl that he had seen with her nurses many years ago, in the distant past when, as a youth, he used to deliver the morning milk at the country estate. Did she know of their past?

Could he be the one to take Julie to physical, mental and sexual maturity? Danny had past experience, as she knew, but now he might bring her pleasure by being the teacher!

Could he patiently watch and help her to grow up and develop a loving relationship, at her speed, and make it a lasting one with their complete trust in each other? He had 'flown his kite', but now he might be visually undressing her. And she didn't seem to mind!

Danny knew that he was ready for something long-term. He smiled and thought that it might be a case of 'horses for courses'!

Julie's breeding came through in her elegance and sophistication, and Danny recognised the barriers between the Manors family of landowners she came from, and the poor farm herdsman he represented to her parents. Danny decided that he could not be the initiator of any close relationship with Julie, and despite his keenness, could only react to any advances that came from her. This was a waiting game that he had to adopt with great patience, despite knowing there was a strong physical attraction between them.

However, she did seem to want to help him in buying a horse suited to his build and also to his riding inexperience. She talked easily to him about the horse's age, height, breeding and temperament, and the buying requisites and regulations. She offered to go with him to look at a horse and tipped him about seeing how it reacted to being saddled, bridled and groomed. And so, when they arrived to see it, already saddled for riding, she was suspicious. She politely confided to him that she could tell the horse was better in the company of geldings rather than mares, probably had an unreliable temperament and was therefore not very suitable for mixing with other horses or inexperienced riders.

Eventually it was proposed that a horse from The Manors' stables was the best buy for Danny. This gave Julie's parents the excuse to meet him and ask some leading questions of him. They knew that their only daughter was sweet on him and were concerned, but hoped that it was just a passing phase and that Julie would 'move on' and find a partner of similar breeding, stature and financial resources. The parents were learning that their control over their daughter's life was loosening by the day, as her own activities widened.

Danny was a quick learner once he and the horse got to know each other. Following Julie's demonstrations of her equestrian skills, he soon mastered the straight-backed riding posture, with feet and legs taking his weight. She briefed him on squeezing with the lower legs, sitting and rising at the trot, and when she said, "It's hips forward with gentle thrusting movements," her eyes met his with perhaps the tiniest hint of a knowing smile as to what he was thinking about. This was progress for Danny indeed. And so their friendship developed in a natural way, but both aware of the physical attraction between them, and of her parents' disapproval of him.

Julie was selected as travelling reserve for the county junior two-day eventing team. The three team riders all had a partner to assist them with the transport and logistics to the competition. Danny was surprised at being asked to help her on the trip. It was almost as if it was to' cock a snook' at her parents. It was an onerous task ensuring that all that was needed by horse and rider was packed into the Land Rover and horse box. For Danny, driving the Land Rover with trailer attached, required his concentration. For Julie it all seemed to be an exciting adventure. She was on a 'high', chatting away unreservedly with a youthful innocence. The miles rolled by, and with them came easy, relaxed familiarity. Danny was secretly amazed at the feeling that her close presence and young beauty was having on him. She was like a delicate spring flower, the fragrant petals of which he must not disturb!

Once the horse had been stabled on the site, they went to see about their Hotel rooms, which had been booked ahead by the competition committee, only to find that one twin-bedded room had been reserved for the two of them. Danny asked for another room straight away, but all were booked up.

Julie did not bat an eyelid as she said, "Don't worry, we'll manage." He protested, but she just added, "Danny, it's alright, I trust you implicitly." He knew that her heart was pounding!

"Julie, thanks, but I am not so sure that I trust myself," Danny admitted.

"Oh, come on, let's get on. It's late and we're going to miss our meal," she answered.

What a quandary for Danny. The other couples were partners on the same game and would know and assume things. Also, Julie's parents were thinking of coming to the event tomorrow if Julie was required to compete! Did she know what the 'room share' could bring?

The introductions and the meal and drinks went off all right, with the conversation all about horses and eventing skills. Not a word was said about the accommodation arrangements, but the other couples were undoubtedly familiar with each other and comfortable about their rooms.

The time for early retirement had arrived. The other couples left first. The two of them then quietly walked the hotel corridor to the door of their room. Danny had to open and close it behind them, and then they were strangely alone, but together, and nervous about it. Julie had now gone very quiet. Danny had to say or do something to break the silence.

"Julie, look I'll sit on the balcony for a bit, you use the bathroom first."

Julie didn't say a word but crossed the room, toilet bag and night-ware in hand. It was as if she were dreaming! Danny thought to himself that it looked like an old-fashioned honeymoon scenario. She would soon be in bed waiting for him to come out of the bathroom. Was she waiting for him to join her between the sheets? The teaser was the other twin-bed! And she was leaving the decision to him. What could he do? He had sworn that he would not risk making any advances because of his extra maturity, what people would suggest of him, and their different experiences and backgrounds … and many more factors! It was a win-but-no-win situation. But what was she expecting of him?

He undressed in the bathroom, but kept his pants on, and entered the bedroom. He hoped that she maybe would have turned away and feigned sleep, but she was sitting up in bed, still quiet and looking nervously at him. He knew then that he dare not make any move which might completely spoil their developing relationship or send it down some uncontrollable path, but the temptation was overwhelming him. And then he again felt the same tingling sensation in his shoulders. Someone somewhere was disapproving and cautioning him!

He took a deep breath. "Julie, you look absolutely wonderful. I am falling in love with you and it is crucifying me to not be able to slide in beside you, but I want to love you in circumstances different to this. Please let me just hold you and kiss you, and then you must push me away because I am likely to lose all reason."

He bent over her and held her and they experienced their first real and prolonged kiss. To them both it was something new and wonderfully different. He felt the heat of her body under the silken nightdress and could see her pale, blue-bloodied complexion, the binary nature of her temperament, and his bare chest and shoulders in her arms. Thankfully Julie did seem to hesitate a little about the next natural pleasure and response and he quickly took the hint, withdrew from her arms, and retired to the sheets of other twin-bed.

Longing prevented sleep for them both. Two bodies were lying within five feet of one another, each warm and inviting, but two minds and trains of thought were uncertain and fearful of spoiling everything between them. Julie had seen Danny's form, and they both knew that one word of encouragement from either and 'it' would happen. His arm had brushed her breast and her body ached for him but she didn't know how to handle it. Danny guessed that she was afraid of the unknown, the intimacy, and future implications. And what if her parents showed up?

Sleep finally came to them and Danny woke early, as was his habit. He quietly dressed, studied Julie's sleeping form, and then slipped out to feed and groom the horse. All the other team riders and horses were present and fit to compete so that the reserve was not going to be needed.

When he returned Julie had just finished dressing and was on the phone to her parents.

"No, you don't need to come, I'm not needed, I'll be home later," she said.

"How do you know you're not needed?" Danny asked.

"I don't, but I have to stop them coming! You know what they will think and the trouble they will cause for us. Let's have breakfast, get packed and loaded before we exercise and load High and Mighty. I don't want to stay and just watch the eventing." As they left Danny looked back at the shared bedroom. And then at Julie. Their eyes met and their thoughts coincided. An unforgettable experience!

The aftermath of the shared room was that the experience and the prolonged kiss had brought them closer together. Now deference was removed. Danny encouraged touching, holding hands, hips nudging together, arms linked or the odd quick squeeze or peck on the cheek were natural to them. This was clear for all to see, but the raging desire for more they tried to hide.

Julie's parents saw the change straight away. She had fallen for this young farmer - who had plenty of known history - and it was now looking rather more than a passing phase. In fact, it was looking very serious. On quizzing their daughter, Julie denied that any thing had gone on, or was going on, and defiantly said, "it's Danny who is conscientiously holding back."

Mrs Manors was shocked by these words. "Well your father will have to talk to him. You are going to regret all this later!"

"Mr Ross, will you call for afternoon tea this Sunday?" Julie's father addressed Danny on the phone.

Danny guessed what sort of inquisition he was in for, and was not looking forward to it, but he was now very clear in his own mind what he wanted. And that was Julie. And Julie had fallen in love. Mr Manors did not quite start the questions with, "What are your intentions towards my daughter?" but he might as well have done. His questions were about Danny's past and upbringing, how he ended up with owning the farm, his finances, his prospects, his ambitions and the like.

Danny found some of their questions objectionable, and when they asked about his intentions, he felt like asking if they meant towards the horse he had bought or toward their daughter. He then realised that having their horse was not the same as having their daughter. They were trying to discourage him by discreetly mentioning the differences in age and experience between Julie and 'the self-made young farmer who had previously seduced the wife of another man'. He was beginning to lose his cool and pointed out that the true story of his previous relationship with his beloved Mary was known only to him and her. Their love and his ultimate loss on losing her was immense and eternal.

Anything between him and Julie would be only at Julie's wish.

Danny was proud of his mother and father and their lifestyle and his own upbringing. He told of his time at college and then his arrival at the farm as a temporary herdsman, what he found there, and what he had to do to work-wise.

He talked about his eventual love for Mary and their developing relationship, which was based on the hard work, the planning to rectify the farm's problems, pulling together as a team, and the successes. This was the catalyst for their love and respect for each other, and overcoming Mary's marriage to an absent, no good, dishonest and lazy man. He did not conceal his absolute love for Mary, or his devastating loss at her death, or the apparent reasons for her changing her will with everything good before them. Only at her death did he know that she had done this.

And as for Julie, Danny said that the apparent differences in their situations, maturity and experience seemed to him to be disappearing over time and them getting to know one another. He respected and understood her vulnerability and had tried to give her time and space of her own. However, their love and physical attraction had let them see that the past and the differences in their lives up to now would not be important when and if their relationship continued to grow.

Mr Manors was impressed. But now he had to try to tell his wife how his attitude towards Danny was changing. He warned Danny that Mrs Manors would create trouble for him. She was a bit of an old-fashioned prude and had restricted her daughter's development and knowledge of the ways of life. He actually confessed that his wife had almost forgotten that their own marriage undertaking in their youth included consummation of, and fulfilment of, the marriage rights. He was surprised to hear himself discussing his own marriage with this young man - who had impressed him with his openness and honesty - and confiding that his love-making with his wife had long ago seen her treating it as an obligation, and because of this, a turn-off for him.

But she was still expecting her only daughter to marry in pure virginal white, to a high-ranking man of substance!

Danny knew that he had been right to not risk anything that might lead to the loss of Julie's chastity. She had so much to learn, and this would have to be recognised with the gradual, understanding, learning process of love, patience and care - at the right time. But if Mrs Manors wishes were to be met, then an early marriage was essential for the couple who just could not wait much longer in resisting nature's instincts!

After the exchanges between father and mother, Julie's mother's influence gradually, was diminishing and she had to recognise the situation even if she did not like it.

Danny and Julie were already looking for a suitably expensive engagement ring. Julie was happy, eager, and filled with emotion at the thought of marriage at an early date.

The posh wedding had been quickly arranged; guests invited from all walks of life. It was as if the whole ceremony and reception was for Julie's parents' benefit. Mr Manors proudly led his lovely daughter down the aisle; his wife enjoyed the prestige and the necessary publicity, but still worried about the suitability of the union. The prestigious guests seemed comfortable. No drunken best man's speech and only very subtle hints and jokes about the couple's 'first night'. Danny's words were in gratitude and assurance to all present.

The secret honeymoon hotel and wedding night was for Julie's and Danny's benefit. They were finally alone and together with no restrictions in discovering one another and the ways to Utopia. Danny treated his bride's initiation with the utmost tenderness and patience; both their longing and waiting ended with fulfilment and gentle and loving care. The couple patiently beginning to seek out what their partner enjoyed and what culminated in ecstasy. The groom's past experiences had impressed on him that his consideration of what was right for his partner's enjoyment and fulfilment was paramount in sexual satisfaction for them both. He was now the tutor; she the learner who trusted him to show her the way to the maximum pleasure and fulfilment that was to be part of their happy marriage and all that now went with it.

CHAPTER **20**

Fifteen Years On

The passage of time through the 80's continued to change the world and the people within it; but some characters memories prevailed, even in Yorkshire Dales communities!

Julie's parent's estate and Danny's farming and stabling facility both demanded full-time attention and meant that the couple were both kept busy in different directions, but when Julie became pregnant within twelve months of their wedding day it meant that changes in their relationship were inevitable. Julie became a full-time mother and they did not get a lot of time to be alone. As soon as daughter Marion started to grow into a little girl rather than a baby, then their second child – a son named Johnny - arrived. That was at the same time that Liam and Martha, who played a big part in their farming workforce, also became parents to Shaun.

With these pressures - ageing parents, expanding farm and stabling work, and two children to bring up - time flashed by, and the youngsters, with their fathers exuberance, continued to be a real handful as they reached teenage.

As each year went by Danny never forgot his past times. This particular day, as in every year, was his 'Remembrance Day' - an anniversary of Mary's tragic accident. On this anniversary, Danny stood in the farm yard quietly and privately remembering. He walked over to the small copse where he had scattered Mary's ashes so many years ago, and stood next to the cedar tree he had then planted. The blue bells were out in full bloom and overcome with emotion, Danny wiped his eyes. His thoughts were of the country life with Mary. Their love making and the synergies from it. His memories and their rapturous times, were still there; but also his earlier sexual encounters and relationships. And the necessary farmwork was essential.

He always reminisced about his innocent teenage days, and his initiation with the desirable Charlotte - the feel of her firm breasts through the white silk blouse and then her thighs through the silk skirt. After all these years Danny still felt a lot of gratitude for Charlotte and his first time. Then there was his College life, with Little Mo and her claimed desire to lose her virginity. He knew that Maureen was now a qualified vet in partnership with her husband over in Lancashire.

It had been a fast-developing world of women's contraceptive assisted freedom. Naughty wife swapping parties had become the norm, and Jennifer, Samantha, the Forsets and the like, had made his habitual desire for sex easy to fulfil – with his female partners satisfied. He had heard that Jennifer had remained in the public limelight as a celebrity good-time-girl who got involved in a scandalous affair with a footballer who was 'playing away'. Samantha still had a successful physiotherapy and massage business - which was advertised in Yorkshire Life magazine. Ben Forset had sold the auctioneering rooms and he and his wife were now constant global travellers seeking pleasures afar - memories of youth long gone!

For Danny, the time had flown by, but many memories remained, and a feeling of Mary watching over him and the successful business that they had worked together to create out of a rundown loss-maker. But few knew of the full impact her death (and that of his child) had had on his emotions and his way of life, and that for a time women and sexual relationships had been with a couldn't care less mind set. For Danny they were lonely, sad and reckless times of long gone. Many years of hard work and developing maturity had followed with Julie and their family.

And now Danny was an important man in the community of the village of Hilden Cross in the Yorkshire Dales. His wife Julie, likewise, had turned her 'silver spoon ' adolescence into being a good wife to Danny, a loving mother, and a figurehead in the village's increasing development and prosperity.

Danny was now the owner of Maple Dairy Farm as well as the adjacent Ross Horse Riding Stables and with his wife Julie and their children were held as an example for the villagers to follow. And, as Danny surveyed the wonderful countryside view from his property with some satisfaction, his summarising thoughts, were that everything was in place and going so smoothly.

But was he really happy with his life?

In the passing years he had been a loyal and considerate husband and father to two growing children. When he reflected on his life sensibly, he knew that he was fortunate to be happily married to a loyal wife who allowed him to make all the decisions with respect to whatever he thought best for them all-; except in 'her kitchen'. In addition, Danny and Julie had the trust of ageing in-laws in dealing with their demise and needs of the estate.

Julie was happy with her family, but for Danny, without new physical, mental, and sexual challenges, he was becoming somewhat stagnated. His impulsive ways and his sexual experiences were embedded in his character; he had certainly sowed some wild oats before settling down to courtship and marriage to Julie Manors - with all the benefits of being part of an influential family and their country estate.

However, the day-in, day-out routines of farming, with its milking machines, cows, udders, milk churns and milk marketing wagons, and cleaning out siphons and mending fences morning and night had lost its appeal once it was no longer a financial necessity. He had become complacent with a routine lacking challenges and risks. He was looking for some excitement. He was a man who did not believe that "whatever is; is right." It could always be changed! Secretly, he was disillusioned with farming graft and routines.

Julie dutifully fulfilled her part of a wife, and mother to their two children, and in what had become the routine of their sexual love lives, but seemed unwilling to introduce any variety or initiative of her own. Danny, sadly, was finding more sexual fulfilment fantasising about sex with Mary his first love, rather than with his wife.

Julie had been brought up with a silver spoon in her mouth, but with her mother's thumb pressed down on her to protect her vulnerability, thus stifling the development of a little wildness in her character and personality- which was probably unknown, even to herself. Her sexual experience was with Danny alone and he was aware that she retained some shyness and modesty. She nearly always acquiesced to Danny's need, but really with very little eagerness, and all she could bring to the party was something that he had taught her.

'Come on! Fight me, resist me, hurt me!' Danny once said to her in the bedroom, but her demure seemed to prevent her from letting go. It seemed that what was more important to her were her children, and then her 'untouchable lady' image in figure-hugging riding gear – the full outfit with jodhpur breeches with the classic half-cut seat, inner thigh padding and zip closure. Under her tailored riding jacket with its velvet collar, were pull-on Long Johns, seam-free briefs, and anti-bounce bra. Julie's imposing figure astride her hunter was taken for granted by Danny now, and maybe to him she was just beginning to look a touch'aloof'.

Sometimes he felt he would have loved to have passionately and roughly ripped each item of clothing from her, break down her modesty, expose her nakedness, and overcome her reticence, but he guessed that the repercussions of his wife's shock and dismay at such actions would be detrimental to her, and possibly their comfortable marriage. They didn't talk much these days, probably because each of their daily priorities were unimportant to the other.

Expansion of the estate kept Danny fairly busy, but his long-standing ambitions were now wrapped up in horses and racing. He was developing a stabling, riding and training business for hunters, hurdlers and race horses on the flat, and was interested in their breeding. He had succeeded in getting his licence to train, and was beginning to gain inspiration by events on the racing scene and the people involved.

The horse racing business took his mind away from predictable routines and into a world of new discoveries, costly but new lessons, and excitement in abundance. People of all backgrounds - from those 'up to no good', through to aristocracy, and everything in between – were involved, and race tracks were alive with colour and every emotion born of failure, love, greed, hope, expectation, success, and more.

CHAPTER **21**

Lady Sylvia Scerton

anny's ambition was to rub shoulders with famous trainers such as Henry Cecil, Sir Michael Stoute, Dick Hern on the flat, or McCain, Pipe, and Henderson over jumps. With this in mind he was desperate to develop his stabling and training facilities and the standard of the racehorses in his care. This ambition would obviously be jeopardised by any unfaithfulness or destabilising of the family bonds and the finances he needed from that source.

However, Danny had heard on the racing grapevine that a local, well-known rich lady owner of race horses - Mrs Sylvia Scerton - was seeking a trainer for Highlight, a three-year-old filly of excellent breeding. (A Group 2 winning stallion called Edson, and out of Angelis, an already successful mare.) The horse was broken in and trained ready for the flat race track. He had been told that Mrs Scerton was somewhat of an enigma in that, for an aristocrat of culture and breeding, she had a reputation of being a bit of a 'wild card'. She used several different trainers, but the tittle-tattle was that she was disenchanted with the performance of one in particular John Calloway who trained near Newmarket. Danny had difficulty in believing the rumour that she had wanted more than just training her filly. He had casually met 'Lady' Sylvia at York Races and from a distance she looked a beautiful lady full of character and personality. She seemed to Danny to be a confident lady when he met her; they both had horses entered on the same race programme. On the last occasion, over a cup of coffee in the owners and trainers stands, she had asked to be introduced properly to him and had been quite forward and enticing. When she invited him to call on her and to 'have a ride' with her, Danny's imagination ran riot. Did she mean just on the horse, he wondered, because he guessed that she wanted some excitement injecting into her life and this was what was getting her 'talked about'. Rumour had it that her late husband, Lord Scerton, had suffered from cancer, which ultimately had led to his early demise - leaving a rich, sensuous, unfulfilled lady. Affluence was not providing her with the pleasures of sex. She wanted the excitement that a man like Danny could bring, along with the calm after relaxation, instead of the harrowing, lonely, disturbed, sleepless nights.

A business proposition for training Highlight was presented by Lady Sylvia, and it appealed to Danny as he had vacant stabling to fill, but unbeknown to his wife Julie, the stabling and training business was now being heavily subsidised by the other farm activities. Danny found the excitement he was looking for in the racing business, with the accompanying travels to various tracks, and the gambling and gathering of inside information as part of the socialising. He imagined himself as a potentially successful and famous racehorse trainer.

At first his better judgement was to decline any proposition for fear that the rumours about Sylvia's undoubted affluence, erratic lifestyle and desirability would promote gossip which she did not seem to care about. But his own frustrations and yearning for some excitement in his life were instrumental in him agreeing to take her business proposition further, and he agreed to meet to assess the filly's physique, potential, temperament, fitness, breeding history and the like. This meant a visit to the Manor House, farm and stables to see the horse that Sylvia had brought home from Newmarket.

Danny drove in through the arched gateway and made his way up the long drive to the impressive house. He gazed admiringly at the orderly yard and stabling block; the good housekeeping was obvious by the tidiness. He rang the doorbell, and Lady Scerton quickly opened the door and welcomed him into the living room with both a hand shake and a peck on the cheek - as if they were old friends. Sylvia was looking forward to Danny's visit. She was starved of intimate relations with younger men and saw this as a chance. She had taken great care with her image and had dressed especially for him.

Close up Danny became intensely aware of her beauty. Unlike their meetings at the races - when she was well-dressed in a practical country sporting rig out - she was now in a sophisticated, figure-hugging flowered dress - which was obviously expensive designer-wear. Jewellery was in abundance: diamond rings and diamond-edged watch, but more noticeable was the necklace dangling down into a very low and revealing cleavage. Danny thought that perhaps she was going out to some expensive function, but she appeared to be in no rush to show Danny the three-year-old filly he might be allowed to train. He was invited to relax on a deep-seated settee, and she proffered a sherry with the comment that her housekeeper was 'out for the day'. She asked if Danny was comfortable, offered him a cushion 'so that we can have a really good chat'. She refilled his glass. She is pampering me, Danny thought, she would literally breast feed me if she could … He wondered if there was a 'catch'. She obviously wanted to know more about him, and her questions were clearly meant to get him to open up - but Danny was sure she was asking questions she already knew the answers to. He tried to keep his mind on why he was there: his horse breeding and training ambitions, but when she 'innocently' leaned over him, he was suddenly aware of the perfume she was wearing.

"Have you any runners at the Uttoxeter meeting next week?" she asked him. It was as though he had a large string of horses in training such that he had regular entries in the imminent racing programme. In fact, he had just two entries over the next three weeks from his four horses in training. She probably knew that too, he thought, but she was talking to him as though he was on the same footing as she was - with several horses with other trainers ready to run, and one or two prospective winners amongst them. He felt that Sylvia was doing this so that he might feel confident and above his real status. It really was the first stages towards seduction, and Danny - who was now no novice at dealing with female wiles, but not used to aristocracy – knew that he must be careful … or was he getting the 'wrong end of the stick'? He was here for business after all. But when she used the phrase '…" if she was satisfied that he could perform" the hairs on the back off his neck stood up. He responded by asking if he could have a 'close look at the filly in question to assess her fitness and attitude'. His response accidently revealed what he was thinking about; and at this moment it was not the horse. Was it his mind, or were they now both thinking the same intimate thoughts? When she knew that he was 'attracted' to her she broke off any intimacy by reaching for her telephone and asking her stable master to collect Danny and show him the set-up and in particular, walk out Highlight the filly in Box 3. She asked that Danny think about terms and a training programme to fulfil the potential that the horse's High breeding line implied, and inform her in writing about charges and suggested training routines and reports. He left the well-bred Lady Scerton and went to see the well-bred filly.

He observed that the filly looked top-class - in keeping with her blood line. She was a well-proportioned developing horse, with a look of intelligence and alertness about her. He had never seen a young horse with eyes that seemed to emit quite such a kind of alert yet telling look in them, and such a burning intensity. As with the owner, maybe, her horse had an intense but vulnerable double character as well. Left alone together, he stroked the horse and felt for a very slow, steady heartbeat. As he was about to move away the horse tossed her head and poked his arm with her nose as if to say 'don't stop'. He was strangely moved by the horse's action, it was as though they were old friends, and he could not fathom the uncertainty in his mind. And then he felt a tingling sensation in his shoulders; it was the sensation he had felt at other times in the past when something important to his future was imminent. He believed that his beloved Mary was trying to warn him from above. He badly wanted the stabling and training business at his yard, yet some premonition made him unsure. He wanted time to think about both Highlight and Mrs Scerton, and he avoided becoming entangled with Sylvia again by explaining to the stable master that he had other business to deal with that morning. "Thank Lady Scerton for her hospitality, and say that I'll be in touch," he said as he left.

He delayed in sending his quotation and terms in writing to Lady Sylvia, despite his need of the stabling for income and positive cash flow - and a new quality horse for his stables.

No contact was made until they met again at the Beverley race meeting. He approached her, intending to wish her luck with the horse she had running in the first race, in which he also had a running declaration - a novice maiden filly which he was training for a syndicate of local solicitors. This time he did not find her demure and sophisticated, but slightly drunk and boisterous, with a tall and seemingly aggressive male companion clinging to her, trying to touch her. Danny didn't like the looks of this guy. Was he an associate of John Calloway, who had been employed as the horse's current trainer? He walked away. Time would tell.

"Who's the guy with Lady Scerton?" Danny asked one of the other owners in the ring.

"That's Shane Kerne; he's a bad egg," was the reply.

"Why? What's his business" Danny asked.

"Keep away from him, Danny, he's bad news"

Sylvia was accepting this man's familiarity as though she knew him well and was being guided by his instructions. Danny backed off and decided to watch the race from the stands where he could also see on the wide TV screen how his own horse was travelling. He was pleased with the run into fourth place, confirming what he had seen of the horse's progress made on the gallops. Sylvia's entry – Highlight - finished well down the field, not showing any of her previous form. Danny next saw Sylvia in the unsaddling yard, putting on a show of disappointment, criticising both her trainer and the form of the jockey booked for the race.

She saw Danny and she spoke loudly to him in an alcohol fuelled manner in the hearing of her trainer, her companion, and the entire group of owners present in the enclosure. "Mr Ross. I haven't had your quotation and programme for Highlight yet. You know that I want to put some of my horses with you. I would like your invitation to visit Ross Stables as soon as possible."

Danny only gave a nod of acknowledgement and hoped she realised that this was not the time or place to respond. His lack of enthusiasm with the attention that Mrs Scerton, and those with her, was creating, was interpreted as showing his disapproval. He could tell that the tough-looking guy was asking her about him and her exchanges with him. Was he a suitor, or a mentor who was a little curious or jealous of her exchanges with him? But then he wondered what had made him think that?

While driving his horse box on the way home, Danny's mind was in a quandary. He started to think about both his financial problems with Julies' purse strings on the stables, and about what Lady Scerton could do to solve these with a good fee and maybe a share of potential winnings from an undoubtedly well-bred filly. Both females would need the right handling, but he was confident that he could improve them both with the right care and attention. Would there be adventure and excitement on the way to success and achievement with an intimate experience thrown in? But what was the downside? Where did Shane Kerne fit in? Why had he taken an immediate dislike of him? The journey home passed in next to no time. He parked the horse box, bedded down his horse with a pat and feed for her good performance, and went to the house. As he expected Julie had not waited up for him to enquire how his day had gone; she was asleep tucked in on her side of the bed ... and clearly not to be disturbed at that late hour.

Danny was up and dressed early the next morning. Whilst making coffee his mind was planning the day's routine and programme for each horse, and what to get his stable staff to work on. The mixed bag of horses he had stabled with him 'highlighted' the need for better quality, well-bred racers and less social hacks. An omen perhaps?

He checked his phone for messages. He had one recorded message from 6:40 that morning. There were no introductions, just:

'I'm coming over to look at your place today since you haven't invited me, and since you haven't agreed to take my money with a contract to train Highlight. If I like what I see I am prepared to give you complete control of Highlight's training and racing activities, but I want to be involved so that we both get maximum enjoyment from any investment I make' … Sylvia Scerton.

He had another message from even earlier – from a phone number he did not recognise - again no introduction: "Just a warning to you. Keep clear of Mrs Scerton and her horse. Don't bite off more than you can swallow because you will certainly regret it. Take heed and be warned, or else we can ruin you.."

Danny wondered what was going on! Out in the yard and in deep thought, Danny immediately noticed a car coming up the lane towards the stables. His heart missed a beat as he saw it was a white Jaguar saloon - he knew straight away that it was Sylvia here to 'vet 'his set up. Compared with her stables she would at the best think it small and unpretentious. He had never advertised for business, preferring to rely on locals and word-of-mouth recommendations through friends. He had always thought it would be nice to call it a 'boutique' stabling and training facility - 'boutique' as per the dictionary: 'Small, but expert and skilled to success'.

He stood nearby as she slid graciously out of the car; long legs first, and then a short skirt that permitted him a peak at shapely calves and ankles and expensive high-heeled shoes. She stood up - as tall as him in the heels - a mature and beautiful woman in an immaculate outfit. The boisterous character he had witnessed at Beverley had gone. In its place was a quietly confident and elegant lady. Danny was overawed and now a bit nervous with her as they walked round. He wondered what she thought of him and his yard. If she was a little embarrassed at his modest training facilities, horse walker, trotting ring and gallops, she did not show it or linger on it as she produced a large envelope. Graciously thanking him she said, "Here Danny, I want you to read this. It's a draft contract over eighteen months. You enter the monthly upkeep charges you need for the horse to cover its training and medical needs."

Danny tentatively asked, "How does £5,000 a month sound?"

She immediately replied, "No, I'd double that. I don't want us scraping around in our days together."

What could impulsive Danny say? He signed the contract without further thought.

Sylvia said "You will get the down payment and the first monthly cheque tomorrow. Highlight is entered to run at Windsor's evening meeting in three days' time. If you'll come down we could stay the night and get to know each other better. I will be interested in what you think of the horse, and perhaps make some plans for her."

CHAPTER **22**

Highlight's Windsor Run

Danny wished he could have had more time with the horse before signing the contract, and even to let Highlight settle in at her new home. He wanted to get to know and evaluate the filly properly, but because of the generous contract, did not feel able to say no. Also, breaking the news to his wife was going to be difficult. Julie didn't usually take a lot of interest in Danny's racing days, but the news would have to be followed by him telling her that he needed to be away from home for two consecutive days.

He went in for breakfast, expecting Julie to be engrossed in their children's school programmes and activities: Johnny's games day and Marion's exams, but she pushed the local newspaper towards him, folded to show a small article on the sports page:

'Lady Sylvia Scerton has enlisted Danny Ross to train the three-year-old filly, Highlight, that she bought for 40,000 guineas as a yearling at the Irish sales. She said that she hoped that this may be the start of a growing business relationship with the small Yorkshire stables.

Surprised and embarrassed, Danny said, "It was only signed up yesterday. I was just going to tell you. It's valuable income for the stabling and it'll be the best horse in our yard. I have to go to Windsor to see her run."

Julie was quick to respond. "What about the farm and the milk yields you were monitoring? I thought they were very important to you? You were going to go to see Liam and Martha at the farm. You know they need some help. Are you going to leave the farm and all this to me? Who says you have to go to Windsor?"

"Well, Lady Scerton wants my opinion on future entries for the horse. Liam, Martha and Shaun are in charge for now."

Julie grimaced but said nothing, and Danny quickly made some toast and changed the subject by asking about the kids. (Neither mentioned the fact that their son Johnny wanted to become a jockey.)

Danny journeyed alone down to the Windsor Evening meeting. Lady Scerton was being chauffeured in her white Jaguar by Connolly's boy - who had supposedly prepared the horse for the race. It was the last race of the evening and Danny was dawdling, trying to avoid too much of her company. He eventually met her in the saddling enclosure. She seemed concerned as to where he had been, and was pretty keen to see him. She looked fabulous. Sophisticated, understanding, interested in the horse's well-being, but disinclined to interfere in the preparations for the run, she was a highly desirable owner. When the runners were galloping down to the start, she came to him to seek his comments on Highlight. He had watched Highlight as she was being prepared for the race; he did not care for what he saw. The horse looked ill at ease, unsettled, perhaps even agitated, and the jockey looked as reluctant to mount as the horse did to race. He had casually put his hand on her to feel her heartbeat; it was racing. The horse seemed to be spooked. Danny could not understand Highlight's restlessness.

As they walked from the ring to the viewing enclosure, Sylvia casually linked her arm in his so that as they walked together it appeared that they were close partners. Danny felt quite proud and the couple did not go unnoticed by other owners, trainers and press. She stood out as an immaculate, beautiful woman in her prime, and she gave off an air of confidence, while also giving the impression of willing dependence on her man. Danny could not help feeling exhilarated by her closeness and the warmth of her on his arm, or with the envious glances. A knowing reporter - with a large, flash camera on his shoulder - approached wanting an interview with them about the horse and Silvia's new trainer. Danny brushed him off saying, "Not now. We have a horse running." The reporter backed off but not before he snapped them with a dazzling flash. Danny had seen this reporter near the horse earlier, and wondered if the flash had been used to unsettle Highlight. What was going on? Stable security was supposed to keep unauthorised personnel away from the horses!

Highlight seemed reluctant at the start of the race, losing ground on the others, but she made a good shot at getting into contention with two furlongs to go. However, she was unresponsive when the jockey started trying to ride her hard, losing by some 10 lengths down the field. A disappointing run, but Danny was not surprised - the horse was never there to win – its race was run long before the finishing post. Sylvia looked quite unconcerned.

"We're booked in at the Old House Hotel and I booked a table for 10 o'clock," Sylvia said. "Collect your car and I'll see you for dinner and we can talk."

He arrived at the hotel and checked the restaurant: Dinner for two booked for 10.15pm. He then checked in at Reception: He was booked in Room 11; Mrs Scerton? Room 10 …

He went up to the room. There was an adjoining door to room 10, which was unlocked. He cracked the door open and could hear Sylvia's shower running. He could just see a half-empty bottle of red wine on the table. He quickly pulled the adjoining door closed again.

He showered, but as he dressed, he started to feel a little uncomfortable at spending the evening in the company of Sylvia - and the dangers of any adverse publicity. But why? She had been a pleasant and very reasonable companion at the race, but thoughts of the reputation that she had, started his shoulder tingling. A premonition perhaps? What had he got himself into? Was he up for it? But what of his wife Julie and the kids?

The adjoining door opened and in marched Sylvia in a white towelling dressing gown - pulled together at the waist but opened enough to reveal a fair length of bare leg as she strode in, long hair still wet and brushed back from her face. "Oh, I thought I might have caught you in the shower," she said, laughing loudly. " Well, I'm sure that you're ready for a meal. It won't take me more than ten minutes to get dressed. I will see you in the bar. Get the drinks in." With that she walked straight out again through the adjoining door.

As Danny ordered two gin and tonics, his intuition told him that he would have a problem resisting any possible invitation that the open bedroom door inferred. Should he, or could he escape without losing the finance and support of this beautiful woman? Did he even want to? Never before had he experienced such a situation.

Sylvia entered the lounge looking fabulous in a shimmering and transparent silk blouse, a tight, short blue skirt and matching blue high-heeled shoes. She leaned over and kissed him as if it was the most natural thing on earth, and he just knew. Any holding back was pointless with the generous contract involved; and he finally relaxed - with the intention to enjoy the meal and anything that followed. The conversation over the meal was very amicable and Sylvia's choice of red wine was flowing by the bottle. When Danny went to the men's room, unbeknown to him, Sylvia slipped a tablet into both his and her own glass. This desperate means of gaining extra impetus and pleasure with her ailing husband had left her with this stimulating habit. With the combination of alcohol and the sexual intensity drug, out went any remaining reservations for them both, eventually leaving a couple desperate to make the journey as if the destination had never been reached before! They were soon keen to curtail the meal, the wine, and the chat about the horse, and head for the bedrooms - with a very intoxicated Sylvia clinging to him as if she was afraid he might disappear. The hotel corridor was very quiet, but a wine-influenced and drug-stimulated Danny heard Sylvia's words: "You're going to be good for me, Danny, aren't you. The fact is I badly need you. It's been so long since I had a real man that I'm going crazy." It was quite clear what was expected. So here goes!

At her bedroom door Danny swept her into his arms, pushed the door open with his foot, and carried her in. His alcohol-fuelled hands felt the warmth of her body. He sat her down on the edge of the bed, leaned over her, and roughly kissed her. With both hands he pulled the silken soft blouse up from her waist, expertly slipped the buttons, and massaged her full, heavy breasts and hardened nipples. She just had time to undo the waist button before he roughly pulled down her short skirt Then he pushed her legs apart and stood between them. He unbuttoned his trousers and let them drop to his feet and stepped out of them. She saw from his bulging pants that he was up for it. "I'm ready for you, Danny," she cried out. Feeling his forceful entry, she was thrilled with his deep thrusts and rhythm. She locked her legs around him to get every inch of him, as uninhibited she got closer to her climax. A frenzied Danny gasped at Sylvia's ploy, until they both surrendered in exhilarating completion. With a shudder he collapsed on top of her. They lay together, their hearts pounding. He pulled her onto her side so that they could face each other. There was no retribution, as they fell into a drunken and drugged sleep with just the sheet over them.

Danny was pleasantly dreaming, in his befuddled sleep, of female hands upon him. - something his wife Julie had seldom done lately. Then suddenly his befuddled brains realised that this was really happening, but the effect of the drugs left him mentally unable to waken. Sylvia was trying to manoeuvre herself for another ' five furlongs' with him. Danny, although still struggling to wake up properly, started to realise what was happening, but he was unable to resist. Sylvia's thoughts were about making the most of her chance. Her determined squeeze asked the question of him and his reactions answered it. He finally pushed her away exhausted and with a sudden fear of the likely repercussions that this night would bring. He rolled out of the bed they had shared, leaving her barely conscious, face down, and went back through the adjoining door to his room and dressed quickly. Then, still dazed and in a great panic, wrote a note on the memo pad for Sylvia to find: 'Had to leave. Needed urgently at home. Fault on the Horse Walking Mill. Accident danger'.

He knew that she was not going to be happy!

On the drive home he realised he was going to have to face terrible recriminations; he was going to be in trouble up to his eyeballs. In haste he decided to text the lady.

"That should not have happened. Don't send the horse. The deal's off."

About five miles further on the journey his mobile rang.

"Get a Life, Danny," Sylvia cried. "Get real. You know you loved it. Read the contract you signed. You made me a Happy Bunny! Thank you!"

As his head started to clear, Danny realised that he hadn't just been drunk, his drink had obviously been 'spiked' and this had clouded his thinking, making him act impulsively for enhanced pleasure, but removing sense or reason. As the after-effects started to wear off, he felt lethargic, mentally weary, and barely able to drive safely. He pulled off the road and put his head back. He slept for about three hours and awoke to be shocked at the passage of time and the realisation that Sylvia had drugged them both.

When he got home the first thing Danny did was to find the contract he had signed; he had pushed it under some files so that Julie would not see it. It was so long-winded and complex that he had to read it twice and make notes on his contractual responsibilities. With some dismay he looked at the list. In addition to the training and upkeep of the horse, as he expected, it appeared that the cost of the jockey's fees, getting the horse to the races, entry fees up to £2000 and keeping the owner fully-informed were his to meet! And the end of the list he had impulsively agreed and signed 'To undertake and to fulfil the owner's best interests, as defined at her discretion, for a period of two years'.

His head was in a spin! He now knew that he was playing with fire! If he withdrew, he would be burnt financially. If he met the contract's terms, his family life would be 'roasted' if this came out. What if someone was noticing their relationship! And what were the implications of the sinister warning voice on his mobile?

The kids were glad to see him when he got home, and he sat with them and asked them about their day. Julie was distant, as though she was sulking about his trip and leaving the farm management to Liam and Martha. He went to find Liam for an update on events.

Later, when he went to his office, he opened his computer and found an email from Sylvia. It was the reasonable and understanding Sylvia this time. She had obviously sobered up: 'Sorry if you're concerned about the hotel booking, and about the reporter nosing for info. I can be very discreet if you're worried. Owner/trainer relationships are common, and business successes follow. If we pass it off as a 'business arrangement', we don't have to hide things. Open a direct email link with me with a secure password. We can then 'talk' in private. Get the best out of the horse, Danny, and you get the best out of me as well!'

The next day, out of the blue, a horse box arrived, bringing not just Highlight, but another horse as well. The driver's instruction was to unload both.

He rang Mrs Scerton. "Two horses! What's this?" he demanded to know.

"See your emails," she replied. "I've sent you Madame Fatale. Highlight is more relaxed when she's with her. She's a good brood mare, but not in foal after being covered at

Harvandon stud by an expensive stallion, Hereldem. The costs for Madame Fatale are for my expense. I am also sending you another horse walker, so make room for it."

Danny shuddered. What could he do? He had space for the mare, but a new horse walking mill for equine exercise would have cost him a fortune.

Early the next morning Danny decided to muck out Highlight's box himself. He needed Highlight to get to know him and be comfortable with him. He talked to the horse all the time as he cleaned out, and gently touched her when he wanted to move her around the stall. He stroked her and held her head next to his, before reining and walking her out along with Madame Fatale. The two were obviously relaxed together, rubbing noses and shoulders as they walked. He wanted to let the horses relax and get used to the life at his stables. Plenty of horse walking was needed. The filly's poor performance - after showing good form earlier - was hard to understand, it could have been an off day, but with his own drug-induced evening still on his mind it suddenly struck him. Could Highlight have run above her peak on earlier occasions after being illegally treated? Could she then have been in a state of withdrawal, running poorly at Windsor. Some explanations were necessary about what he had got into now that the horse was his responsibility.

CHAPTER 23

Training Contract

D anny decided to ask Samuel Long, his veterinary surgeon, over to check the health of both horses, as was the routine followed with new horses to his stable. He did not mention his suspicions and waited in the yard for the preliminary verbal report as he would usually expect.

"The brood mares in good fettle and it looks like you have two good additions to your team, Danny," the vet said. "I'll send my full report to you tomorrow." He made no specific comment about Highlight, which left Danny wondering and in limbo.

That evening, Sam Long phoned him at home. "Danny, has Highlight been injured recently?" he asked.

"Not that I know of," Danny replied. "As you know I've only just taken her under my wing. What's the problem?"

"I found minute traces of an ephedrine-based compound in her bloods. I didn't want to put it in writing without talking to you first. As I am sure you know, ephedrine is a stimulant, and while it also helps a faster recovery from injury and is permitted in some situations, it is banned from use to enhance racing performance alone during the racing season. If you are thinking of racing her soon, then it would be wise to wait a bit so that it has cleared out of her system. Just what exact drug has been administered, or when, I don't know, but all sorts of derivatives of ephedrine and anabolic steroids are coming onto the market by the 'back door' as you might say. They're a bit like those reportedly used illegally by Olympic athletes."

"Well it's not come from my yard I can assure you. She's new to my stable. Don't send a report just yet, Sam. Give me time to try to find out more. I had felt that the horse was unsettled in some way before you looked at her. She has been lethargic on the gallops and nowhere near her previous racing form."

"Let's forget the tests I did this time. Leave it for a time and then I'll do an official test. I know that you would not get into this sort of business, and do have routine dope testing visits."

Danny did not want to believe that Sylvia Scerton would be foolish enough to be involved in a drugs racket, but got an answer fairly quickly. His mobile rang one evening, just as the night was closing in. It was the same sinister voice as in the previous recorded message:

'You'd better come out to your barn if you don't want it to go up in flames'.

The hairs stood up on Danny's neck. He locked the door behind him and crept forward in the shadow of the house. He picked up a hay fork on his way and moved slowly and quietly across the yard to the barn door. He pushed against it forcibly, and it opened with a bang, but then he stepped back a pace. Someone rushed forward expecting Danny to step in. There was a couple of seconds' delay as the intruder realised that Danny had not charged into the barn - it was all that Danny needed to act quickly. Instead of being backed into a corner by the two men he saw, he noticed that they were quite close together and a feint towards one of them was rapidly followed by a vicious swing of the heavy fork at the knees of the second one - who went down clutching what might well have been a broken knee cap. Danny then spun him round ending up behind him, the fork handle pulling in across the guys throat, holding him upright. The second man, a scarf over his mouth and a baseball bat in his hands, slammed the barn door shut with a kick and then turned to face Danny. It was a stand-off between just the two of them. Danny now backed into the corner, jerking his captor with him by the pressure on his throat. The second intruder, seeing the determination and lack of fear on Danny's face, realised that he had lost the initiative, backed off a bit and changed his attitude.

"Calm Down, calm down. No one needs to get hurt," he said. "We're just the messengers. Let him go and listen to me. We're here about the horse and be sure that you're listening. Okay? Are you listening? Our bosses have been following Highlight's career while they were at John Calloway's yard. Now that she's here we are going to ensure that she is properly looked after, especially when she is due to race. You don't need to know any more, only that you keep yourself and your people out of the way when we turn up to check the horse over. You just train, enter and run the horse as you normally would. Don't ask questions or get curious and everything will be fine. You don't have to do anything else. Bear in mind that that's not illegal for you. Your alternatives to complying would be bad news for you."

"You can get stuffed. It is illegal! You can't do that here. I'll have the police onto you. There's no way that you are going to get at my horses," Danny responded.

Kerne's man then said, "You'll be wise to keep quiet and go along with what you're told to do, otherwise things could get nasty for you and your family. Calloway found that out. Don't get out of your depth or you will regret it. We're only the messengers for the men who always get what they want. Take heed! And just so we understand each other, Just imagine what might happen if the brakes failed on your wife's car when she was taking your kids to school. And have no doubt that if things go wrong the Scerton woman will be exposed as having a 'doctored' horse take the prize money.

We'll be back when the time's right. We know what we are doing. Just think it through and act sensibly and we can all be quids in. Remember, my bosses can be vicious, and ruthless. Too powerful for you, mate. They can hurt you and your farm all ways. Let go of my mate and we leave quietly."

The man Danny had by the throat was choking and barely managed to limp away when the pressure on his throat was released.

Danny had to do some thinking. Crooks, drugs and stimulants had now impacted on his life. Where has all this come from? How could he keep this from his faithful wife Julie and protect the kids from it? She was sure to say "Go to the police," but he had to see Sylvia first and find out her side of the story and what explanations she had to offer.

He went back into the house, not mentioning the phone call, but told Julie, "I'm going to the village. I'll lock the door. Don't wait up if you want to go to bed and I'm late." He did not reveal where he was going, but drove off as slowly and quietly as he could, before hitting the accelerator on the road to the Scerton estate.

When she let him in, Lady Sylvia's face and tense manner gave her away, and her concerns at Danny's arrival and the determined look on his face were obvious.

"You know that what went on at the Windsor hotel was not right, don't you" Danny said. "My drink was spiked, and come to think of it, you were under the influence as well - and I think you were 'on something' on other occasions when I met you - like at Beverley for instance. This can't go on, contract or no contract, horses or no horses. If you don't start telling me the truth about the horse you sent me, then there's no way we can work together. I have just been threatened by Kerne's mob and all of my family are now in danger." He described what had just happened and finished by saying, "So come on, Sylvia, start talking."

Lady Sylvia was visibly shaken as he talked, and tears welled up in her eyes. She then broke down and cried freely. "Oh, Danny, I'm in a mess, please don't abandon me. I will tell you the whole story."

Her story poured out in between sobs which could not fail but to get Danny's sympathy.

"The drugs started because of my husband, at the start of his illness. As you know he was older than me, but I was happy and content until his cancer appeared and with it his anxiety to still have a normal relationship. When I discovered that he was on stimulants and that they sometimes helped us together, then I started to use them as well. But the last four years of my life with him gradually became purgatory for us both. We had money, an estate, riches and assets such that we could have done everything and gone everywhere. But we could do nothing, only watch and wait for his suffering and mine to gradually come to its inevitable end."

"On the day it was all over, at dusk, I was so relieved that I went out on the moor and shouted out over and over: 'I am free! I am free!' That sounds terrible, I know, but I knew that the years I had lost I had to make up for in full. My desire was to catch up on what I had been missing in every sense, the racing, the spending, the loving, everything, Danny. I had become desperate for company, for activity, and for a full life. Buying horses and the competing was the outlet for me. And then John Calloway came to me with the confession, the gambling syndicate, the bunch of thugs, the violence, the threats and trickery, and the blackmail. They forced their way into John's yard, beat him up and knee-capped him, doped Highlight with a drug stimulant to make her run faster, held John's daughter prisoner to make him run the horse in the race, and placed a massive bet on the colt and collected a fortune when Highlight won. Then they blackmailed John with threats of exposure if he 'squealed' and attempted to stop them doing the same again."

"Highlight was never able to perform with any consistency. When they suspected that John Calloway had split on them and the police might be investigating, I think they made him tell me to move my horse to another trainer. I didn't know all this at the time, and it was only when John saw that they had introduced themselves to me, and the danger he had put me in, that he confessed about what was happening and how it had turned him into a nervous and physical wreck. John is trying to move away with his family and has left someone in charge of selling the yard and moving the other Calloway horses. They're dangerous people, Danny, and criminally clever. They pretended that they were respectful city bankers wanting to enjoy the racing scene. They were polite to me and considerate, until they thought things might go wrong. But it was all a sham. They turned nasty and will now stop at nothing. I just don't know what they will do next! Shane Kerne is ruthless"

Sylvia had won Danny's sympathy, and she clung to him as though she was barely able to stand. "I need to lie down, Danny, I'm fainting!" she said. He carried her to her bedroom. "Don't leave me, Danny, I'm afraid of what I might do," she said, with fresh tears.

He lay with her on the bed, hoping that she would settle down. Half an hour passed and it seemed that she had fallen asleep. He was exhausted after all that he had been through and just couldn't keep awake. Half-asleep, he felt for her body to see if she was alright and still there sleeping, but when she moved closer to him it was as though they were under a spell again. She pressed her body to his. Then he thought about his wife Julie and his family. What was he doing? He must get away right now!

Finally, she spoke: "You are wonderful, Danny. Such a good person. And you know what? We are good for each other."

Danny immediately jumped up and headed for the door, before being tempted by this beautiful and duplicitous woman.

It was sensational, he could not deny that, but where was all this going to end? Many hurdles lay ahead with wins and losses along the way, no doubt. His conscience was pricking when he thought of his wife Julie and how he was ruining their marriage.

Danny had some hard thinking to do. It looked as though he was being drawn into being a pawn in a big gambling and fixing game where the Kerne gang, and other powerful people like them, pulled the strings, while their puppets desperately carried out dark and murderous crimes to ensure that large amounts of money were being accumulated by 'gambling' or worse – money was being made illegally from drug dealing, and being laundered through bookmakers, betting operations and the racing scene.

CHAPTER 24

Highlight's Dilemma

Shane Kerne imagined that he was top of the pile. His influence and control of activities in their 'Precinct of Lower Life' was rigidly maintained by a posse of people who were either dependent on Kerne for their survival, or held in his grip by some blackmail about their past criminality. They were unable to break away from the threats and reminders about what would happen to them if they showed any reluctance to carry out Kerne's demands.

James Cross and Thomas Spindle were two of many in Kerne's employ. Below the surface of the sphere was violence, intimidation and law-breaking - all to achieve what the 'boss' demanded. Above the surface, the gang wanted to use the financial spoils of their crimes to mix with the upper-crust of society, who, they were finding, were in some cases just as vulnerable to manipulation if practiced subtly. The gang were out for more power, cash and influence by any illegal means whatsoever. The Horse Racing business was their vehicle.

While Kerne and his man, James, sat drinking fine wine in their office behind a local bookmaker, and making plans for their next moves in their racing, blackmailing and gambling coup, Danny was realising that he had a decision to make.

Should he try to ignore what was going on by acquiescence, only to be pushed by these people in the future? But Danny's instinct to face the danger and not turn his back on it was coming through. He now knew that trainer, John Calloway, had been ' persuaded' to turn his back once, but had thereafter been forced by their threats and intimidation.

He had to find out more about the crooks at the top. Sylvia Scerton was now embroiled in it; he had seen Shane Kerne talking to her at the Windsor meeting. He now knew how smooth Kerne could be, but also how ruthless and vicious when it suited him.

Sylvia awoke the next morning feeling well, but the realisation of what trouble they were in soon made her subdued and worried.

While she was having breakfast, she remembered about the meeting with Shane Kerne at Windsor. She knew who he was from John Calloway's description. She had been a bit afraid, knowing that under the surface was a vicious man who when he did not get what he wanted, was more than capable of violence. Despite intruding, he was at first very polite to her, and appeared respectful of her position as owner of Highlight. He said that he was interested in investing in race horses. However, his manner could not quite conceal his rudeness and ruthlessness and attempts to influence her and she began to realise her predicament. After talking with Danny, Sylvia could now piece together a likely scenario of what had happened and of Kerne's doings with the racing business.

Highlight had run well, into third place, on her race debut - although a little 'green' and inexperienced. It was on her second run in a maiden filly's six-furlong race at a small mid-week country fixture that Kerne became involved. Highlight had won easily at a price of 4/1 after opening at 8/1 - reflecting the considerable amount of money backing her. Sylvia now suspected that Highlight had been given a drug before the race. At the Windsor meeting Kerne had appeared in order to ensure that this time the horse was spooked and the apprentice jockey 'leaned on' to make a poor start; and, would not be the winner. After the meeting, John Calloway had offloaded the horse onto Sylvia and then disappeared 'into hiding'. And now Kerne wanted control of Danny and of Highlight's performance for another prospective betting coup, which explained the henchmen turning up at Danny's stables. The fraudulent plan all seemed to fit into place.

What could they do? The police would want evidence, and any reaction from them would be too slow to protect Danny and Sylvia and their properties and families.

Should Danny try to stand up to the Kerne gang, refuse to co-operate and face the consequences? That would be a difficult battle to win; odds against.

Sylvia chose to lie low for a bit, to stay at home, avoid the races and any public appearances, and improve security at the Manor. Danny would wait to see what would happen next, and would be constantly on his guard and ready to react.

But right now Danny had to provide some explanations to his wife and family - and then try to prepare for the thugs next visit, demands and actions.

Before he could do this, a call came from James Cross - who was messenger for Shane Kerne - and a request to enter Highlight in the seven furlongs Maidens race at Beverly in ten days' time. There was a veiled threat of trouble if he did not do so, and a reminder that Danny was not being asked to do anything illegal (at this stage). Danny could ignore the instructions, but waiting to see what they would do to him or his family, if he did, was too risky. He entered the filly as instructed, and then waited for the race day to see what they would do. On the race card there were seven runners declared to run.

Danny had been spending a lot of time with Highlight and Femme Fatale, often grooming them himself, cleaning out adjacent stalls, stroking, talking, and walking with them in the yard areas. He could tell that they were relaxing with the 'pampering' that he was personally providing, and the familiarity of the training routines. He was confident that Highlight, in particular, was responding well She was coming into peak form. They were gradually forming an intuitive relationship and friendship. She had got that confident look back in her eye and she would 'nibble' his hand and nudge his arm with her nose as if showing off to him. Her form on the morning gallops was looking and timing exceptionally well.

Danny was there in the early morning stillness and mist. The thunder of galloping hooves as Highlight and Madame Fatale approached, the heavy breathing of the horses as they passed him at speed, sent shivers down Danny's spine. They weren't going to drug this horse again if he could prevent it! He expected them to turn up any time now and he was on his guard both for the horses, and his family as well. Suddenly there was a surprise phone call from a young apprentice jockey, Simon Simms, confirming that he was available to ride Highlight in her race, and asking could he gallop her out to familiarise himself with the horse!

"I haven't booked you to ride," snapped Danny said.

The jockey merely replied: "I've been instructed to contact you."

Again, Danny had to decide. Better the Devil you know, than the one you don't, he thought, and arranged the gallop, He just might learn more from the jockey and what he was up to. When young Simms visited and galloped Highlight out, Danny rode Madame Fatale out with them and watched his every move, but nothing amiss was seen. Danny's son Johnny was also enlisted to watch Simms very closely on the gallops and afterwards in the stable yard. The young jockey seemed innocent and not involved in Kerne's manipulations … yet.

The next time Danny looked at the Beverly race programme, three of the original seven entered runners had been withdrawn. That was surprising, since the ground conditions had not changed. He phoned one of their trainers.

"You've withdrawn your horse from the Beverly programme. Is she not ready?" he asked. There was a very long pause and he could hear some background discussion going on. Then there was a brief, hesitant reply – 'We have other plans for her' - none of the usual chat. Finally, it dawned on him what might be going on. The Kerne's syndicate was not just manipulating Highlight, Danny and Simon Simms, the jockey. None of the horses involved were from the big trainers. The crooks were now trying to manipulate the owners or trainers of other horses in the race, in order to fix the winner! He warned Liam and Martha at the farm and he set up a security field around Highlight and even slept in the stable next to her stall on the last two nights before the race, and driving the horse box to the meeting he was on the alert and did not leave the horse at any time. He guessed that if anything unusual happened in the race there could be a stewards' enquiry, drug tests, interrogations and the like.

In the parade ring Highlight seemed very alert, but relaxed and settled. She remained a 4/1 outsider of the field of four. However Danny watched as the price of Saxonade, an almost grey filly, started to drop from 7/2 through 3/1, and then 2/1, representing some large wagers placed on her. She was certainly on her toes going down, and the jockey had to rein her in with some force. Highlight entered the starting stalls first, without trouble, but they had to wait as the next two horses needed hooding before reluctantly entering the gates. Saxonade was also difficult, kicking out behind and bucking in the gates. The starter was getting impatient. Many a horse would have been withdrawn by the starter for hesitation, so that the race would not be delayed further, but the fact that only four runners were starting, the late withdrawal of one - particularly the favourite - would make a mockery of it.

Finally the gates shot open and the race was on. Sure enough, Simms did not urge Highlight forward. It was as if she had got tired of waiting in the starting stalls and was left some three lengths behind. Saxonade was flying along at a terrific speed, while the jockeys of the other two were trying to set a reasonable pace so as to have something left for the finish. The order did not change for some three furlongs, except that Saxonade was drawing clearer and the result looked a foregone conclusion.

"Five to win one ON Saxonade!" shouted a bookie jokingly, not expecting a bet. Five grand on Saxonade! A punter had taken up the offer! At this point, with some one-and-a-half furlongs to go, Highlight finally shook herself out of Simms' reining with an acceleration that took the young jockey by surprise. She really was flying now and passed the other two! The gap between Highlight and Saxonade was closing, but it still looked as though the winning post was too near … but was it? Surely it was … Highlight was up-sides now. They were neck and neck, and the greater will to win was the only factor now. With her last stride Highlight thrust her head forward. The crowd roared! It was a photo finish! Wow the short-priced favourite had been beaten! Danny looked round at the crowd of punters in the executive stand. Shane Kerne was there, unnoticed before, but unable now to contain his spontaneous anger at the result, arms flailing, face as red as a fire, he stormed across the stand. He was moving quickly towards the exit.

Highlight had won a race on finishing speed, free of drugs, and had beaten a horse that probably had had stimulants. Kerne's gang would have lost a considerable amount of money. Danny hugged Highlight's face and saw that knowing look in her eye!

There was likely to be some trouble now. After a quick wash down and blanket for the filly, Danny wanted a fast exit from the race course. He rushed to the gents' room on his way, but at the urinals, looking down, he was aware that sidling into the next stall was Shane Kerne. Also looking down, Kerne spoke to him … "You'll be lucky if you and that lady bitch even live to regret today. I'll have you for this. You're a dead man. The horse may be a good'un but I'll nobble her as well. You're a fool. Nobody crosses me and gets away with it!" Danny was the first out of the 'stalls' this time! And was quickly speeding away in the horse box!

Danny was very concerned about the criminal's threats. At home, he didn't dare tell Julie the full details behind his horse's win. He just told her and the kids to be sure to lock up properly and make sure all the security systems were switched on, and to watch for any strangers hanging around the stables and the farm premises. He dare not tell her the full danger to which he and his family were exposed.

CHAPTER 25

Julie's Escort

The estate's legislation and her family did not divert Julie from her interests and responsibilities with the local Hunt meetings, social occasions and the forthcoming Annual Ball. Danny had started opting out of escorting her, not being prepared to change any of his racing plans to fit in, and Julie knew their relationship was beginning to fall apart. It was only when their growing children or her father's estate was involved that the couple were involved together. Her interest in the sexual part of their marriage had changed from the initial wish to have children; to satisfying Danny because she loved him; to a disinterest and the opinion that it was now an inconvenience. The 'flame' in their marriage had flickered down to a token glow, but possibly one to be reignited. But she found it awkward when she needed her husband as her escort at the Hunt's social events. She never knew whether he would be available or not, and twice he had slept in the stable barn with his horse, but she had decided to ignore the local gossip about Danny's absences at the Hunt social meetings. She would try to hire a male escort.

This proved a little more difficult than she was expecting, even with money being no object. References and CV's from the list of escorts was accompanied by restrictions and dates of their availability, and also a request for her own references! Her enquiries did, however, eventually result in the hire of Roberto - a handsome young man of her choice - squeaky-clean apparently, very fit, and aware of all the protocol of the regular evening functions. They quickly became easy social partners and he immediately began to impress her with his younger outlook. They developed a fairly intimate relationship - despite the 'no sexual favours' contract - and she knew that he was aroused by her presence and closeness when on the dance floor. She was a bit amused at first, but pleased – he made her feel good. Much suggestive talk went on between them - and boy, could he talk – and she became curious of him and his prowess.

Roberto recognised the signs. She was gradually becoming curious and interested in Roberto's 'Sexual Intimacy' contract. It was an arrangement that he kept secret, exclusive, and separate from his normal escorting. Roberto's sales patter kept the matter of sexual attraction to the forefront, and Julie gradually confessed about her sexual modesty, and rebuffing Danny's sexual foreplay.

The price of the 'sexual favours' contract was exorbitant, but as Roberto's impressive sales pitch explained:

"The sex act in married life is a pro-creational ritual, with foreplay and fulfilment for reproduction the mind-set to govern its practices. Recreational sex rituals are on a different plane, and emphasise unashamed and natural uninhibited pleasures of all kinds being given and received freely by both parties. At these times, foreplay routines are now the practiced art of modern-day sex-play. It is the younger woman's secret weapon. It allows both partners enjoyment together in their relationships and keeps the men considerate, appreciative and loyal. This art needs a little time to acquire and practice, and just like many sports, physical fitness enhances the pleasures and the mutual love of the partners for one another."

However, Julie, with a teenage family to see to obviously did not have a lot of free time, but Roberto's contract sounded intensive! Practice would take place at his 'studio' when her husband was away, he'd said. He was very convincing, and Julie signed up without further thought.

Whether or not it would be worth the money, she didn't care, but she was immediately taken aback at the foreplay routines of his so-called 'modern-day sex-play'. On the very first lesson Roberto dimmed the lights, and emphasised that any embarrassment should be forgotten. His smooth, low, relaxing voice helped to teach her how to enjoy and be excited by his touch, and the slow removal of one another's clothing, in a sensual way so that eventually she relaxed, half naked, and completely unashamed - with pleasurable thoughts at the touch of hands on bodies and of lessons to come. He said, "Relax and understand that the aim is for pleasure without any embarrassment," and spoke quietly to her all the time. His teaching of massage of her body with perfumed oil, taking his time so that her anticipation of the movement of his hands became quite exciting. She was enjoying it now!

Then he said, "Now it's your turn to learn how to give your partner the same pleasures in the same relaxing way," and oil was applied from his six-pack down. She had only limited experience of men's parts - and generally, since her shyness was always to the forefront, her husband had provided the action. However, amazingly, she found it easy now that she was relaxed and unembarrassed. But she did think that she might have managed things more comfortably if it had been Danny. Time was getting short though, and soon the sensation at what Roberto was teaching resulted in relaxed pleasure that she had not before experienced. Roberto kept saying to her, "Be aware that you are giving pleasure to your partner and enjoying his actions in response."

The assigned time was up and the lights brightened again, despite her offering to pay for more time there and then! The next appointment was to be the main lesson. In the meantime, her homework was to eat a healthier diet, lose a little weight, and work on her fitness and stamina!

CHAPTER 26

Danny's Discoveries

Danny decided that sitting around waiting for the repercussions of Highlight's beating of Shane Kerne's gambling and fixing syndicate was not an option. He couldn't just do nothing when he expected some revenge. How could he bring this all to a head and have a showdown with Kerne? A plan was needed. What could he have up his sleeve for bartering with or defeating these crooks? He did not know enough about them and how they worked – or how they got away with what they were doing. And where were the drugs coming from? Sylvia had a suspicion that a 'mule' was being used to smuggle them in from the continent, because John Connelly had told her that he had seen an airline ticket that Kerne's man had thrown away. He decided, almost by instinct, to leave his countryside moorland home and go to Leeds town centre, where Sylvia had said that Kerne had an office. Danny was in the vicinity from early morning just watching for any comings and goings and looking for any leads that he could follow up. After a little while he saw a man he recognised climbing the steps to the office door; it was the man who Danny had grappled with and held with the pitchfork handle when he had been confronted in his barn.

Danny stepped back out of sight. The man was followed into the office by a smart-looking and well-dressed woman, high heels and all, carrying a bulky travel bag - as well as her fashion handbag. He waited, partially concealed by an alcove, and pretended to read his morning newspaper. Ten minutes on and the two came out again heading for a parked car. Danny moved quickly to his own vehicle and was able to track them from a distance in light traffic. Where were they going? They took the Bradford road out of town. Maybe he was wasting his time, but following a hunch he continued to tail them and then he guessed - having seen the woman's travel bag and the road they were taking – they were heading towards the local airport. They were clearly going to catch a flight or meet someone. He decided to risk passing them on the dual carriageway to get ahead and park up at the airport.

The young woman was dropped off alone and had made her way to 'Departures'. Danny looked at the flight timetable board. The only departure from the airport in the next two hours was for Amsterdam. There was something about her body language … sometimes looking overly casual and then glancing over her shoulder as if afraid, and tightly gripping her camel-coloured travel bag, that made him wonder what she was up to. He whispered to himself, "I must be mad", as he got his passport from the pocket in his car, went to the airline reception and booked a ticket on the Amsterdam flight. He hung back while waiting for the flight to be called. It was about two-thirds full, with some eighty or so passengers, and he obviously wanted to remain unnoticed. The casual short flight passed uneventfully, and after arriving at Amsterdam he followed the young woman at a distance. He was becoming a regular sleuth! With the price of the flight ticket in mind, he was not going to lose her now!

She seemed in no hurry to leave the airport, and instead made for the airport restaurant - keeping her travel bag close by her at the table. Danny stayed watching outside. He did not want her to notice him, but her mannerisms suggested that she was nervous and uncomfortable. She finished her food but did not move, and constantly looked at her watch and glanced over her shoulder. Then suddenly she stood up and headed to the airport toilets. He waited just out of view until she came out five minutes later, still carrying her travel bag. She walked over to the escalator and glanced behind her, before stepping onto it. The bag unexpectedly dropped from her grasp on the escalator and she started to panic as it bounced down a couple of the moving steps. She tried to race down the escalator after it and fell heavily in a heap and was being dragged forward. Fortunately for her the bag came to a stop at the bottom and she hastily grabbed it and hurried on, with scant regard for her own bruising and discomfort. The observant Danny noticed the girls panic, realised that the bag must now be pretty heavy, because she did not easily lift it - whereas before it had appeared light and easy for her to carry. She glanced back and now quickly headed for 'Departures'. He looked at the flight departure board and the return flight for Leeds/Bradford was leaving in about an hour. Was she a drugs 'mule' for Kerne? Danny rushed to the airline ticket office to book a flight back. Now he wondered whether the young woman would get through customs at Bradford.

It was, thankfully, another uneventful flight, and on leaving the plane the woman now looked very composed, beautiful and relaxed. She headed straight through the 'Nothing to Declare' exit with an enticing smile for the casual custom's officer who did not check her luggage and she climbed quickly into a taxi. Danny saw immediately a change in her body language. She now walked with a sprightly step. The enforced seductive smile for customs had changed to relief and relaxation. Why was she taking such a risk? What hold did Kerne have over her? What about

Customs & Excise at the airport? Not all hand luggage was checked, but what a desperate risk. Danny picked up his vehicle and headed straight to Kerne's office. He knew now where the drugs for the horse had come from and had more proof of the crimes. He could threaten to 'spill the beans' if Kerne did not lay off.

His mobile rang before he could enter the office block. It was Sylvia Scerton, sounding quite hysterical, and shouting down the phone, "Oh, Danny, where have you been? I need you straight away! I've just run somebody over in the car! He was trying to grab me as I got in and pushed a chloroform rag in my face. The engine was running and I set off and swerved and the car door slammed shut on his arm and he fell out, and my back wheels ran over him. He had a broken leg and couldn't move. Somebody got the ambulance and they took him to Leeds hospital!"

"I'll be over as soon as I can. Go straight home, lock the doors until you see me. Lie low and try to relax. It's not your fault. You'll have to say that you can't remember anything. Do you know who it was?"

She answered: "James Cross. He's one of Kerne's men. He was out to grab me!"

Danny went up the steps to Kerne's office, opened the door and walked straight in. Security was lacking as the young lady shared a joke with Shane Kerne, while he was leaning right over her in a seductive manner. The travel bag had been opened and various articles of clothing and toilet accessories were scattered on the floor leaving the remaining contents, in packages, exposed. They were completely taken by surprise by the 'visitor'. Kerne was the first to react. His hand automatically went inside his lapel. Danny guessed that he had a gun holstered.

"Ross! What do you want? Looking for trouble? You getting scared now, Ross?"

Danny was quick to reply "Your man Cross is in trouble. He's in hospital!" And that's where you'll end up for messing with me and my friends. I know more about your doings than you think. Your woman bringing drugs from Amsterdam for a start. I've got photographic proof, and if you really want more trouble you can have it from us any time. Do you want more of your lot in hospital, or would you like police and customs officers in here? I can put you behind bars! The choice is yours. Lay off us or take the consequences. I will do it if you don't lay off." Kerne moved first towards him, but then towards the drawer of his desk. The gun was there. Danny lifted his foot up and hit the desk hard, pushing it towards Kerne and sending him staggering backwards - but not before he pulled the trigger. The blast echoed through the room and Danny felt a searing pain across his upper arm. Danny immediately tipped the heavy desk up and let it fall onto Kerne's sprawling figure, trapping him beneath it. As quick as a flash Danny kicked the gun from his hand. The girl had rushed out of the office.

Kerne was flabbergasted. Danny had him at his mercy. He grabbed him by the throat and held on as if to strangle him. He eventually let go and as he walked out, he picked up Kerne's gun, and hit him with the butt., "Think about it. Keep out of my business or somebody's going to end up in jail or get killed. And it won't be me!" He left Kerne struggling to get his legs from under the heavy desk, blood running from his mouth.

CHAPTER **27**

Julie's Choice

Julie was unaware of Danny's escapade. She had Roberto's plan on her mind. She had started power-walking in the countryside every day. Her next appointment with Roberto was due and she was already feeling fitter than she had for a long time. She was amazed at what she'd already done and learned and enjoyed. She hoped that Danny was going to be away on the day rather than on the estate, and she looked at his timetable of racing dates and saw that he would be at the Ripon meeting. She bathed and attended to her bikini line and underarm hair and looked in the full-length mirror at her figure. She felt some satisfaction and no embarrassment because suddenly her fitness had become important to her again - and to Roberto. She had to admit that she'd let it go a bit recently. Now, with Roberto's emphasis on seeking and giving pleasure unashamedly in sex-play, and having the stamina to achieve this for the full 'six furlongs' her expectations of a better life with Danny were high. She had drawn the money from the bank to pay Roberto for the next contracted lesson.

Roberto summarised her first session by saying that the main aim of it had been to rid Julie of any embarrassment in fully exposing herself to a partner by thinking of both giving and receiving pleasure. The titillation for both at the way each item of clothing was removed and the following massage were arts to be practiced. Today was the day for the theory and then the practice of sexual intimacy prior to the ultimate act of fulfilment, and the timing. Julie was entranced by his every word, every action, every demonstration and every response. She had started to realise what she may have missed with her lack of approval and response to her husband's foreplay and his desire for more of this open intimacy in their bedroom. She was an excellent pupil for Roberto and in another world until suddenly she realised that Roberto had stopped his preliminaries at the time that she thought she was more than ready. He had paused and started talking on another plane and she had trouble in returning to reality and understanding his theme.

Roberto was talking to her, not in his smooth, relaxing voice, but with more urgency. "Julie," he said, "we met because you needed an escort for your hunt functions. We got on okay together. Now I need you to think and tell me why you wanted to sign up to the sexual intimacy contract. Are you looking for better things to aim for within your marriage to Danny? Or is your marriage beyond repair such that you just need gratification, which can be, but only if you have clearly thought through your needs?"

"Don't stop now, Roberto," was what she was thinking, but what he was saying, and the way he was saying it, eventually got her attention. He was asking her if her marriage to Danny was at an end! He was asking if she was sure that she wanted to proceed to the next stage of the sexual contract she had agreed to, to maximise the pleasures of the practical act with positions from the Karma Sutra?

Had she already been unfair to Danny in going so far and should she be having second thoughts? The crunch question was this: Was she there to learn for Danny's benefit and better sex relations with him? If so, how far should she be going with Roberto without later recriminations? Or was she there paying for gratification and excitement with Roberto - both the provider and beneficiary. In which case the next sensations were coming up right now!

The question, when it sunk into Julie's mind, stopped her in her tracks; her marriage would be at stake if what she was going to do with Roberto left her dissatisfied thereafter, and perhaps even addicted to it. She had begun to realise what Danny's desires for more pleasure in their bedroom were about. If she gradually used the foreplay techniques she had learned, maybe the two of them could together, as a couple, learn more of the pleasures of the next stages. She became grateful to Roberto for asking the question before ploughing ahead with the next stage. Roberto had got to know Julie and her family and circumstances pretty well, and had hesitated at the possible repercussions. His occasional sexual contracts were not usually with ladies such as Julie, who he had already escorted to prestigious functions, and whose husband Danny, he knew. He tried to keep this activity quiet, although it paid well for him, and he prided himself with the knowledge and experience of the intimacy that he used to send his clientele into raptures of ecstasy. He assured Julie of his discretion about the help he had provided in removing her modesty, and showing her the part that she could play in the marital bedroom.

Julie left Roberto with a shake of hands and with his advice clearly in her mind. Roberto had said, "Be patient and reveal your new enticement skills very slowly so that the change in you is not too obvious. Lose a bit of weight and get fitter with the exercises, and your husband will think that this is what's changing your presence!" Julie's intentions were in place. Danny was in for a pleasant surprise!

From Kerne's office, Danny wrapped his handkerchief round the wound on his arm, and drove straight over to Lady Silvia's. He found her sedated after her ordeal, and saying, "I want to sell Highlight, Danny. I want to get out of all this racing business. I want to sell the horse."

stride length, rhythm and ease of movement. Highlight stood out compared with the other horses he had had in his stable. Her effortless and economic speed showed in particular. His thoughts were moving towards a longer distance, maybe even a one-mile race. By winning at Beverley, Highlight had shown that she had good speed, acceleration and determination to get her nose in front in a tight finish. She obviously would be a short-priced favourite in grade 5 races over six furlongs, and would be hit by the extra weights from the handicapper. But maybe, in the future, she could qualify for bigger prize money and better odds in a longer race where she was not yet proven. However, Danny was convinced that he had an exceptional horse, able to perform on any reasonable ground conditions, with a rare determination to win, one that could reach the top, and he could not let her go at any price. If Sylvia Scerton was adamant in wanting to sell her horse and rid herself of the threats and drug issues, then he had to find the money to buy Highlight himself. The owner had to be consulted on entries, but she was now distancing herself from decisions on the horse and was 'wanting out'. Danny knew this was because of the traumas and threats from the Kerne gang, but he hoped that Kerne would go elsewhere to easier pastures now, having witnessed that Danny was capable of a response to their violent tactics.

Danny knew that Lady Silvia would tell him to do what he thought was best, but he rang her anyway, and then entered Highlight in a six-furlong Selling Stakes - this time at Ripon's evening meet - that meant that the winner of the race automatically went up for an auction sale. Danny needed enough finance to make Sylvia a reasonable offer in the bidding for Highlight if she won and went up for sale. A winning purse from Ripon might be used to soften Sylvia up on his plans, but he did not have the cash. Julie still held the purse strings, controlling the finances of the Manors' estate, and his relationship with her at the moment was cool to say the least. Highlight's turn-of-foot excited him every time he saw her pushed to full stretch, be it on the gallops or at the races. She was developing into a big, powerful and intelligent horse and he could see potential in her that others, including the Handicap Committee, had not yet seen.

CHAPTER 29

Racings Rhythms

Danny's conscience was pricking him. He felt guilty about his misdoings and how he had neglected to give attention and consideration for his wife and their family life. He should try to do better, he knew that, but Julie now seemed to distance herself from him - with a hint of disapproval at most things he did. Maybe she suspected that he had been unfaithful, but if she did, she did not seem to care and still gave him little encouragement in the sexual side of their relationship; that is, until last night when he was very late home after his unbelievable day. He was not sure whether she was asleep or not when he slid quietly into bed, but she had snuggled up to him instead of keeping her distance. And she had changed her normal nightwear to a more enticing silk negligee. He had been exhausted and maybe had missed an opportunity to improve relations.

It was a bit of an enigma, though, and he did not know if it meant anything - but time would tell. He couldn't stop thinking about it as he got on with the tasks in the stables and then the work he did for the estate.

That night Julie cooked a meal for him and the kids and with no meetings with the hunt committee - for a change – they all enjoyed a homely night in. Danny hoped that the conversation would help to relax the tension between himself and Julie. An early night was on the cards for them after another long day, and Julie wandered off to shower before going to bed. Danny was the first into bed, complete with the Racing Times to read, leaving Johnny and Marion downstairs watching television. Usually when Julie was taking a shower, she closed the bathroom door for privacy. Danny could never forget Mary and their unbridled sexual happiness when showering together. The contrast of the closed door behind Julie and her modesty was always a disappointment to him. But surprisingly the door had been left wide open so that he could see her nakedness under the shower, instead of the fleeting glimpses of her body as she dried herself. Even more, as he stared at her, he realised that she knew he was looking and appeared to proudly exhibit her body instead of turning away. He knew that she had started power-walking. He had wondered why, but now he realised that she was looking slimmer and fitter. He was being turned on by the sight of her body. Dare he quickly join her under the shower? No, it might not go down well. And then it was too late!

But now Julie was thinking about the advice that she had paid for. To be more favourable towards her husband's approach, instead of avoiding or ignoring him as more recently was the case.

His mind was in a spin when she walked into the bedroom, and without a glance at him slipped on a flimsy negligee, got into bed close to him, but turned away from him. He took the risk of moving over towards her and put his arm gently round her waist. Julie felt his closeness and didn't rebuff him, in fact she moved slightly closer to him. Danny was encouraged, and he slowly moved his hand to her buttocks and started gently massaging. For the first time in years he sensed that she was feeling pleasure from his touch, and she eventually turned onto her back, pulled him to her, took his hand and in a short time– much to Danny's amazement – proceeded to slide close to him in response.

He couldn't believe what was happening, his sexually inactive wife - who for so long had kept her distance in bed - had become, by some miracle, sexually pro-active and was happily giving him long-forgotten pleasure. But more than that – she was now indicating that she was conducive to his fondling in return. He was in shock, almost panic, but then in ecstasy too. It was like it was a first time ever!

Julie was pleased that what her escort had taught her was working. She remembered his last words about taking things slowly so as not to arouse suspicion. She stopped massaging Danny and moved even closer to him and held him tight. He was too amazed to want to take things further, but he needed more of her responses to believe that this was really happening. Where had this come from?

They heard their kids coming upstairs to bed, and kissed and clung together, just as newlyweds would do. Julie wondered if she had gone, too quickly, for him to think that this change was natural. She wanted him to be curious about what had transformed her, and how she was now more comfortable with her own body and his, and so efficient in arousing his interest and giving him such pleasure.

They remained close until they both fell asleep with happy, wondrous thoughts and expectations in their minds.

Johnny and Marion were up and breakfasted by the time their parents woke up. Johnny stuck his head around the door to see if everything was all right, as his parents usually were up first. They had both slept very well and now had to get a move on with their work and plans for the day. Their thoughts throughout the day were about those precious moments the night before, with both of them pleased that it had happened.

There were unanswered questions for both of them and Julie had some of the answers.

CHAPTER 30

Highlight's Future

At lunchtime, Danny, in desperation for the money required to bid for Highlight, approached Julie on the subject. "If Highlight wins next week, I will lose her," he explained, "she will be sold to someone else at the auction sale. Will you help me to buy her using the estates finances?"

His timing was good because Julie seemed to be in a friendly mood. "You love that horse, don't you?" she said. He just nodded. "I wouldn't want you to lose her. Let's wait until the race day and see what happens before doing anything."

Highlight won the Seller by a length, despite having a poor starting draw. The jockey hardly needed the whip. Highlight was hardly off the rein. Danny hoped that it was not too noticeable and that none of the bigger trainers and owners were at the meeting. He had scraped together £6000, which at 7/4 brought the young man who had discreetly placed a bet £10,500 by return. The auction was a low-key affair as Danny had hoped. His bid of 20,000 guineas was successful. He had news for Mrs Scerton: she was rid of Highlight as she wished, and had received the best part of £20,000, The new owners were Danny and the Manors' estate. The new owner and trainer couldn't get home fast enough to report that their yard had acquired a prospective Group 1 or Group 2 winning horse. There were big prizes to go for - which would hopefully bring a fine and profitable racing record - and also enhance her breeding status in years to come.

Julie, having provided some of the finance, was now beginning to understand the bigger picture, and seemed to develop a new faith in this horse and show an interest in the racing and breeding programme Danny was following. Their son, Johnny, was also now beginning to show more interest.

"Why does this horse rank so high in your expectations?" Julie asked Danny later that day.

He thought hard before answering. "She has intelligence, and because of this, her character can be developed more than the average filly. We know that her will to win is already there, but she will need treating like a child: regular times spent talking, training, pampering, influencing and developing her relationship with humans; regular time-out with other horses where she will be free to roam and develop her character and determination. A Horse doesn't get this by being locked in its box all the time. She needs an active life just like us all. If we put the time in with her, she will reward us one hundred-fold." A convincing answer!

Danny studied the coming race meetings, hoping to see Highlight going up in both class and distance. Newmarket, the home of racing, was one meeting where Highlight's ability could be tested. She would also gain valuable experience at a bigger track which drew a much larger crowd - with all its distractions. It would be a seven-furlong maiden on the historic straight and wide stretch of turf for Highlight, against some thoroughbreds and older horses with previous winning records among the entries.

Danny and Highlight had worked hard and trained well and was one of the outsiders of fourteen declared runners, drawn also in the outside starting stall against the far rails.

A fast and even start saw all the horses drifting across to the centre and inside rails - except Highlight! (The jockey said later that he wanted to guide her across the track towards the favoured ground, but she seemed to be resisting him, and so he let her go down the outside rails.) All the attention was on what looked like a very tight, close race, with several horses in a line disputing the lead. Highlight was barely noticed racing on the far rail of the wide course and seemed to be well out of it. The watching crowd roared with excitement, though, and then gasped in amazement as the finishing line was rapidly approached, and then was reached first by Highlight on her own on the far rails! In a breath-taking moment she had, almost unperceived, accelerated to a tremendous speed to hit the line first by a short head on the photograph - and at a price of 20/1!

Danny, excited and elated, rushed down to the unsaddling enclosure to Highlight. He hugged her face and rubbed her nose – but the understanding developed between him and the horse enabled him to see in her eyes, some distress and fatigue. She had flared nostrils and was tossing her mane. She was also badly overheating. He shouted to Johnny - who was acting as stable lad – "Get buckets of water, quick, this is urgent! And bring sponges too! Please move away everyone. No interviews now. Away please!"

They poured cold water over Highlight and sponged her down, and she gradually seemed to recover. Danny threw a thin sheet over her and led her quickly to her stalls, and said to Johnny, "Represent me at the presentation, will you. Apologise and say that the horse's welfare comes first." He stayed with her alone, stroking her and talking quietly as he did in the stables back home. Only when he was satisfied that her temperature was okay, did he put her in the horse box, and without any formalities they set off for home.

Johnnie was clutching the fillies' trophy and the winner's cheque. He was as proud as punch.

It was very late by the time they got to the yard, and Johnny turned in straight away, but Danny fed and watered Highlight and bedded her down. He crept in quietly, once again expecting Julie to be asleep in bed. He was exhausted. He undressed very quietly and slid into bed so as not to disturb her. However, the new Julie had been waiting for him, and she was anxious to know how the race had gone (she was also amenable to Danny's advances). "How did she run?" she asked, as she snuggled close to him,

"She won … she was brilliant," mumbled Danny, already half asleep, as Julie slid her negligee-clad body on top of him.

"Just relax, Danny" she said. "If you're tired, just relax. I'll do the work. The exercise will be good for me." No embarrassment shown!

The sheer surprise of her touch and slow movement enabled Danny to respond. It was like he was in a dream, in the controlling hands and body of a seductive expert. In his exhausted state he relished his wife dictating the rhythm and soon found relaxed satisfaction. Julie realised this, and although not herself completely fulfilled, she knew that a new love life was opening up for her and for Danny. She had this time taken the active role, where in the past she had been unable to do so. She thought, I can now be ready anytime for us both to enjoy and reach ecstatic places neither of us has been before. The past indifference to each other had gone, to be replaced by loving anticipation, intimacy, and the open message of real love it conveyed. It was a marriage reborn. The flame rekindled for them both!

CHAPTER 31

Prix de la Forêt

Julie, vitalised by her new knowledge and experience, was up early, leaving Danny to sleep on. He needed to recover from the exertions of the previous day. He eventually surfaced to be told by Johnny that Highlight had not eaten up and seemed a bit stressed. Danny went to see her, stroked and pampered her, and whispered and quietly sang to her as he walked her round the yard. He could tell that Highlight was glad to see him, and visibly began to relax with his presence. After a while Danny gradually moved away a bit, still talking, and he left the feed bag in place in the stall.

When he eventually returned, she was calm had taken the remainder of the feed and water.

"What did you think was wrong with her, Dad?" Johnny asked.

"Just a maturing ladies' temperament and prerogative, I think, Johnny."

If Highlight could get one more win in a classic race, Danny could benefit tremendously in a two -fold way: a big money prize and a betting coup, with Highlight then being a top-class young breeding mare with a black-type rating and vast potential. He would allow Highlight a let-down for a while, and come back after she'd rested, to top form for her next run, stepping up to maximum racing fitness. Danny searched the racing fixtures and made alternative entries, hoping to find the right race and good going for her to run on.

Danny couldn't stop thinking about the ultimate thrill of running Highlight at the prestigious Longchamps meeting on the banks of the Seine, near Paris in France. The famous history of the course went back to 1857, and it was a favourite haunt of Emperor Napoleon the Third. The race? Possibly the Prix de la Forêt for three-year-old Fillies - a six-and-a-half-furlong downhill course with a prize of 171,000 Euros and run on the same day as L'Arc de Triomphe. The prestige from this sort of record could ensure that with Highlight, as a young mare, breeding could possibly outweigh the option of her staying in training for another year.

On her three-week holiday from training, Highlight was turned out for a short time each day with a small group of horses - including Madame Fatale. She enjoyed the break and once she had established her leadership of the small group, she became relaxed and happy. Every day Danny would go down to the paddock and spend an hour amidst the group, and particularly stay close to Highlight, just to maintain the intuitive relationship between them. Highlight always seemed pleased to see him and have him close, despite him keeping her on her toes by making sudden unexpected noises and movements such as clapping his hands, and running forward and back for her to follow him. He needed her to be alert and unconcerned and confident in dealing with such minor intimidations – it was all part of her one-on-one training.

For now, their new lifestyle at home included: no race meetings; no contact with Sylvia Scerton (who had gone abroad to Monaco looking for a change in environment); a far more comfortable atmosphere and a relaxed relationship in the bedroom (restricted to quiet talking, gentle foreplay and silent intimacy due to the presence of their offspring in the two adjacent bedrooms!) Both their kids were sexually aware - thanks to the school curriculum and emphasis now aimed at educating developing teenagers - and they were happy when they realised that Danny and Julie had found a new consideration for one another around the home! Their kids had also spotted Julie's new lingerie and nightwear in the family laundry! The nights when the kids were away from home or on sleep-over evenings at their friends, were the nights Danny and Julie looked forward to, where they introduced a variety of new pleasures - all the better for their delayed arrival.

"Highlight has made the acceptances for the Prix de la Forêt!" shouted Danny one morning, when he got the mailed information. The entry and expenses would hit their racing finances hard now they had plans and reservations to make, however the experience and possible rewards for success drove them on.

Danny's last visit to France was via the ferry with Liam, all those years ago, and he remembered it well. The cost and uncertainty for Highlight of flying to Paris, was out, but now, of course, there was the Channel Tunnel. Just a one-hour journey and you were on French soil, and no sea sickness for horse or travellers! A special horse box was needed for the journey, with fresh air and emergency supplies, and drainage and cleansing facilities. Highlight could now quickly be at the races in a fresh and fit condition to show her excellent form.

"We can do this, Dad!" Johnny cried and Danny was convinced.

"We have one month to have everything ready and in place, son," he replied, and together they got to work preparing the special box and travel details.

Their race entry brought plenty of press and publicity for Highlight and the Boutique Training Stables. The media's verdict was: "A deserved entry into this prestigious race on breeding and on winning performance at Newmarket, but an outsider in this class of field". But they didn't know the horse like Danny and Johnny did, or about the intuitive relationship that had developed between the owner and horse using Danny's methods. A careful relationship between the horse and Grant Gibson - the jockey hired for the ride – had been developed too. Danny had enlisted Grant for the race on the understanding that he spent time with Highlight, and followed Danny's technique of gaining the horse's friendship, understanding and trust.

The day before the race they travelled by road to a friend's farm in Suffolk - where Highlight stretched, exercised and rested in Danny and Julie's company. Then it was an early morning 'Chunnel ride' to France - never done as late as on the actual day of the race before, with arrival at Longchamps to schedule. First-class treatment and facilities awaited them on their arrival; they were really beginning to feel like celebrities. Excitement was mounting, and the press and the racing public were following the tale of the horse's and stable's history. After the news on the Arc de Triomphe prize - with some of the world's best horses, jockeys and stables competing - the next story that caught the attention of the racing public in France was the interest in the performance of Highlight, trained by a new, little-known, little boutique stable in the English Yorkshire Dales, which had made the accepted entries list by some means or other. The non-arrival on the day before the race had made some of the racing press wrongly assume that this unknown horse must be a non-runner, as she could not possibly acclimatise so soon after the voyage. Danny kept quiet on their journey and whereabouts, saying only, "We're here now, aren't we? And we'll be ready to race when the starting stalls open."

The unknown horse with the little-known jockey was quoted at 40/1. And when L'Arc was won by the favourite from France's number one stable and richest owner - who also had a runner in the Prix de la Forêt too - Highlight's odds went out to 66/1. Johnny and Grant spent all their time walking Highlight as far away from the enclosures as possible, quietly talking to her, stroking her and pampering her, and telling her that her very best would be needed, but that with her determination she could put these temperamental nags in their place. And they were going to be behind her at the finish!

When Julie saw Highlight saddled up, and Grant was legged up on board in the new, wind-resistant Lycro silken colours of the Ross stable, she looked a dream. She wasn't the biggest or longest striding horse in the race, but she looked at the peak of fitness. The betting odds dropped slightly to 50/1, and the press and pundits could not decide whether it was just silly money from betting mugs, or whether the discerning experts had realised from the approach of the horse's trainer and his son, that they were all in a determined mood. Most of the punters were keenly watching the odds on the two joint favourites. These were Normandy-bred, Aramise, and Lunership - drawn No 6 and No 8, spectacularly placed on each side of Highlight, drawn at No 7, in the field of sixteen. The tense atmosphere, energy, and the excitement of the spectators honed into the Commentary Box as the race began.

"They're off!" the commentator cried. *"The early pace is not very fast. The expected front runner in the field has started badly from the gates. The three horses at the centre of the field are having to spearhead the race in the first two furlongs. Highlight has taken an early lead with the two favourites alongside. She's certainly getting maximum exposure for her run. They are at the three furlongs mark ... the established front runners are now coming through. Aramise and Lunership are tucked in behind. As expected, Highlight is dropping away now. The pace is hotting up a bit. Five-furlong mark, the field is beginning to string out, Aramise still easily tucked in with Lunership now under a bit of pressure. Highlight still surprisingly hanging in there, about sixth, five lengths back. Aramise is beginning to stretch out now, a lovely, long-striding horse and beautiful to watch pulling away with half*

a furlong to go for the in-form Normandy filly. Oh my God, the little English horse is trying to stay with her. A plucky, but probably unsuccessful effort. Oh mon Dieu! She's upsides of the champion and it's going to be closer than anyone expected. NO! I DONT' BELIEVE THIS! It's a photo finish at the post and it's very close too. In fact, the bookmakers are cheering. They may have made a small fortune! And goodness knows what the Head Establishments will have lost. The English filly has shown amazing speed and determination in the last few metres and may even have got her nose in front!"

Then came the announcement over the loud speaker: Photo finish; " *Le gagnant es Highlight d'Anglais! ... numero sept!"*

A hush fell over the crowded enclosure. The only noise to be heard was from Danny, Julie, Johnny and Grant - cheers, whoops and laughter! Highlight was garlanded and covered with the special winner's sheet. Grant unsaddled her and went to weigh in through a gathering of official witnesses - disbelieving and suspicious of the circumstances.

"Weighed in! Satisfactory."

Fait accompli.

Danny did not want any limelight, asking Johnny, Grant and Julie to attend the presentation while he tended to Highlight. He knew that the horse, the stable and the team would now be famous ... and rich. And under the Spotlight.

En voiture! Next stop Yorkshire! And then-Celebrations!

CHAPTER 32

Echoes of the Past

It was now the end of the flat racing season for the year and Highlight was turned out in the daytime with her friends. They were stabled at night, though, as the weather grew colder. Rest and quiet recovery were the modes for horse and family. Both Madame Fatale and Highlight were retired from racing, as planned, and were scheduled in the future breeding programme. Plans were made for covers at stud from high-ranking stallions. These were Julie's choice after lengthy research into the various bloodlines and success rates of available stallions and records of their offspring! And the stud fees of course! Madame Fatale had been covered by a high-class stallion whose offspring had already achieved successes. Highlight's 'appointment' and visit had been pre-arranged, and was due very shortly, but Danny was now hesitating about Highlight's racing retirement.

She was still a precocious young female to him with more races in her, and hardly seemed ready to be a broodmare. Was it worth it to gamble on more race successes? Could Highlight retain fitness, speed and enthusiasm for another season while having to beat the handicap weights as well? Choices and decisions to be made!

In the village it was now the socialising season, with Hunt meetings and the forthcoming Hunt Ball. Julie was a prominent figure on the organising committee. Guests, seating arrangements, menus and entertainment had all been arranged.

Danny had more time now, although dealing with a press anxious for racing success stories was not easy. They were all after the training secrets that had led to the creation of a 'wonder horse', and which he was not going to divulge. "There's no secret," Danny responded, "just dedication to the task." But nobody would believe that. Danny and Julie had eased the task in front of them by giving Liam, Martha and their son Shaun more responsibility, and reward, for the running of the dairy farm.

Danny and Julie Ross were resting together on their bed; a brief afternoon respite before dressing for the evenings Hunt Ball. They had been prominent and influential figures in the Yorkshire Wolds before, but now the growing fame of the racing stables and the win at Longchamps had rocketed them to almost celebrity status - and in a much wider area.

Theywere looking for them;and then started gesticulating loudly in their direction. They started rushing towards them, both of them looking bigger and more intimidating as they approached the table.

Danny also saw the couple were chatting animatedly together, and they both turned in their direction and began to charge towards them. And Sam Long was rushing in too, his face as red and raw as a beetroot. Both Danny and Julie ducked together under their table, with their own thoughts! Julie on how she had bared all to that man's touch and how she had touched him, supposedly in learning how to actively participate in sex! And Danny's mind was on the drug-induced intercourse he'd had in Sylvia's hotel bedroom, and the vivid memory of her hands on him and the response to his hands on her!

They were both sweating, shaking and panicking. This could shatter the newly-found faith they now had in one another! And then they were both playing out the prior events again: Danny had Sylvia's legs round his waist, while Julie watched them. And Julie's hands were on Roberto, and Danny was watching. Both felt hot and breathless and were completely consumed by fear of what might happen next! Danny saw Highlight galloping across the dance floor, nostrils flared, being chased by Sam Long and she was now rearing up on her hind legs near them. Both man and horse struck out at him. Suddenly everything was in darkness and someone who Julie could not see was viciously striking both at Danny and at her face, and she could not stop them! She started to stumble, grabbed at Danny and they both fell to the ground in a paralysed mode.!

And then the emergency fire alarm was suddenly ringing loudly and very loud voices were shouting to them in their bedroom.

Danny and Julie were both now lying out, breathless, shaking, sweating and going crazy trying to understand all this nightmare they were having!

With a start they both came to their senses. And as they did, Danny was sure that he felt a slap from of the hand of his beloved Mary …Shades of the psychic!

Back In reality, their son Johnny was shouting loudly to them from the bottom of the stairs, and why was their bedroom alarm clock ringing loudly? Danny and Julie stared at each other.

Had it really been a nightmare to surpass all nightmares that had consumed them both? They looked at one another with a lost expression in their eyes. They saw the obvious distress in each other's faces as they tried to understand what they each had just experienced! Shades of the past!

Their Past Misdemeanours were now surfacing at this unexpected time. Conscience Pricking? What had they been doing?!

CHAPTER 33

Repercussions

There was a great commotion in the yard. Flashing lights from the local Fire brigade. Firemen w.

"Were shouting and walking in and out of the buildings. The couple sheepishly emerged half dressed and still shaking." What's happening "they asked, confused and disoriented"

The chief officer was scratching his head. "We've just extinguished a small fre. It could only have just started. The funny thing is that we got a call at the fire station about thirty minutes ago. We thought it might be a hoax. It was a woman insisting that we deal with a fire at your stables It was only when we searched around that we spotted it just starting to blaze.

Danny looked at Mary's Cedar tree near the wall and then kneeled in tears and prayers.

Julie joined him. They had both learned their lessons today. There would be no more indiscretions, even as a means to an end.

They were bundled into a taxi which fairly rattled down the driveway..

When they arrived they took their seats at the top dining table and looked at one another and stared out on to the floor and all the people looking up for them to start thr proceedings.

Johnny sensed that his father could not speak and so he stood up, raised his hand for qiet and ' on behalf of his father welcomed all, so that procceedings could commence. Within an hour a waitress brought a obile phone to Danny.

"A call for you Sir"

"Oh What now. " It was the stable girl who was bedding down the horses.

"Mr Ross, Highlights gone! She's disappeared! She was in the little paddock where she's been kept each afternoon. I went to put her in her stall as usual. When I couldn't see her, I thought she must have walked in herself after the firemen had left, but she was not there! I've looked around and can't find her."

Danny groaned and then shouted down the phone "Get Liam out, look down the fields behind the farm where the colts are out. Was the Gate opened? Have a good look with Liam. She must be somewhere. Ring me back in half an hour." Now Danny really was agitated. He excused himself from the dinner table and went to the men's room with mobile phone in hand.

"She's gone Danny. We've looked everywhere. All the Outbuildings, down the meadows, all the stalls. Nowhere! I'm just going to look on the CCTV that points towards the yard. Just hang on. It's playing back now - when the firemen were here. Highlight was in the paddock."

"Run it forward. I'll hang on the phone while you check it."

Julie was getting worried by Danny's absence from the table. She asked her son to go and see if he was alright.

In the men's room Liam was just telling Danny that the pictures on the CCTV were no longer clear as it was going dark. The security light had not lit up but the faint outline of two men had seemed to cross the edge of the pictures on the screen.

"Ring the police, ask them to get to the stables urgent and keep a look out for anything or anybody unusual on the way there. I am coming home if they will pick me up on the way, as they pass the Hall."

Johnny had to return to his mother at the dining tables with the news that Highlight had gone. Julie was distraught and Danny had gone home! The festivities obviously had to go on but with Danny's absence raising eyebrows and fanning a rumour that the famous Race Winner had gone missing.

Subsequent police investigation found a lock on the paddock gate sawn off, identified tyre tracks, and a 'shadow' on the playback screen - from what was probably a small horse box. Not much other local evidence, no sightings of horse or vehicles and so the urgent local search for Highlight became a National one with diminishing expectations of success.

Danny and all his family were at first traumatised by their loss and worried for the horse's safety. This gradually turned into frustration at the lack of any clues or information. The various theories deduced by the police at first were that the horse and box could be hidden away somewhere fairly local so that sightings on major roads were avoided. Searches were made at random remote farms and buildings on the moors. Nothing found, no clues or evidence unearthed despite a small reward being offered for information.

As the weeks started to roll by the whole family were slowly coming to terms with the financial impact of their loss, but harder still was the worry about Highlights wellbeing and safety. She was like a spoilt child to them and not geared to rough handling, neglect and perhaps even cruelty. Thinking about her and what she might be going through was tormenting them all, particularly Danny and Julie who would not just 'move on'. They spent hours looking for leads. Local thieves, horse box owners, and transport companies any type of person who might be up to doing this; and of course, Shane Kerne and his gang. Where they striking back?

The 'younger generation' Johnny and Marion, seemed better able to look to the future and not let the event rule their lives forever. Johnny worked hard taking over the management of the other horses and keeping the yard going. Marion, still doing the work of a stable hand, wanted to pursue a career in other directions and was studying travel and languages at the local college. But Danny still had plans to confront the Kerne gang again in his quest for answers about Highlight.

CHAPTER 34

Johnny's Progress

At the Hunt Ball, when the evening was coming to its close, Johnny had a secret hope and intention that he might get a chance to 'chat up ' Kathleen Parkinson. He had met Kathleen several years ago when they were younger and she lived with her parents in a country cottage on the outskirts of the village.

With the horse missing, the whole atmosphere at the Ball had been clouded by the news, and Johnny missed his chance when he was required to join the searchers. People had seemed to be going through the motions of the event without much heart or enthusiasm and excuses were being found to leave early. Kathleen had been working as a waitress for the evening serving drinks to the next table and when Johnny saw her, he could not take his eyes away. She fulfilled her reputation as the most sexy, beautiful waitress ever seen.

A smile on her face and a joking response to the wants of the guests. Her high heels could not have been very safe for carrying full trays of drinks, but 'Boy' did they show off her figure in her short waitress uniform revealing the full shape of breasts and buttocks, 'shapely' calves and ankles.

Johnny kept thinking about Kathleen. There were not many eligible girls living in the village and when he went into town on a Saturday night, he had difficulty finding a girl to his liking. Some looked good but when they had drink and started mouthing off and acting drunken stupid any initial attraction was soon lost. At the other end of his spectrum the daughters of rich Racehorse Owners were a bit intimidating to him. He had more experience with racehorses than with temperamental women.

One particular morning he saddled Marcella, one of the stables 'hacks' and rode out across fields and country lanes. His sister Marion was in the yard.

"Where have you been; you've been a long time with Marcella! Will you turn her stable over"?

"I just fancied a longer ride out today."

Have you been out to Copside?" Marion could read him like a book.

"Why don't you go to The Red Bull in the village. Kathleen works behind the bar there on Tuesdays and Wednesdays. There's entertainment on. Be careful what you drink if you're driving."

Johnny made a point of going for a drink at The Red Bull on a Saturday night. Kathleen was pretty sure why he was there, and was still there when it was nearly closing time. Like quite a lot of girls she was pretty streetwise and could handle' being chased' by suitors and keep control of things even if she was up to a bit of ' getting to know one another'. She was excited by his presence and more than receptive when Johnny asked her if he could give her a lift and save her dad coming to pick her up. On the way home Johnny stopped the car in a lay-bye. Looked at her, leaned over and tried to kiss her. She did not resist. And then she said" let's get in the back seat, its more comfortable". It was enough to have Johnny already hard. Kathleen was familiar with interest from the opposite sex. Their kiss was prolonged but then she ended it and wanted to chat. He wanted more. His hands found a way under her top coat. Her breasts were firm and nipples raised, but she was thinking that she was not about to be stripped off in the back seat of a car, on the first ' tete a tete'! She pushed him away. Enough for the first time she was thinking as she purposely backed off. A girl has a reputation to protect!

"Dad will be wondering where we are. I have to get home now. "She knew that Johnny was snared now. When Kathleen said "I'll see you around perhaps". Young Johnny's quick response was "Hey, can I see you again when you're not working in the bar. Give me your mobile number."

CHAPTER 35

Search for Highlight

Danny was STILL searching for Highlight. He refused to accept that she was gone forever. Maybe put down by the thieves with all evidence destroyed when they realised that a massive search was underway and publicity was not abating. He was continually breaking his car journeys to detour and look round remote farm properties on the moors, just on the 'off chance' of finding any evidence or clues of a horse or horse box's presence. He spent hours on the new computer trying to study various routes that a horse box leaving his yard might have taken to remote areas on quiet country roads. He spent hours on the telephone to the police to keep their searches alive. Shane Kerne was often in his thoughts as well. Was revenge a motive for him after Danny's visit to his office? Maybe being taken down a peg or two still riled him but this kidnapping was in another higher league.

Most of the people involved in the searches and investigations when Highlight was stolen, had 'moved on' to other things as the months rolled by, after no real leads had been discovered. But not Danny, who felt something urging him on. Maybe again it was some psychic influence with the tingling feelings in his shoulder which always made him think that perhaps Mary, his first love, was looking over him at some crucial time. Or maybe it was just his love for the horse, but what could he do? There seemed to be just nothing to go on, except this urge to not give up on Highlight.

Madame Fatale was not long off foaling. She had separated herself from the other horses which was one of the first signs that the birth was imminent and she was brought inside and the time and her condition was being monitored and extra nutrition and care given. The Ross family were all a bit nervous and wanted to stay around. They were prepared in case the birth of Madame Fatale's foal encountered any problems.

As is often the case the birth was natural and during the night, with just Danny there who ensured that after the birth the bonding of foal and mother was good. By the morning Julie and Johnny were soon on the scene to see that the foal was on her feet and already suckling hungrily.

"What name is he going to have?" asked Danny.

"Monsieur Dramico; from both mare and stallion s parentage? He's a beauty. Four white socks and a perfect white diamond on his face. A good 'lanky' look. That promises a big long striding colt."

A quite emotional and happy family; but for Danny, Highlight's quality could never be replaced!

The horse training business was in need of some reorganisation and addition of good quality race horses to live up to the reputation they had now established. And some cash was now available to modestly buy into ownership of another horse as well. Danny decided to learn more about the breeding side of the racing game and to make a trip to the site of an Irish Bloodstock Sale. He wanted to buy a yearling colt with a good pedigree at a reasonable price. He chose to travel by Irish Car Ferry, rather than flying, and planned for Julie and Johnny to manage things. Everything was prepared with food and drink for the journey as he was planning a very early start, driving the horse box over the Pennines, through Wales to the Holyhead Ferry and on to Dublin.

Conscious of this, he did not sleep well. He was not sure whether he was awake, asleep, or half asleep. His memory brought him to the meadow and bottom field where Mary, his first love, had died. He thought about this scene often in his sadness since the accident. And then he was suddenly besieged with the tingling in his shoulders and a presence in the room that he somehow knew was his beloved Mary. He could smell her fragrance. He was trying desperately to see the face, and the long smooth black hair that she used to comb out for him to touch. His memory was gradually allowing him to see the outline of her face and then hear the whispering anxious murmur that he used to know.

"Danny. Start from the Key." she whispered. He lay still, trying his utmost to hold the vision and see more, but his memory was losing the moment and she was gone. Danny felt dizzy and befuddled as if he had been given an injection of some sort which affected his brain. And Highlight was near. He gradually became frustrated with being unable to make sense of this mindset and he stumbled into his clothes, grabbed his food and drink climbed into the cab and eased into his journey. It was a journey where he could not remember passing the various landmarks, or taking the correct routes on the way. His mind was only on trying to make sense of the words he thought the spirit of Mary had whispered! "Danny. Start from the Key". In all his past efforts he had not found any real lead to follow, or key to open or any avenue worth investigating in his yearnings for Highlight.

Once on the ferry and with horse box parked in the hold, he had a snack and a drink and then managed to relax and get a little rest. He awoke to hear noises of cars and vans being started, and clanging of the drive off doors. He was near the front of the roll off queue and had to get a move on.

"So this is Ireland the home of racing bloodstock". He was talking to himself. He had only a rough idea where he wanted to head for. He had the town of Naas, County Kildare in his mind, but he stopped once he had cleared the ferry terminal, intent on looking at the maps. The weather was dull and dark with a heavy mist. Where am I now he wondered and he wound down the driver's window, could see very little, and so he leaned to the passenger window and wound it down. All he could see was a road sign for the opposite direction, which said "Quayside". Not much use to him. He decided to proceed further. After a little while he felt uncomfortable with where he was and stopped again. "Not many road signs in Ireland" he said to himself. The only one he had seen so far was the one pointing back to the Quay.

"Start from the Key" he had heard Mary say. Key or Quay? His whole body shook and shivered as it dawned on him what Mary may have whispered. He started off again in a trance just driving anywhere as he tried to absorb the meaning of this séance. He was ultimately on the N81 but he left it by impulse at the first exit on to a small side road. But what forced this undeniable compulsion? He got out of the car and stood looking about. He was consumed by some sort of spirit drawing him forward and he stumbled on the grass verge, lost his balance and fell to the ground. The impact shook him out of the trance he was in. He scrambled back trembling to his car, slammed the door, hit the starter and accelerated away at speed. Finally, at a fork in the road he followed the sign, indicating the road to Naas and he pulled in at the first lay-by feeling that he had returned from some unreal world. Some fantasy of his mind.

He found a B&B on the outskirts of the town and was glad to get his head down and try to relax and rid himself of the tremor from the apparition.

The following morning, he found the Bloodstock Auction Sales Dealer that had advertised the well-bred yearling in the auction lists. He watched the sales for a time before locating the horse in which he was interested. She looked interesting, seemed advanced for a yearling, good conformation and movement, and calm in the surroundings of people, horses and noise. All the paper work seemed in order but the dealer was suggesting a part cash pre-sales deal, obviously to receive undeclared money to avoid taxes and fees. Danny had cheque book ready but put it away when declining any improper arrangement, where upon the dealer finally agreed to the cheque. All a bit "ropey" thought Danny; but the colt looked a fine prospect if handled right. He loaded him and secured him in the horse box. He had time to kill now before his return ferry. And time to think. His recent apparition was still on his mind and on his return for the evening ferry he decided to tempt fate by going via the little side road of last night's happening. Driving very slowly, looking all around, even before he reached the spot of his stumble, he saw a smallholding just off the road and a knock up sign with" Horse for Sale" on it. The place exuded an atmosphere of fearful unreality. He exited his cab, warily crept forward in the darkness and mist. And then he instantly became a believer of Mary's 'life ever after'. From his previous apparitions with Mary he just knew that this secret location was the place where he was going to find Highlight, his beloved horse! The shape in the shadows became clearer and the horse lifted her head and they simultaneously recognised each other. Danny for a moment collapsed to the ground in a shock reaction. But a greater ' hurting shock' for Danny was the state that the horse was in. Bedraggled unkempt, damp sack as a cover; and swollen in foal! She obviously had been stood up for a stallion fairly shortly after her kidnapping. What had gone wrong with the criminal plans thereafter, resulting in Highlights demise, was not known. Maybe Kerne had taken his revenge in seeing the horse stolen and had then offloaded into Ireland.

Danny looked around, could not see anyone at the cottage, grabbed the bridle and ran with the horse towards the road to his horse box. Highlight followed with 'horse sense' in complete co-operation as if her confidence in Danny was unimpaired by all that had passed. He quickly dropped the loading ramp of the horse box down and pulled the horse in, next to the yearling he had bought earlier. He raised the doors, slammed the bolts, and ran towards the driver's seat.

A giant of a man, unkempt and threatening, had appeared from the cottage and was barring his way. The only way that Danny could pass him to get to the driver's door, was to distract him and Danny went right up to him with his money pouch out." This is for you", he waved the open pouch at him and then dropped it to the floor when he was about to close in. The giant bent over opting for the money rather than Danny, who jumped into the cab, locked the door, crashed a few gears and was off away at speed. Three miles further on he stopped to think about what he had just done and the resulting impact of it.

Horse rustling carried heavy penalties and he had wished those penalties, and more, on whoever had stolen Highlight from him. Now he had just 'bought' her back for a few hundred quid! Should he return to the smallholding to find out more but risk the dangers he might meet? No way! That place, off the beaten track, exuded a crime scene. An atmosphere of corruption, poverty and mystery prevailed. The giant of a man looked capable of violence in the third degree.

On his way to the ferry he stopped near a goods yard and found two empty wooden pallets. He separated and roped the horse box into two rough compartments to keep the horses confined for the sea crossing. Getting aboard the ferry, was accomplished without problems. He stayed in the driver's seat as long as he could, threw feed to the horses and then found a quiet corner in the lounge to think about the way forward.

First and foremost he phoned Julie and the family. "Listen. You'll never believe this! I've found Highlight." He stopped there and unsure what to say next, he said no more.

"Are you alright Danny? What's the matter with you? You're going out of your mind with keep bothering about Highlight! Where are you? Whatever are you doing?"

"She's alright Julie. I should be home in about four hours." Danny rang off. He did not know where to start explaining. His phone rang. It was Julie. He did not dare to answer that the unbelievable had just happened!

CHAPTER 36

Breeding Programme

When Danny drove into the stable yard the family were all waiting for him with questions. Julie gave him a hug and asked "Are you alright? Your call worried us! Whatever is happening to you." She really wondered if he was going out of his mind because of the Highlight saga.

"Yes, I know this is beyond belief but come and look."

He dropped the horsebox doors and first brought out their new yearling and led him to the stalls. Highlight was then brought gently down the ramp. She looked in really bad shape. The exuberance that Julie used to know was gone, but she recognised her features.

"Get plenty of warm water, let's wash her down and get her inside the barn as quick as we can. Warm blankets, food, drink and nutrients. Send for Sam Long and see if he'll come straight away."

Highlight foaled a filly that night. It was a difficult birth for her. She had no stamina or strength and Danny, Johnny and the vet had to work hard to assist the birth of the foal. The vet predicted that Highlight may be unable to survive in the condition she was in. Highlight was barely able to stand. She was presented to the filly, nuzzled her a little and managed the important first colostrum's and feed. She wanted to bond with her baby foal but she was nearly spent. She was given a little time but, in order to stop her suffering further, Sam Long had no option but to put her down by injection in the early hours of the following morning. The whole family were distraught. Julie and Marion took their sorrow back inside the house. Their past grieving over the first loss of Highlight, when she had been kidnapped, was tinged with hope and uncertainty. Now the sadness returned and they grieved once more, but now they had her baby foal to love. For Danny, Johnny and Sam Long there was so much to be done for the foal. Monitoring her temperature and heart rate and. taking blood samples for Sam's analysis. Encouraging her to suck from a bottle for milk substitute and nutrients at Sam's instructions and then his registration of the birth and the like. They moved the Irish yearling that Danny had bought back from Ireland, close to her in a divided stall for comfort and companionship. As the days progressed it was regular two hour feeding from a bucket. The next stage was to introduce Madame Fatale and her own foal. The company of the other horses was to awaken interest and progress interaction between the foals and the mare.

Danny and the family buried Highlight not far from Mary's Cedar tree where Danny often lingered. Her foal had become known as Pamperlight. This was mainly because the amount of time that the workforce at the stables found vitally necessary for her wellbeing, was seen by some as 'pampering 'her. In the months to follow, it did however begin to show some reward as, from a terrible start in her life she was beginning to 'grow' in every respect. Any lack of a mother was being overcome by the bravery and curiosity she showed when sometimes left alone. They all could see in her, some of the character and determination of Highlight her mother. She would canter with neck arched, tail up, and exaggerated knee raising as if deliberately showing off. It was soon clear that the 'unknown' stallion that Highlight had 'visited' must have been a thoroughbred. What schemes had gone wrong thereafter with Highlights welfare, was not known. Madame Fatale must also have smelled or recognised something from Highlight, her 'best friend', in the foal and she was now unofficial mother to two foals; in their protection, education and wellbeing. And she took her 'duties' very seriously.

the house. Buy some bottles and bring them to Andrews with you. We're going in a minute. It's just further down the road."

Danny and Marion tagged on. The sound of the loud music left no doubt about which house the 'party' was at. A big detached property was in its own grounds. A strobe light had been set up and couples were dancing, some together, some apart with bottles in their hands. It took a little time to get used to the noise and the darkness and flashing lights. Shortly Kathleen came over to them. " Hello Marion, I remember you from our college. Are you still working with your horses and with Johnny? I'll see if I can fix you up with Andrew for the night. He's on his own tonight I think." Kathleen spoke to Andrew and they came over to them.

"Hi, this is Marion and Johnny: Marion meet Andrew". Come on Johnny let's have a dance." Marion thought that Andrew looked a decent sober boy. A bit quiet perhaps. They were both stuck for words at first having been 'thrown together' but they managed to find two empty kitchen chairs and converse a little above the noise of the music. Marion felt a little bit like this was not really her scene and that they were both a bit reserved with the opposite sex in this party situation. They tried to keep the conversation going as they watched figures being openly intimate together on the 'dance floor'. Among them was Kathleen whose body was completely draped around Johnny whose hands grasped her buttocks. After a couple of drinks to the good, Marion spoke." I'm not much good at dancing, but we can give it a go if you like."

Andrew replied "Well to be honest, I am not either. Would you like a breath of fresh air? We could walk in the gardens for a bit." It seemed like a good idea to Marion and she was glad to escape the crowd. They walked a bit. Andrew made a clumsy attempt to kiss her. She wasn't exactly surprised at this. After a while she tried to break away but Andrew was now gripping her very tightly, leaning on her so that it was difficult for her to move. His hands were now on the move. Now to her breasts in a clumsy but insistent way. It was more like a brutal assault than an amorous advance. Marion might have been naive in relationships, but she was not naive in everything and she' kneed' him as hard as she could and hit the right spot because he was hurt enough to go down on one knee in pain.

Marion shouted "I didn't want your company for this you know."

"So, you're not up for it. O.K I'm sorry."

He just walked away, limping back to the house.

It was all unexpected and she was agitated with it all. She tried to compose herself when he had gone, wondering what was expected of her, and slipped back into the house looking for Johnny.

There was no sign of Johnny among the dancers, in the lounge or the kitchens. An intoxicated Kathleen had been doing her best to drive him to utter depravity. On the dance floor she was moving his hands to parts of her body swaying in and out, grinding him to her, with thighs into his crotch and then breaking away to drink from her glass of mixed cocktail, and then quickly again draping her body over him hips working into him. Johnny was becoming recklessly desperate for more. Kathleen grabbed a bottle of vodka and a glass and dragged him to a door, opened it, pushed him in and closed it behind them. He quickly realised that it was a bedroom. She was laughing at the look on his face as he watched her dive onto the bed." We might as well be comfy, come on. Bring the vodka bottle with you."

Johnny was both amazed and dazed at the opportunity that seemed to be laid before him. What was happening to his ideas of getting to know a girl, courting her, snogging and careful working up to a mutual desire for a relationship that would lead to the fulfilment of both his and her longing?

He climbed on the bed ready for the action to begin. But Kathleen was not for taking part. She was only wanting to chat and drink. She was not responsive to his love making when he was expectant of his opportunity. She stopped all the action at this critical stage. She was just playing games with him and his desires. Danny was' deflated'. What an anti- climax! What was her idea in coxing him on when she knew it was only to eventually deprive him? She was playing a game with his desires when she wanted to just chat and share the vodka with him. He was angry when he realised, she was not serious; in fact, it was just a funny game to her. He left Kathleen in the bedroom and immediately saw an unhappy Marion looking for him.

"I'm not stopping here Johnny. Let's go back to the Red Bull." It was pretty quiet at the pub with lively Kathleen away; and the two were also pretty quiet as they headed for home with differing thoughts of what might have been! Marion knew that Johnny was obsessed with Kathleen, and she did not mention her 'contra -temps with Andrew's actions and words. She wondered how she might find 'old fashioned ' decent, patient young men interested in a long-term relationship and not just a one-night stand.

Marion still made a point of befriending Kathleen for what she might learn because her personality made her the 'hub' of activity. She was well known locally behind the bar at the Red Bull. She knew about the city night clubs, holiday jobs, and careers, and Corporate Entertaining opportunities at Race meetings. In fact, all the wider aspects of 'living the life' as a teenager. Marion admired Kathleen for her friendly personality and the way she could manoeuvre herself into the limelight. Marion's 'day job 'remained at the family's stables but her thoughts and interests were now also engaged elsewhere with an eye for clawing her way out of village life and sampling the whole wide world.

The Horse Race meetings were put on to attract and entertain punters, visitors, company sponsors, owners, syndicate members and the general public. All had money to spend on the entertainment being provided and Kathleen knew this.

Kathleen introduced Marion to the Landlady at the Red Bull and, when they were short of staff behind the bar Marion started collecting empties and helping with food orders. She loved the job and the company and friendly atmosphere. Always something new to talk about or someone new to joke with, in contrast to the routines at the stables. Working late at the pub and then an early start at the stables was hard to do, but cash and the variety of additional nights work, attracted her.

Corporate Hospitality and catering at Doncaster's Evening race meetings were her next ambition.

Marion wanted to have a free choice of career and her friend Kathleen had now become a Race Day Hostess. Kathleen's personality and friendly obliging nature in entertaining' well to do' guests at the meetings seemed to make her' in demand' with clients. She was there to bring their drinks, place their bets for them in their quest to find a winner or two, about which she had gained a little knowledge. However, a few of the rich and young clients wanted the festivities and the drinking to continue into the late evening after the race meeting had finished. As the 'hostess with the mostess' Kathleen was in demand for the meals and after. Money was not an issue with most of the clientele. Marion gradually started seeing what was going on for Kathleen and one or two other girls. When she 'quizzed' Kathleen about it, she admitted that the money was more than excellent for just being around and serving drinks. Marion agreed to give the work a try at the current race meetings evening party. What Kathleen did not tell Marion was that occasionally in some circumstances she might convey a suggestion that in the evening she was amenable for more, and If" she liked them" she might "let them". She was leading them on, as they became intoxicated. Playing with their alcohol fuelled emotions and desires, only to back off and frustrate them, so leaving herself richer but intriguingly deceptive and elusive.

Marion realised that Kathleen was playing a dangerous game. Ever more dangerous as the evening progressed and the drinks flowed and when the guests were not necessarily English. This appeared to be another ruthless side to the popular Kathleen's personality. Marion could see Kathleen's desire to both make money, and make things happen in her life by not always conforming to the norm. This again contrasted to Marion's routines, stable habits and relative 'inexperience'.

Amongst a party of French Racing enthusiasts supporting the French trained second favourite in the big race,one man called Pierre had introduced himself and in particular had 'befriended' Kathleen in the Bar, tipping well when drinks were brought and while there to enjoy himself, seeming to be a quiet, polite, considerate and sensible, but naive personality . After the French trained horse won its race in a gambling coup, there were loud celebrations and during the late buffet Pierre invited Kathleen to have a drink with him in his hotel room, 'not as a hostess but as a friendly date'.

"Please bring Drinks with you from this money I give you now. For you this evening." The amount of money he gave her was in excess of that required for drinks, and Kathleen was slow to grasp any inference in this. She was quite prepared for a little familiarity in return from this rich and handsome young Frenchman and she thought she could' control events' as was her experiences with her dangerous game! She had tantalised many young men and benefitted in popularity and in various other ways from their desires. Now there were rich financial 'pickings' to be had in the job as she played the 'very friendly hostess' whose charms and personality were a delight.

She was not surprised that Pierre was alone and waiting when she knocked quietly on his room door. He poured them large drinks and the language translations and understandings made conversation slow and difficult. She began to sense something urgent and perhaps sinister about his manner as he sat very close to her. With the alcohol his advances quickly became more sexual but she went along with it for a little time, but as things progressed, she found that this time she could neither 'talk him off, ' or 'fend him off'. Her protestations and her usual ' hold off' and excuses were ignored. He pretended to not understand what she was saying and his insistence was demanding. He was now physically overcoming her resistance, pushing her on to the bed, using the weight of his body to hold her and prevent her wriggling free while his hands were brutally dragging away her modesty. The talking had finished; to be replaced by a silent physical struggle. He wanted her almost naked, and was using his considerable weight and strength in what became a prolonged silent and desperate fight between them, until he was forcibly down on her with no apparent thoughts for the consequences of the action. Thoughts only for his need and satisfaction. In the struggle Kathleen's stamina had ebbed away. She was physically helpless to stop his prolonged action until he was satisfied with his fulfilment. When he was done with her, he rolled aside lying in 'recovery' on the bed. Kathleen had never been treated ruthlessly like this before and she was in panic. She thought that she had been raped. She eventually grasped her clothes, started screaming at him as she tried to dress. Now he lay relaxing on the bed and was still ignoring her words. Kathleen was so distraught, and upset and maddened now by his disrespect and in this state her anger and panic at the situation came to the fore. She grasped the heavy wooden bedside lamp and with strength from her panic smashed it down on the side of his head, where he lay, with as much force as she could gather. He never saw it coming. He never knew what hit him. She saw blood from his face and he had not moved. At this, she grabbed her remaining clothes, rushed across the room to the door, unlocked it, and then ran out into the corridor slamming the door behind her. She saw the lift, but thinking about avoiding any witnesses of her dishevelled and mindless state she took to the stairs, ran down two floors, stopped for breath and to complete her dressing and now, walking slowly and carefully, left the stairwell avoiding the reception area and away. She was bruised and battered and now distraught and panicky, worrying about what he had done to her and then, what she had done to him with the heavy table lamp and the resulting spurt of blood from his split forehead. She was transformed from the confident couldn't care less personality into a nervous and introverted, frightened young woman. Kathleen walked a little way from the hotel trying to calm her nerves before managing to stop a taxi, directing the driver to the village. Sat in the taxi she looked for money to pay the fare and counted the notes she had been given 'for drinks'. It was in twenty pound notes amounting to nearly two hundred and fifty pounds. Oh my God! This was not 'drinks money', it was money in expectation of rather more favours; and she had taken the money from him. No wonder he had 'forced the pace' unremittingly. It was what he expected, and her struggles had invigorated him.

What if she became pregnant? What if his injuries were serious? What if he rang for the hotel staff? What if they then called the police? Would they be able to trace her? She stopped the taxi to let her out near to the Ross Racing stables, paid him, waited until he was gone and then slowly walked the rest of her way home. What had she got herself in to with her dangerous game? She crept up to her bedroom without wakening any of the family. Her turmoil prevented sleep. What could she do? Her fear of all the consequences had broken her spirit.

had left before Marion. She did not speak. The policeman was waiting for an answer to his question about the taxi driver.

"I am not sure. I might be able to."

"What were you wearing? Could we have a look at the clothes you wore last night?" Marion went to her room and brought down her coat and waitress uniform, which the police man inspected and returned to her. "We will need to ask you further questions later. Please keep yourself available, rather than us holding you in custody at this stage. Some of the French guests were apparently quite drunk late in the evening. Did you see any arguments or incidents as such?"

Marion shook her head. She thought that she had to be careful what she said. The inspector looked very hard at her for some moments before indicating that was all for now.

Do they think that I had something to do with the crime? Was Kathleen involved, she wondered to herself. After a time, she decided to ring Kathleen on her mobile. There was no reply on that number.

She tried her home phone number. Answer phone message —not available. Kathleen seemed to have disappeared. Marion could not settle down to the stable work. She could not rest until she knew more about the incident and Kathleen's whereabouts and her part if any, in the incident that led to the man being critical in a coma. She decided to risk going first to the Hotel and then, perhaps to Copside village.

The full investigation team were busy taking fingerprints, photos of the crime scene, searching for evidence. The Press reporters and photographers were active and some of the hotel staff and guests were rushing around and asking questions. A good deal of the commotion was made by one of the French guests who would not book out until the story had unravelled and the attacker of his friend Pierre had been arrested. Supporting him in an aggressive manner was a big rough, tough looking man with a limp. He looked familiar to her but she could not recall why. When he was talking on his mobile, she edged carefully closer to try to hear what he was saying. She only heard an odd word but it was enough for her to be horrified." Yes Mr Kerne." It was one of Shane Kerne's henchmen. She had learned only a little of her father's dealings with the crooked gambling syndicate and that name sent a shiver down her spine and she quickly faded in to the distant background. 'Without Kathleen's presence she was at a loss to assess whether or why she or Kathleen might be possible suspects. And her friend had disappeared! She would have to tell her father what she knew and assure him that she was only involved as a waitress bringing drinks for the French party. However, Kathleen had disappeared, and the police were asking Marion some leading questions!

The two policemen were soon back knocking on her door while she was still talking to Danny. They had now established from the Taxi firm that at slightly different times before midnight two journeys had been made from the town to Ross Stables and one of the journeys's Marion had admitted to and the other probably was Kathleen, who had completely disappeared! They would not believe that Marion did not know more than she was saying in answering their questions. But they did not have enough evidence to apprehend her. Kathleen's disappearance suggested to Marion that she was involved and in trouble.

The telephone rang and Danny answered it. The threatening demanding voice of the early troubled days with Highlight and Kerne's manipulations, was back again.

"Has your daughter told you how much trouble she is in, Ross? Could be murder of a French visitor to the Races! We'll need a couple of favours from you if you don't want us to incriminate her. We'll be back to you shortly." Murder is a serious business you know!" Danny was worried, but his days work with the horses had to continue.

CHAPTER **39**

Generation Genes

The young colt Danny had bought in Ireland, had been named Gingerbread and had been developing quietly over the months, away from all the attention surrounding Highlight's protégé Pamperlight. The colt had also benefited from the equine company of Madame Fatale and her own protégé in the early days, but with more maturity, and more intensive training, education and gallops, she was becoming ready to experience the Racecourse. Gingerbread had shown some speed at home but was a bit temperamental among other horses and at the starting stalls. Danny entered him in five-furlong novices' race at Kempton Park. Marion said that she wanted to accompany Johnny to Kempton Park. She had in mind to stay overnight in London after the race meeting. It would be her first chance to contact an Employment Agency that

line to Soho. Her heart was pounding as she surfaced from the tube and feared the sight of the man again.

She was looking for an Employment Agency that Kathleen had mentioned. It was getting late with the darkness and drizzle setting in by the time she found it.

Yes, Kathleen had registered there! No, they had been unable to find her immediate work but on questioning, admitted that she had left a contact address of a bar in Soho, but with instructions not to divulge it. More wandering in strange little streets in the dark and the rain until she finally found it. The barman's response to Marion was. "No! She left. Try back Chapel Street Flats." More directions, more streets in the rain. She finally ended climbing up three flights of dark, damp narrow steps to a door with graffiti all over it. There was no answer to her knocking. With heart beating she decided to push the door open and she could just distinguish someone lying on the bed in the dark. It was Kathleen! But not the Kathleen she had known! She was in a bad state; bedraggled, dirty, shivering and afraid. She cowered back. When she realised that it was Marion she burst into sobbing and crying. When Marion put her arms round her she gripped her and would not let go, with broken hearted sobs and wails. The embrace lasted for some five minutes before finally Marion managed to disentangle herself. The room was 'mangy'. Dark, damp and cold. And Kathleen was shivering in fear. Marion threw Kathleen's bits of belongings into her small case, wrapped her in her own topcoat and almost had to carry her down the steps to the street below, where she managed to hire a taxi cab to her hotel. She left Kathleen in the cab while she booked in, and then 'smuggled 'her up to her hotel room by the back steps.

Still breathless, she ran a hot bath for Kathleen who just sat there, gaunt, head down, fatigued and despairing. Seemingly she was incapable of doing anything. Marion had to strip her damp and dirty clothing from her, help her into the bath and wash her. Then she shampooed her hair, just as one would look after a small child. While she let Kathleen soak in the hot bath, Marion relaxed a little after all the happenings and tried to assess the situation. As she helped Kathleen out of the bath, she, for the first time noticed her perfectly lithe, slim and beautifully perfect naked figure. The hot bath treatment had transformed her, but it was Marion's protection and strength of character that was the main factor. Marion herself thoughtfully compared her own far more ample breasts and muscular body honed by the physical labours of the stable work she did. She wrapped Kathleen in the bath robe, and sat on the bed with her, hugged her and then dried, brushed and fixed her hair, as a loving mother would do to her child, before helping her into the double bed and covering her up with the duvet, where she quickly was asleep.

Marion composed herself, made a cup of coffee and ate the biscuits provided by the hotel. She too, was tired and hungry. She hot showered, dried and donned her night wear. Comparatively, Kathleen's beautifully perfect, lithesome, but vulnerable figure was still in her mind as was her vulnerability of character. She slid into bed next to Kathleen but the presence of her at first somehow prevented Marion from sleep. She turned, closer to her friend and rested her arm round Kathleen's waist in a protective gesture before finally finding sleep.

As they awoke early the following morning, they both in turn needed time to recall where they were, and the trauma they had been through., and then absorb the warmth, comfort and security of the shared bed. Kathleen again pulled Marion closer. She knew that she had been her saviour out of the awful existence and disparaging episodes of hiding in the city. She had tried unsuccessfully to earn enough money to live off, while keeping herself unnoticed by the law and in fear of men who were just after her body for their selfish plans. The admiration and her dependence on what Marion had done for her when she was at her wits end, and the awareness of her warm well- muscled bodies strength and dependability told her that what she needed was this woman's love and friendship instead of the struggle to resist men's frenzied, selfish demands of her. In a confused state of shock, she pressed herself as close to Marion in every way she could. And then she gradually began to relax contentedly.

Marion awoke, remembered Kathleen's presence and what she had been through and what it had done to her. She raised her arms to her in a comforting embrace. The first 'closeness' between them had been because of Kathleen's panic-stricken need and Marion's need to protect and comfort her. Now in the comforting warmth of the bed, the embrace introduced other feelings. The friendship and the admiration of Kathleen's beautiful body was what attracted Marion as a better alternative to the perplexity of men's selfish approaches she had so far experienced. The kiss which followed naturally for them both was prolonged until it was interrupted by a banging on the bedroom door. Kathleen rushed into the bathroom and closed the door. Marion waited quietly. There was no sound now from the corridor outside. She put the safety chain on and then started to open the door. It was immediately pushed hard from the outside. Through the open crack she was suddenly eye to eye with James Cross. He violently elbowed the door again but the chain held.

He spoke in a sarcastic manner "It's O.K. I was just checking that you were both still in there!" Had a good night, have you both? I have a proposition for you both". He disappeared from view. How were they going to get away from the hotel and from him? Marion dressed quickly,

CHAPTER **40**

Dead Heat

B ack at the Ross stables Danny was desperate to hear from Marion. She had not been in touch since the Kempton meeting and when Johnny arrived back with the horsebox and without Marion, he was vague about her plans in London.

Brother Johnny's head was now full of other thoughts. At the Kempton Meeting where he was in charge of the running of Gingerbread, he had been formally introduced to Samantha Jacobs, the daughter of Darrell Jacobs, the successful Entrepreneur and Irish owner of the winner of the Laurel stakes over in America. Johnny had secretly admired Samantha, a gifted, beautiful girl who seemed to have everything to look forward to. And now, what's more, a friend of hers had told him that she knew who he was and that 'she had been enamoured by him' and wanted to get more of his company!

Ross Stables was going through a busy time with the up and coming young horses, Pamperlight, Gingerbread and Monsieur Dominic ever nearer full fitness. Gingerbread was entered for his second run shortly, this time over six furlongs at Doncaster. It was not like Marion to not keep in touch, and with the threatening telephone calls from Kerne's mob and the daily publicity about the Hotel incident and the Frenchman's fight for life, Danny had a very uneasy mindset. He tried to concentrate on the stabling work but decided, later in the day, to go and see Liam and Martha at the Dairy Farm to see if their son Shaun could give him a hand with the stabing.When Dannyl arrived at the Dairy Farm, he found a heated argument going on between Liam and his son. Young Shaun had grown up to be a bit of a hothead. Many of his ideas differed from those of Liam and Martha, as many of the younger generation's ideas did in a fast-moving world. Poor milk prices were making it difficult to make a good living and Shaun was impatient to get decent rewards from the hard work he put in.

Both men were shouting angrily, but the row stopped when Danny entered. Shaun was quickly on his way with an angry and determined look on his face and the farmer's shotgun in his hand.

An uncomfortable Danny asked "What was all that about"? Neither Liam nor Martha responded.

"How is the workload going? I was wondering if Shaun could give us a few hours at the stables."

Again, there was a delay in responding. Liam looked at Martha and then spoke. "Shaun has a lot on his mind at the moment. I wouldn't want to ask him at present ". There was no further explanation. It was unlike Liam, but Danny left it at that. He walked out with nothing more to say. Liam followed him out and now spoke.

"James Cross has been here."

At the mention of James Cross being at the farm the alarm bells were ringing in Danny's ears. Concern and absolute fury at the thought that something was going on there behind his back. No wonder Liam was not answering his question. This man Cross was now amongst them, and his links to Shane Kerne spelled of crime and violence to achieve his way. His presence meant trouble. The phone demands from Kerne's mob; Marion's secrecy about her time in London. The incident at the hotel, and Kathleen's possible involvement and disappearance. He felt like it was a grip being tightened round his throat. His fury abounded. Shane Kerne was out for further revenge and to ruin him.

It was Danny's nature to react to adversity!

James Cross's threatening presence and attitude with Shaun at the farm, and his avoidance of Liam and Martha had now also alerted Liam as well as Danny. He knew his own son well enough to recognise when he was in trouble, because he was easily pressured into taking hasty and rash actions. With Cross and another thug turning up, Liam had just wrung the story of what was going on, from his son, when Danny had arrived.

The story was that, with money on offer, Cross had enticed Shaun into passing on a parcel containing drugs to another contact who was a driver of the daily milk collections from the farm. Once incriminated, Shaun was blackmailed into being used to distribute further drugs. Packages arrived at the farm from the Continent via a Feedstock Delivery and were being moved on via the milk collections wagon. Shaun was next being incriminated, when a cash payment was missed. He was being 'roped in' by the Kerne gang.

Suddenly, Liam and Martha heard loud shouting and were then shocked by several loud gun shots being fired in the yard. Martha now feared for Shaun and also her husband's safety if he went out into the yard. She rushed to Danny." Danny, Cross is here and there's shooting outside. I'm phoning 999 for the police."

Danny was already on the way to the yard, with his Smith –Weston gun in hand, and when he got there, he and Liam cautiously crept out towards the barn. Shots had been exchanged. A body could be seen lying near the bales

alongside. Marion and Kathleen together. Julie smiling in happiness to suggest that her future was calm and safe.

And then as Julie held him, his mind and body relaxed. He was gone from the world he had fashioned for himself and all those close to him.

He entered another place where he saw his beloved Mary, still a youthful smile on her face. Floating with Arms outstretched awaiting him to drift with her. No pain, no anguish, no worries, no fears, as they contentedly drifted in an embrace. Together again in the Universe of After Life.

No tingling in his shoulders now!

End of Part 1.

PART 2

Julie's Fortune

CHAPTER 1

Julie

I t was the day of the Wedding of the year for the village of Hilden Cross in the Yorkshire Wolds.

The young and innocent Julie Manors, was the only child of Mr and Mrs Manors, principles of the village and owners of the large county estate. She was marrying Danny Ross, renowned farmer at Wallace farm; who had a pretty long history according to the village gossips. As an only child, and of the rich and much respected Manor's family, Julie was envied and sometimes jealously shunned by her age group at the Pony club and the Local Hunt. When Julie showed an aptitude to horse riding, the little pony she had learned to ride on was sold and her parents bought her a magnificent well bred mare of fifteen hands, appropriately named 'High and Mighty', also new top of the range, saddlery, red jacket and jodhpurs.

In growing up, Julie's lack of boy friends of her own age was because she could do nothing without her mother's interference and influence. The boys of the village were put off by the family's privileged position and wealth. Her love was for the horse and horse riding and not really for amorous young men of little standing. When in the saddle, with the wind in her face, the feel of the power in the horse beneath her seat, was a sensational experience for her and an equine means of escape from her frustrations.

In contrast to Julie's innocence and naivety, she knew that Danny certainly had reputation and history enough for someone to write a book about it.

Julie had heard from the village gossip about Danny's troubles, joys and sorrows. In contrast her persona was of beautiful big brown eyes, innocence and inexperience, such that what she may be thinking was there for all to see.

It was her intent to break away from her parent's control. Julie felt a physical attraction to Danny' which was based on what gossip she kept hearing of his prowess .Eventually the first meeting with Danny was when, after the Local Fox Hunt, he stepped forward from the mulling crowd of spectators arms out ready to catch her fall as she slid down from her horse, and then provided her with the traditional glass of sherry. As the relationship between them gradually developed, she would not listen to her parent's concerns about Danny's "Lower Pedigree "and reputation.

The naive Julie was intent on attracting Danny's attention to her riding prowess on High and Mighty.

Not content with showing the locals what a magnificent pair Julie and her horse made, she wanted to show how she could ride the horse 'bareback'. No saddle and girth straps! Just her feet, thighs, heels and hands telling 'High and Mighty how to respond. She had been training the horse to recognise and respond to her touch and pressure signals and she knew Danny would be in the group of spectators at the annual Show on the village green.

She mounted the big horse bareback from off the paddock fence. Horse and rider both sensed the freedom and relished it. High and Mighty literally flew over the ground. So fast that all Julie's body shook, arms clinging to the horses neck; thighs and heels tight as she could, round the horses girth; relying on the horses ability to just sense what she wanted in direction and speed. Could she bring the horse to a stop, right in front of the crowd and in front of Danny, whose face showed concern and then amazement at her feat?

And then, Julie wondered; would she ever have such a marvellous feeling if and when she was intimate with the right man? And that man would be Danny Ross!

Mr Manors knew what was happening to his daughter and her infatuation. Her mother could not and would not accept that her expectations of the man marrying her daughter, were not to be. Julie's thoughts and actions were consistant in her priorities towards Danny.

When the relationship became common knowledge, Julie's father 'interviewed' Danny' ; and admitted finally to Julie's mother, to being 'somewhat assured'.by the man's words. His honesty and sincerity about his past history, and now his love for Julie, was strong. Nothing her parents said, was going to stop their union.

And so, the bride was dressed all in Virginal White attire which must have cost her parents 'the earth'. In the 1980's, the bride marrying in white, still signified accordance with Christian principles.

The Manors resistance to their daughters desires, had crumbled into agreement with some haste, as the young couple had made it clear to the parents that their insistence on a ' white wedding' meant an early date. That they could no longer go on preserving their daughter's chastity. Julie was madly in love and her choice of partner was hers and not one of theirs. Julie and Danny would not wait longer for the events of that 'honeymoon night 'to bring them together.

So Mr and Mrs Manors had their desired White Wedding Day of pomp and ceremony. The reception went well with the groom and his best man "behaving themselves" in the privileged company. That very night the Manors daughter

Julie would be taken by Danny Ross for both of their needs and satisfaction.

In the Hotel bedroom Julie knew that Danny would gently and considerately show her the way forward, as the desperation within them both was released as they undressed. They were both thankful that the ceremonies were at an end and the guests were leaving. Danny's mother who was staying overnight at the hotel, had retired to her room. Julie's parents were going home as they preferred. The best man had drunk his full and been helped upstairs to sleep it off. The newly -weds needed to calm down and relax after the occasion. They were both conscious that this night would be a future memory. Changing into nightwear together was a bit tense as they both remembered the one instance of them sharing a bedroom before. It was at the Junior two day Eventing contest. They were brought together in a shared hotel room, booked at Julie's planning, but they had changed separately in the bathroom and slept separately in the twin beds available. Danny's conscience and Julie's hesitance had helped them to resist the temptations before them..

Now they were married, in anticipation of sleeping together, and both were pleased that they had resisted temptation the last time.

Both were now relaxed and comfortable. She felt his arms around her gently holding her beside him and she was ready to respond. Julie had yearned for these moments many, many times. She felt the shortie nightdress she had carefully chosen, being lifted right up to her neck, his hands fondling her body. Her own hands were responding naturally now in invitation. His boxers were quickly removed .She willingly accepted him, and they became as one.That Julie's fears may overcome pleasure was not to be, as he treated her lovingly. They were experiencing utopia together. Breeding instincts and sexual pleasures were being satisfied and when Danny eventually showed his fulfilment as they climaxed together they were both overcome with happiness and passionate love for each other..

Julie slept contentedly in her husband's arms. She was no longer a virgin. The wedding night was nearly over and now they were a married couple, a happy couple, looking forward to a new life together as a family.

In her deep sleep Julie was dreaming of her childhood, and the culmination of the developing life that had led her to this day.

Unfortunately she cannot decide on what she is going to dream about! Dreams are not always pleasurable manifestations even when sleep is reached with a relaxed, contented feeling.

CHAPTER **2**

Julie's Adolescence

Julie's dreams would go back to events that occurred when she was growing up under the thumb of her mother and conscious of the expectations that her parents held for her, as privileged through wealth and authority. Every natural event that occurred on her progressive way to womanhood seemed to have been made into a crisis by her mother's concerns for her standing and wellbeing. Her ability to' mix ' with other children from the village was hampered by her parent's status, within the community. When dreaming, she very often recalled a nightmare time when she was just an immature fourteen year old. She was convinced that she had been verbally and physically abused.

The tramp had appeared from the deep woods as from nowhere, unshaven and dirty. He had confronted her when she had been walking down the field with her new puppy.

At first she had not been afraid. She was in her own fields on the Manors Estate which her father owned and was worked by his employees. She would tell this man that he had no right to be there!

However he ignored her words completely and came right up to her and picked up her new puppy and sat down with him on a fallen tree trunk. Now he instilled some fear in her. She must get her puppy back off him.

"He's a bonny little dog isn't he. See, he likes his belly rubbed. Here, your puppy wants you. That's it, come sit on this log with us and talk to me .I mean no harm. I'm hungry, can you get me some food or some eggs, or some loose change. I'm hard up, and I'm hard in seeing you as well you know, cause you're a bonny little girl. Nice new clothes and a lovely puppy! You've come a long way from home. Would you like to have your belly rubbed as well ?" His hand wandered rapidly across her developing bosom and quickly to her thigh. She was slow to understood what he was trying to do. She quickly scrambled to her feet as she realised. But to the young 14 year old Julie it was as if the hand had left its imprint on her, never to be erased. Remembered with some horror ever since, as she realised what his words had meant. She had managed to grab the dog and she had started to back away petrified as he laughed and pretended to unzip his front. He just laughed louder as she ran away stumbling and sobbing.

In her dreams Julie remembered that laugh for most of her young life! It had influenced her demeanour all through her adolescence.

Julie awoke from this bad dream. She hoped that now she could forget this part of her past. She was safe with Danny and still in wonderment at how their union had come about.

She recalled that she had first seen Danny Ross at the Hunt socials. She was then nearly 17 years old when nature's attraction to young men grew on her, but some of those she met, were clearly immature. She had developed a crush for Danny Ross which was new and secretive. He was a mature man, but with an impulsive nature. The village gossips said that he, had been having an affair with Mary Wallace, the wife of farmer Alex Wallace, when he was absent working abroad. When Mary Wallace had lost her life in a horrific farming accident, she was expecting Danny Ross's child. The tractor she was driving had overturned on rough terrain crushing the life out of her..

Julie knew that Danny was devastated. The double loss of a wonderful partner in 'work and play,' and unborn child,had left him bereft and inconsolable; and then needing comfort.

Julie desperately wished that she could provide that comfort, but her imagination of being in his company used to send her nerve endings fluttering and sensual warmth to her belly and thighs. And she feared that she might not be able to respond if he did speak to her, and her mind always held fear of the effect of what the tramp did many years ago..

Julie eventually discovered that the hearsay was that Danny was not short of female company from 'contempory ' women who were inviting him to 'drown his sorrows' with them. But this gossip did not deter her hopes and desires of a future relationship with him.

One day, as the local Foxhunt returned to the village green, Julie had reined in her stallion, High and Mighty and Danny had stepped forward from a group of onlookers, this arms catching her slide from her horse, but then he had held her tight for a few seconds before lowering her and releasing her to the ground. She remembered the feeling of security that his arms around her implied. She was aroused by the close contact between them. Both Danny and Julie liked it! He had released her and handed her a glass of wine and then they were again a part of the crowd.

Would he pay Julie any attention again? He had recognised her maturity by giving her a glass of wine. That improved Julie's confidence. She did not care about rumours of his boldness in seducing a married woman or to having several women for company after Mary's tragic death,. Julie began to quietly try to attract him, but he did not seem to notice her again until the time came that Danny was wanting to buy a horse and to take up riding and hunting. Julie' waited for him to seek her advice about a suitable horse for him and now she was receptive to his questions. However Danny was very careful with his advances and conscious of his own history and of her immaturity.

With Julie's help and her parent's permission, Danny purchased a horse from their stables. Natures instincts were now at play as if Julie's mind and body were being shaped in his direction. She was in love! It was clear that other people's views did not matter to her, but Danny's did!

Julie was picked as reserve for the Two day county Eventing Team. She had plucked up courage to ask Danny to accompany her to the competition and assist with horse and equipment. It would need an overnight stay at the course ready for the morning events. Julie had booked,but concealed the knowledge that the reservations had been made with only one bedroom for each couple in the team.. She had to appear shocked; as was Danny!, Julie had said to him" We can manage can't we. I trust you implicitly". She was thrilled to hear him mumble "But do I trust myself". When the time came for reaching the bedroom, the intimacy of her feelings suddenly overwhelmed her. She thought that she really wanted 'things' to happen, but as Danny came towards her from the bathroom she was suddenly afraid that her virginity and inexperience would being exposed to him. The tender' good night kiss and hold' between them, and his restraint thereafter saved matters.. She was not sure about the sensations and the strange feelings within her body, as they calmed down.

He had known that she was willing, but just expressed his feelings for her with a kiss before he had retired to his own bed. She had seen a side of him that she had not recognised from the gossip she had heard. The following morning, they were more relaxed and familiar together having both endured the night in the same bedroom, in their own twin bed just five feet apart. However, no doubt their intimacy was being assumed by the other competitors in the team.

The couple's friendship was established and gradually a courtship followed. When Danny proposed to Julie, as expected, he was then summoned to see her parents Mr and Mrs Manors. They were worried about Mr Ross's previous 'history', but were 'won over' by Danny's assurances, his confidence and sincerity of his love for her. Julie and Danny then had to fight for the early marriage date that they wanted.

That date had finally arrived. Married life was underway. Julie was a happy girl! She had got her man! Her life would be different now.

CHAPTER 3

Julie's Married life

J ulie quickly became pregnant. In the early married
years a daughter Marion, and son Johnny were born
to the couple and bringing up a young family left their
marriage and own sexual relationship suffering with routine
and lack of quality time. Julie became a good wife and
mother,and had very little spare time.The Hunts Social
evenings were her main chances to relax. However Danny's
increasing commitment to his horse racing business, with
its occasional overnight absences from home and actions to
avoid racings criminal schemes, were usually tolerated by
Julie. It was only when his 'working away' caused his absence
from the Hunts Socials that Julie was embarrassed at having
no partner. She had, in a fit of pique, hired Roberto, a
young male professional, to act as a dance partner and
escort. The intimate role that Roberto played took her by

surprise and she was to be persuaded by Roberto into a private and 'broader' sexual escort contract.. She had, in confidence, admitted to Roberto that while she loved her husband, with the passage of time, she did not always know how best to please and satisfy him sexually. Roberto was quickly showing her how to remove any embarrassment in order to bring back the enjoyment to her marriage relationship. All this as part of the terms of contract and done in a professional manner. Roberto showed her in strict confidence how to forget embarrassment; and try taking the initiative. Get fit, wear more slinky underwear, don't just play a passive role. That was just what he said and just what she did for Danny! The practical sessions she had paid for were tried on her husband; and certainly recharged both their batteries! Julie's constant desire for physical pleasures and living married life to the full, was maintained as the kids grew up with a happy mother who they all relied on.. Julie did however retain some embarrassment on occasions when Roberto showed up at the village social!

CHAPTER 4

Aftermath to a Duel

A double shooting, resulting in the deaths of two renowned figures, hit the local Yorkshire County Press headlines. That was at the farming estate adjacent to the Ross racing stables where in the past a famous racehorse called Highlight had been trained for its spectacular racing successes. The two men were well known in two vastly different communities but their deaths were attributed to the same incident and location.

The police, the news reporters, the Health and Safety Inspectors, the Racing Club Committee, in fact everyone, wanted to know about the links that brought a popular community figure and a dangerous 'underworld' criminal to both die by gun shots in a ' Duel in the Sun'. A bitter struggle came to a climax with the deaths of Julie Ross's husband Danny, a well known figure; and Shane

Kerne- a proven criminal gang leader. It left a wife and her family sad and grieving, and a gang of Betting Sharks in complete disarray without their leader.

For many years Julie had been reliant on her husband Danny in most business aspects of their married life and the management of the land and the racing stables.. Now she felt that her whole life had been turned upside down. She felt so helpless to try to continue without him. Julie felt that she had lost everything.

Both her son Johnny and daughter Marion had responsibilities in the racing business that her husband had built up, while ' old hands' Liam and Martha ran the adjacent farm from their cottage nearby.

The shock of Danny's loss meant that adjustments were necessary and both sides of the business were neglected in the short term. The daily jobs had all to be done, by son Johnny and daughter Marion who both had ambitions elsewhere. Her husband's loss, meant changes for Julie. Many jobs were being 'left for another day', and the media's prying into the crime scene and the background stories, was incessant.

The vulnerability that Julie had shown in her adolescence, before her marriage to Danny many years ago, had returned with his death. She had become nervous and again lacking in confidence. An abstract woman again, after always having a husband for support when she needed her partner.

With Danny's death, Julie really needed to make a lifestyle change. And this was difficult for her to do. She was also missing the marital bedroom style that she and Danny had re-found and which had rekindled their marriage relationship and given them the synergy to fulfil their life's obligations. This pleasure was gone. She missed Danny's comforting partnership in both work and play.

She mourned his absence; had not even been seen outside, leisure walking or riding her hunter stallion High and Mighty. She found it to be a real effort to even step outside the house. This was in contrast to the confident wife and mother she had been over many years.

One morning when looking out from her lounge window a nervous and depressed Julie, caught a glimpse of wisps of smoke coming from the edge of the copse down the valley on their boundary with the forest. Looking longer, she imagined a crouching figure moving in the shade of the hedge.

Maybe a tramp living rough. Maybe it was a racing fan trying to approach the gallops to check on the horses in their training run. Or maybe a poacher after rabbits or grouse. Or anything he could pinch? Now with no Danny to go down to the wood to investigate and 'see off ' intruders, the sight of a tramp in the copse had made her nervous and Julie was ever more nervous because it brought back to her troubled mind a nightmare of the distant past when as a mere fourteen year old girl she was accosted by a tramp.

Julie was in her lounge again the following evening when she again spotted traces of smoke rising from the copse. Trespassers were there with a fire lit and they were camping down there without rights. Her son Johnny was away at the Jacobs stables and she had nobody else that she felt able to call on. Suddenly there was a loud knocking on the kitchen door and she was half afraid to open it. Knocking again, and she cracked the door open to peep out.

"Is that you Julie?. Aren't you going to let me in?" With some relief she recognised that the voice was that of Roberto.

"I'm sorry I have not called before, since the funeral. I kept meaning to call and then something always seemed to happen to keep me busy. More young ladies needing escorts for their parties and jaunts, you know."

Julie was surprised, but on reflection she was pleased that someone was visiting her socially, who could chatter away instead of always offering her their sympathies at the loss of her husband or demanding business answers.

"Are we having a drink then?"

Roberto was helping Julie to relax a bit and gradually realise that the grieving had to end sometime and future planning for happiness was required. He did mention the Hunt Socials in the past when he was her hired escort. The Hunt Club gossip, the joking and tittle tattle they were part of. The future events, social evenings, the 'old times'. He hardly ever stopped talking! To her, he always was a 'sweet talker', but one who you never really got to know or absolutely trust about his activities.

After a while, and quite a few drinks at Roberto's pace, Julie was able to mention her concerns about the men who were camping in their copse and, what they might be up to.

"I'll have a walk down there and see what 's up before it goes dark if you like."

"Well be careful. I'd be afraid to go down there"!

"O K, give me that double barrel shot gun off your kitchen wall. And a couple of cartridges. I'll scare the living daylight out of them!"

He was off without a fear in his manner, heading down the fields and entering the copse where he went out of her sight. She stayed at the window but could see nothing of him in the gathering gloom. She thought she heard gun shots from the copse or deeper in the forest and she was worried. All she was inclined to do was to draw her curtains and move away from the window, lock the door again, and wait nervously. Roberto was away a long time but eventually he was back to report.

"A gang of them. A couple of young girls as well. I crept up and frightened the bloody life out of them when I shot into the air." They have a camp down there and have been setting rabbit traps, camping overnight, living rough on the bottle and the drugs, and collecting any rabbits in the mornings". I don't think that they will bother you again now they know that I'm around."

Julie was reminded of Roberto's relaxed confidence as shown in their Escort/Client days when a fair degree of familiarity had developed between them. Now he was here again with the same proactive attitude! He was already beginning to help her to stop looking at the past and perhaps start thinking about the future again.

As he was leaving she felt his arms round her. He held her to him in what was almost an embrace, knee 'accidently' between her inner thighs, and told her . "Don't worry. Try to relax and move on. I'll call again shortly I promise you." There had been never a word about Danny at all. Roberto seemed to have never a trouble in his world; only an interest in the future, and not in the past.

Now, tonight Julie again could not sleep, for thinking about Danny the husband she had lost, and about Roberto the entertaining escort! Her bed was now a lonely place. And how were her 'grown up' children coping without a father? The next morning Julie's thoughts were racing. She somehow had a feeling of a worrying unease and apprehension.

She recalled that it was the day for the Village Fox Hunt.

CHAPTER 5

The Hunt

The huntsmen, Pony club members and their entourage had all gathered as usual in the centre of the village, just outside the Red Lion Pub. The villagers were out in force to see the spectacle of the Hunt on its way.

Snorting, stamping, stallions. Riders aloft in full dress code, and full of Port and Sherry. Hounds everywhere around the horse's legs. They stamped and whinnied. They wanted to gallop. Young riders and their Ponies also raring to go as soon as the scent of a fox had been traced and the Leader showed them the way.

This particular morning Julie's psychic was telling her that her management of the Ross farm and the stables routines were to be rudely interrupted in some way..

From her farmyard, Julie clearly heard The Fox Hunt and it seemed to be coming her way. The shouting. The baying of the foxhounds, the sound of the bugle, the thud of the hooves and the shouting of the 'Whippers In'. Unlike the usual crossing near the bottom of her land, it sounded as if it was coming much nearer. She realised that,they were now approaching the farm buildings and the paddocks where the horses were tethered and the farmyard where the cows were gathered waiting to enter their milking stalls.

The fox was desperately seeking shelter in the out buildings as it fatigued from the chase. Julie saw it as it ran straight across the stables and the paddocks in front of her. The hounds were on the scent and about to follow in amidst the cattle and her race-horses that might bolt in fear. And who knows what the following huntsmen would do! Julie had to stop any potential damage to her property, cattle and racehorses, and the Hunt appeared to be out of control and oblivious of the dangers. The Hunt Master, galloping ahead of the hunt, had obviously not realised the danger of the situation he was heading into. Julie was at last awakening from her despondent grieving thoughts as she foresaw the imminent danger and the need for action with nobody else around. Her shouts of 'hold hard' to the Hunts Field went unheard and so she again took the double barrel shot gun from her out- house, rushed to the paddock fence and fired both barrels in the air, in the general direction of the oncoming invasion, then quickly reloaded it and fired again.

The four loud bangs seemed to echo around and had the dramatic effect Julie hoped for as she reloaded. The huntsmen behind managed to re-act and divert their galloping horses. Julie quickly slammed the paddock gate shut stopping the dogs from entering the yard, The Hunt Leader pulled to a sudden halt at the paddock gate entry. His pursuit of the fox had been foiled. The hunt aborted. The face off from either side of the fence was between Julie and the leading Huntsman.

"What do you think you are doing?" he shouted. "You'll stampede the hunt with that gun. The dogs had the bloody fox cornered. You've let him get away"

Julie was concerned. "I'm protecting my assets! Keep the hunt away. You were about to be responsible for a serious accident. Are you qualified to lead the hunt? Do you know what you are doing?"

"I'll sue you if you shoot that gun near us again."

Julie responded with" I am protecting my animals : And I've reloaded."

And then, "I'll see you in court,"

They stared each other out over the fence and each made assessments.

'She's a good looking woman, full of authority, capable and aggressive when roused'. She probably knows her rights, he thought.

'He's a determined young man. But young and foolhardy', she thought. But what was he doing? And who was he to be leading the Hunt?'

They were face to face on opposite sides of this situation, and opposite sides of the fence, but each of their impressions of the other, quelled any further verbal's. The Hunt turned away and a catastrophe was averted but both of them registered some sensation. What was it that they each felt? It could have been dislike and animosity, but it was not that at all! It was attraction! Some sort of spark had flashed between them. Julie 'coming to life' again, in quickly re acting to the danger she could see. He in recognising a woman of substance, purpose, and mature beauty he could not ignore.

CHAPTER 6

Pampers at the Gallops

Of the horses at the Ross Racing stables, the one showing the most early promise was surprisingly Pampers, who was the daughter of Highlight,their bereaved 'heroine' and multi race winner. Perhaps without having a mother to protect her, had made the young filly more independent and resourceful and consequently more forward in her development and training. Would she show that she was more competitive on her racecourse debut?

Julie loved the thrill and excitement of horse racing. She was of course aware that Pamper's breeding ' history ' was obscure. So what potential ability could this filly have? Her mother was a Group 2 winner and the subject of a famous well publicised kidnapping story! Pamper's registration had been delayed at Wetherby's for DNA tests but was now, surprisingly cleared, with a little known Irish

On the gallops, the horses and riders were being sent off in small groups. Before the start Pampers was 'acting up ' a little in her exuberant way, impatient to start, but Forshaw picked her out immediately from the other horses by her confidence and some belligerence. She carried her head high with a confidence that was somehow above that of a two year old .Her legs were long and already sound and muscular. When she moved, class exuded from her. Vitality, fitness, potential and a stride that suggested an exhibition. Perhaps Julie's son Johnny had played down this horse's potential and the rumours were true. Pampers was galloping powerfully away, already well ahead of the others with the stable girl riding her unable to really hold her back. The stride length was from what the experts call 'quick feet,' and her muscle co ordination and ease of movement were impressive.

Before he had seen her gallop, Forshaw's scepticism was based on a filly sired by an' unknown' stallion with a mare that had disappeared with a 'fairy tale 'of kidnapping and neglect during the time she was in foal. He was so amazed at what he had seen that he needed time to absorb it all. The filly clearly had 'class' written all over her!

He did not return to see Julie. He just left the gallops in confused amazement at the potential in Pampers gallop. How could he get this filly out of Julie Ross's ownership and in to the Jacobs yard? What Forshaw wanted from Julie was an agreement to sell the horse to the Jacobs ownership. This would enhance his own status with his employers and it would rise further if the horse started winning races. Forshaw began to realise that his relations with Julie were going to be the main factor towards this achievement! And he had just almost ignored her! He had better think again! She was a good looking woman, a widow, vulnerable, and missing her husband's affections and relations. Win her, and he would even win the horse as well!

CHAPTER 7

Gavin

A few days after her 'quarrel' with the Leader of the Hunt, Julie was immediately on her guard with a knocking on the door and a view from her window of a muscular young man in business suit, trilby, white shirt and collar and tie. She was shocked when she eventually recognised him as the man from the Hunt who she had uncharacteristically faced up to with the shotgun the other day. Her heart seemed to miss a beat and she hesitated to open the door to him even though she guessed that he had seen her through the window. He looked so young compared to his impression on his horse. He waited patiently for a few moments in the rain before turning to go, by which time Julie had picked up courage to open the door ready to counter any aggression he might show. The man raised his hat to her and spoke in a quiet unassuming tone.

"Mrs Ross, my name is Gavin Grossman. I was leading the hunt the other day and I am here to apologise to you for my completely irresponsible actions as the Deputy Hunt Master, in approaching your property. I have been told that you have actually led the hunt in the past and I bow to your far better understanding of controlling the chase. I was completely carried away by sighting the fox. I ignored the danger to your animals and did not make a "HOLD HARD" for the Hunt."

"I am relatively new to village life and customs. I have quite recently taken up the role of the village area policeman and I am now living in part of the old police station in the village.

I have blotted my copybook with you and others and I am here to profusely apologise. If there is anything that I or the Hunt can do to make amends then I wish to do so if you will let me."

Julie's guard was dismantled by his polite manner and apologises, also by how young and handsome this particular policemen looked, and she heard herself saying," Oh please come in, out of the rain."

He appeared surprised and embarrassed at this invitation.

"Are you sure? I hesitate to disturb you, but felt I needed to come to see you privately, and without my uniform on, to apologise. Its been explained to me that you have led the Hunt. Before you lost your husband. And when they chose

Marion came in from her early morning labours to announce that her partner Kathleen had heard that the village pub, The Red Lion, was coming up for sale and she wanted Marion and her to try to take it over. Julie wondered what was supposed to happen to the Ross stables and all the work that she and her husband had put into its success? Who were they expecting would run the stables and maintain the racing performances of Ross trained horses, of which Highlights win in Paris was the pinnacle that they might even beat, particularly with Pampers. It now seemed that Julie's own children may not have the same ambitions for the stables that had motivated their father and mother. Opportunities were opening for them that did not need the same graft and dedication. However, life after Danny's death was beginning to put a certain steel in Julie's spine.

And she was still the owner of Pamperlight! She went out to Pampers box and looked at her. The horse tossed her head and looked straight back at Julie with what might be interpreted as nerveless arrogance. Could Julie build a relationship between them, just like Danny had cultivated with Highlight? She guessed that her son Johnny would be having more of the Ross stable horses transferred to the Jacobs yard or they would be sold on. Pampers might be a bit isolated if Julie kept her. Julie would need to keep just a few of her horses so that Pampers had companions; in particular Madame Fatale who had been Pampers 'adopted' mare and companion as she grew up. Julie was still determined to develop her 'one to one' training with Pampers. However, much work on the walkers and on the gallops and the racecourse still had to be done.

It was now becoming a new Julie. She still missed Danny but on her 'good days' she tried to come to her senses with the work and the planning she had to do. Time is a healer but moving forward is easier if life is full of things to do, people to talk to, plans to implement, and younger men to visit her, for whatever reason they give. Her married life had always been active and fulfilling, but she had never really been faced with other men canvassing for her favours.

She went to the next Hunt meeting. Everyone was keen to know how she was and so pleased to see her there. Gavin seemed to be overawed by her presence and reticent to take any lead in the planning of future events and so Julie found herself encouraging his participation. What was he really like if he could be brought out of his shell? What if Julie's friendly approach tried to do this? What about age differences? He was a young policeman. Was it better for them both to ignore the strange spark of electricity and feeling that had flashed between them?

The next day Julie's thoughts were interrupted by a phone call. It was from Mark Forshaw of Jacobs Stables; asking if he could meet her again. She was a bit abrupt in her reply. With a "what for"?

Mark had been doing his own planning.

"I wanted to make some proposals to you now that Johnny is gradually becoming part of the Jacobs outfit through his relationship with Samantha. But more important; I would like to get to know you better if you will let me."

"Well O.K. if I can find the time. When were you thinking of"?

"Do you go into Harrogate at all? I would like to entertain you at the Old Manor House in Harrogate if you would let me, and if you would stay the night after our meal I will book you in one of the five star rooms that the Jacobs Company have priority reservations on. Alternatively I can send our chauffer to drive you to Harrogate and I could meet you there. Also take you home the following day at a time to suit you if you would like to do a bit of shopping while you are in Harrogate."

Julie had previously noticed Forshaw's abrupt manner. Now it had been replaced by an apparent desire to 'please' her. Julie was flattered. He seemed to be a powerful and important man. And he could be pleasant with her as well, when he wanted to. Julie thought that she would give him a chance. Let him ''pamper 'her and see how it develops. Did Pampers come into all this??

On the chosen day, it was not the chauffeur who came to pick her up; it was the 'big man' himself. The white three litre Jaguar drew up on time, Mark was out of the driving seat in a flash to meet her, take her overnight case from her for the boot and offer his lips for a welcome kiss on her cheek.

Was the concern for her comfort real and based on his genuine feelings for her? He certainly was doing everything he could to please her. The hotel room was absolutely fabulous and luxurious to a standard she had not experienced before. Mark was giving her an hour to relax in the luxury of the facilities and then greeting her with compliments on her attractive looks and attire. They were greeted then seated in a quiet corner of the restaurant. The meal was expensively' a la carte'. The service, first class. The wine was vintage and the waiter kept topping up both their glasses. The business proposals Julie was waiting for, seemed to have been lost with the ambience and the effects that the wine was having on them. Attentive Mark topped the evening meal by presenting Julie with a surprise gift. A pearl necklace. How could any woman not be flattered and swept off her feet? He insisted that she tried the pearls on. He was out of his seat at the table to be behind her to fasten them, giving her shoulders a little squeeze while he was there! Julie was impressed. The wine was beginning to have some effect on her and so despite his attentions, Julie was ready to bring the evening to an end.. She declined another drink and made to move.

"You seem to have got me intoxicated", she struggled to say as he assisted her along the plush carpeted corridor to her bedroom door. She was anxious to now be alone but he helped her into the bedroom and then tried to hold her close to him with the excuse of a goodnight kiss and thanks for the company. But then she realised that he was not letting go of her. He was clinging on with his hands upon her in the hope of some acceding hint from her. Tempting as it was for her after the expensive evening,but even in her inebriation, she still did not completely trust this man. His attentions were complimentary to her, but was his real desire to control both her and her horse, be it through her ownership of Pamperlight? When she felt his hands rested on her buttocks it sobered her thoughts and she fought to get his hands off her. He wanted to talk but Julie pushed him to the bedroom door.

"Goodnight Mark. Thanks but no thanks is the answer for me and also for Pampers."

She saw a little flash of anger in his eye and thought that she might have some trouble with him if her drunken state let things happen. She managed to close the door in his face and stagger into her bathroom. She was exhausted and literally fell onto the lush bedding and into a deep sleep. In her dreams she was at the mercy of some sort of aggressive monster endangering her.

Julie awoke next morning vaguely remembering her dream and was in no haste to meet Mark for breakfast. She needed to compose herself and she opened her bedroom window and took a few deep breaths before joining him at the breakfast table. On her delayed entrance she noticed that, his mood was still attentive but subdued and unenthusiastic. He had drawn the Jaguar up to the leaving bay ready to go. On part of the return journey she feigned sleep to avoid a lot of conversation, that was aimed at Pampers welfare, and when nearly home Julie made a point of mentioning her plans to declare Pampers for her first race. She politely thanked him and a rather distant handshake seemed to recognise some of his frustration.

CHAPTER 9

Marion and Kathleen

Kathleen had settled down to country village life again working as the waitress at the Red Lion after some traumatic experiences living in London. The relationship between Julie's daughter Marion and Kathleen had started at the village Pub. Later, Marion had come to her rescue after a desperate London search for her amidst the capital's desperate people. They had both come to realise that 'togetherness' gave them personal comfort of body and mind. Unlike the advances from surreptitious males, Kathleen was finding a loving experience, and a trusting partner. She had regained her job at The Red Lion and for the convenience of being on site she had rented one of the upstairs flats above the public house. Marion had started calling for a drink in the pub after her arduous work at the stables and after closing time they would clear up and clean up together, then would retire to the flat above to relax, with Marion occasionally staying overnight.

Although the room was cold and draughty, some warmth and comfort came for them from a whisky bottle from the bar below and some woolly blankets. Kathleen was the more talkative and the attraction of a' bond' between them was growing with their discussions about their mistrust of men's characters and primary intentions. In contrast they could rely on one another's support and friendship, and the Bonding between them brought about their frank admissions of the safety and comfort that they had together. The warmth of the blankets and their closeness brought relaxation and demonstrations of love. The hug, the stroking, and then, the fondling, and the bonding kiss between them. Afterwards came their thoughts and plans for the future. Kathleen had heard that the Pub was coming up for sale or for tenancy and if this happened her job might be insecure. She suggested that they might be able to apply for a tenancy or even ownership as joint licensees. This would obviously mean Marion looking for an 'out' from her role at the Ross stables and its implications for the future of the racing activities. With Johnny 'playing away' there would be only Julie left to manage the running of the stables; also Marion and Kathleen would have to find the money for a purchase of the Pub tenancy. Both Julie and Marions brother Johnny would have to be consulted on future plans and on Kathleen's schemes. The future of the horses and Julie was seemingly not on the agenda..

Her brother Johnny was obviously besotted with Samantha Jacobs and her family's stables. He wanted more of the Ross horses and some facilities to be transferred and absorbed into the Jacob's yards. This was already happening. Johnny was transferring some of the two and three year olds to be under Jacobs training programme.

Julie insisted that she would retain and train Pamperlight and perhaps just one or two other horses at home.

Daughter Marion's involvement and contribution would depend on her relationship with Kathleen and their plans. The pub was still the central hub of the village and had always been profitable.

Neither of Julie's offspring were growing up in a way that she had expected. She thought that Johnny may find himself 'out of his depth' with the lifestyle of the Jacob's riches. Marion's life, present and future, was even more uncertain. Horse's welfare had become a drudge for her, but a future way of life and a ' relationship' with Kathleen were not easily understood. Same sex couples were new to Julie and she did not know how to react to her daughter being happy in a relationship with Kathleen.

Kathleen phoned Marion with the news that she had been offered the opportunity to run the Red Lion, providing that she could raise the deposit for security, but only if she could have a supporting, experienced partner to work with her. The only way that Marion could provide such a role would be by studying, training and getting practical experience in the role. What it meant was that, as a start, she had to leave the Ross stables employ, solely to Julie; work at the pub and train for pub management.

For Marion the one dilemma was that the pubs clientele of regular customers seemed to be changing. Kathleen in her eagerness to coax Marion into making a move, did not confirm this was so.

At one time the barmaid would have known every customer by name,where they lived,and what they did. Now the personnel was changing, in some cases not for the better. Some of the recent crowd of male customers were barely decent in dress behaviour and cleanliness. 'Countryfied 'would be polite. Scruffy and uncouth would be better. They seldom socialised except among their own and occupied the back room of the Pub with the pool table, and were sometimes accompanied by young girls. Probably not really old enough to drink alcohol and seemed to be associating with men in particular who were much older and mature than them. Marion had to keep an eye on wether they maintained decency in doing what two men in particular called Mansy and Bones encouraged them to do.

This generally rowdy lot tended to be avoided by the established regulars who called them 'druggies', and avoided the back room . Recently Kathleen, when collecting empty glasses entered the back room to find the noisy bunch of men laughing and shouting vulgar comments as if they were not just under the influence of drink, but full of drugs as well. Kathleen was only able to force them to leave by calling the part time Barman who was big enough to make them.

The men were drinkers when they had money but scroungers if they had not. The same two men in particular were the most vociferous when spending money on their pay day but were on the scrounge when they were broke. As they left, two girls seemed to be being escorted by the two older men, They were swearing at Marion as they were asked to leave.

"What's up? You don't provide any good entertainment anyway". How would Marion and Kathleen have managed to cope with this sort of affair without the physical power of a man?

Kathleen knew that the landlord of many years standing was wanting to move on and impatient for the brewery to fill the vacancy. He had started having the occasional day off without caring much about leaving Kathleen in charge with only one other employee, that of the part time barman who lived locally. The work load was also falling on Marion who, after early mornings at the stables, was helping Kathleen for part of the evening opening hours, sometimes staying the night with Kathleen thereafter.

Because the pub was close to the route of the popular West Coast to East Coast walk across northern England, the Red Lion' had customers occasionally seeking Bed & Breakfast at short notice. There was one twin bedded room available for B & B.

Just before closing time one Saturday evening, Kathleen and Marion were ringing the 'Time' bell for last orders when the same two men Mansy and Bones and the two girls, Audrey and Vera who had been drinking and watching TV in the back room were again reluctant to leave and said that they wanted a room for the night's accommodation. Marion was just telling them that they were too late and no rooms were available. One of the two men was saying that they needed to stay or they would have to sleep rough somewhere .Then Kathleen, anxious to increase the pubs takings, took over. They could have the one room for two persons only, available on a Bed and Breakfast basis.

Kathleen said "No food now, it's too late and you've drunk enough. Take 'pot luck' with the breakfast in the morning. Either you two men, or the two girls can have the room. Not all four of you. W'ere not a 'doss' house."

After some discussion they decided that the two men would stay. The girls said that they had somewhere else they could go after all.

bathroom. He was still in a trance as to what he had seen. Mansy was intent on them getting on their way."

"Come on" he shouted.

"What about these two!" Bones shouted back,

"No. We need to be away before people are stirring. Lock them in the bathroom! I've got the takings and some food".They ran down the stairs with the bag of money, opened the pub door aiming to set off down the road.

In no time at all, in the morning mist and gloom, the two men heard the clatter of galloping horses. What was coming after them was like the charge of the light brigade. Horses hooves clattering on road surfaces, Three charging, snorting horses, one female rider with shotgun in hand; firing a shot in their direction. The two men waving riding crops and shouting. One of them shouting Stop! We're Police!

The robbers tried to take to the fields but the speed of the pursuers mean't they were cornered by boundary hedges. With the horses jostling them against the hedgerow, they turned in submission, dropped their bag packs and held their hands up in fear of more rifle shots and the fear of being trampled by the excited horses.

When Gavin showed them his police badge they knew that they were 'copped'. He was off his horse and had them handcuffed together in no time at all.

In submission and remorse, Mansy spoke. "Look ; We have been daft. Just two young women and us in the pub all night with barely any security. They stuck the opportunity under our noses. They tempted us to get our hands on money that we were short of, to get us on our way. We did not harm them. They'll not want to say anything! We have done wrong and are sorry." Gavin and Johnny took them in.

Julie was the first back to the pub and slid off her horse. She shouted Marion's name, heard muffled noises from the upstairs, rushed to the bedroom and unlocked the bathroom door. She gasped and stopped in her tracks at what she saw. "Oh my God! Have they done this to you?" Have they left you both like that? "Get that tape off and some clothes on. I will get Gavin here .He can bring in police reinforcements straight away. The two men have been stopped. I think we have them."

Marion looked at Kathleen, and then spoke "We don't want any publicity!"

"Mother." said Marion. "They haven't touched us; only locked us in the bathroom"

"What like that?"

"Don't let anyone else come in until we get decent. And don't tell anyone!"

Julie gasped as she began to think through the implications of what Marion and Kathleen were about. She just could not understand the business of 'same sex partners ' that her daughter and Kathleen were into! She did remember that both Kathleen and Marion,when younger,both had unfortunate experiences, both mental and sexual, that may have influenced their ways.

Gavin with his policeman's training recognised that the young thieves were contrite, recognised that they had made a stupid drunken error. He also recognised that the lack of security had put temptation under their noses and Kathleen and Marion especially wanted no publicity! Neither did Julie. The two men were handcuffed and taken to the police station and locked away for some time. They were then summonsed,but eventually released on bail. Gavin was disappointed when Kathleen and Marion were reluctant to pursue charges apparently in order to avoid the publicity and the two men were surprised to be released on bail with a return date for consideration of punishment of 'drunken aggression' and intent to steal.

CHAPTER 10

Julie and Roberto

A few days after the incident at the Red Lion, Julie had a visit from Roberto.. He said that he had heard about the excitement at the Red Lion and was calling to see if Julie was alright. However his visits were becoming rather too frequent for her as he was taking some familiarity for granted using his past relationship with her. This time he came with the news about the next Hunt Function, the Spring Weekend social and dance. He seemed desperate to accompany her. Julie thought that she knew what he was thinking.

"I'd like to be your partner again Julie, but not like before when I was under contract at your expense .Escorting you would be my ultimate pleasure and would give the villagers a chance to see that you're moving on after the sadness of Danny and are looking to the future now.". Julie wondered about what the villagers would think, but felt that she should start going again.

So Roberto would again be her dance partner for the evening but with Julie torn between her desire for the company, and her thoughts that he made a living from other women, with money up front. He always had been a glib talker. He was so confident of his abilities where women were concerned. Almost casual about his routines that her memories of his 'lessons' were awakened and the implications thereafter were recalled. She now found herself resisting his attempts at familiarity. Despite him being surprised by this he was in no rush to leave but she wanted him to go and this revealed her inner thoughts! It had somehow not felt genuine. Julie wanted some male company, but not just Roberto. He was so confident of his ability and almost casual about his routines that her memories of his lessons' were recalled. She also felt that she was going to have difficulty with him taking things for granted in the future.

Julie never thought that after Danny's demise there would be prospective suitors for her 'friendship'. It felt embarrassing. "Ah well, its better than being lonely, I suppose!"

The following morning, after a restless night Julie switched on the local radio to be confronted with news that two local girls were missing from their homes. Searches were being organised with volunteers to scan the village and surrounding countryside including her property, the fields, the nearby river, copse and woods. It was established that the two girls had recently been at the Red Lion pub accompanied by two older men called Mansy and Bones. These were the same two men who had confronted Marion and Kathleen.

Being the local 'Bobbie',P.C.Gavin Grossman was now having to play a leading role in the search and Julie told him and the searchers about seeing regular evidence of people camping on the edge of the forest. She omitted to mention that Roberto had gone down there not long ago to investigate, and returned claiming that he had frightened the trespassers away with the shotgun! That was because she was not sure, that she had believed Roberto at the time.

Gavin was under pressure to organise the police and volunteering search parties to cover a certain two square mile area of fields, and woodland and premises. It was his first real assignment organising police from headquarters and forces from other areas. His inexperience showed in that he appeared unsure and nervous.. The search was to cover the woodland, and the area from which Julie,in the past, had seen the smoke coming from. Julie told him that she knew the way through the labyrinth of pathways, through the copse and the thick undergrowth to the deeper forest where she had explored as a child.

CHAPTER 11

Gavin and Julie

Gavin was constantly in Julie's thoughts in that the part she played with him and their horses in arresting the thieves at the pub, had helped them to know more about each other in their reactions to adversity. She realised that Gavin was really a very capable young policeman and her basic attraction to him was enhanced. His improving horsemanship was shown during the recent chase .When not on duty he had time on his hands and Julie was always glad to see him and to develop some mutual attraction. His close presence caused her to start thinking how her love life had been in cold storage; but its 'use by' date was nowhere near reached. Her subtle invitations at a closer physical relationship so far, had him missing her 'friendly gestures'. Julie guessed that he had never had a relationship with a woman before. She had to remember that Gavin was much younger than her and inexperienced with many issues of life. Maybe he should find someone his own age, but there were not many decent young girls in the village that his policeman's job had brought him to.

Julie,the widow, was increasingly missing the sexual relationships that, had featured in her life with her husband. Gavin was shy and strictly reserved when she tried to attract him and she had to stay inside of the dreams that she had started to have.. Even so, she felt that he was attracted to her and he was now calling on her several evenings each week after his work..

Maybe drink would banish any embarrassment or reserve in him?

Maybe her closeness on the lounge couch and her perfume would loosen him?

Julie had tried the 'See-Through' blouse and even an absence of underwear to no apparent effect with him.

She sometimes stepped within his arms, and hugged him casually, but invitingly. When he still did not respond, Julie thought it was just shyness or embarrassment and then she was convinced that he had never been with a woman. A strange situation in the permissive world they now lived.

She was going to have to lead him down the path! Tonight Julie hoped that he might call to see her. When he arrived he seemed a bit tired and languid tonight after a frustrating and uneventful work day on the beat.

Her own day had been certainly relaxing, even boring and she now was looking for some easing of her sexual deprivation. Could Gavin take the hint tonight? She had dressed to invite him, and had 'made up 'to the ultimate. Surely he could not resist her friendly encouragement tonight. She had opened a bottle of wine and she filled his glass, placed it on the coffee table near to the comfy three seater couch, as she settled down next to him. The small talk and her perfume, was only aimed at relaxing him. She snuggled closer to him on the couch and hoped that she could divert his attention from the television.

"I was glad when you asked if you could call. I just needed someone tonight. I've been unable to really relax today. This wine and your company is just what I needed."

She took his glass from his hands placed it on the small table by leaning over him as he sat. She remained in the close position face and body so close to him that as she turned, she invited her lips to his. He appeared a little surprised but eventually responded to her kiss. She took her tongue to his mouth and it was as if that was new to him. He seemed to hesitate. He withdrew from the kiss as if to look at her to see if she was not offended by what they were doing.

Gavin now saw before him the woman that he regularly dreamed about. Beautiful, well bosomed, with the smooth contours of her body possibly available to his touch. The wine was relaxing him and stimulating his confidence to make the move on her that she now seemed to be expecting.

Julie was excited. She pulled him towards her and prolonged the kiss, now with her body in contact with him. He must be able to feel her nipples hardening and breasts firm! He accepted the embrace and kiss. Now it was, in Julie's expectation for him to make the next move. Her blouse was pretty slack fitting anyway and the bra was of the thinnest, finest lingerie. Surely he couldn't resist removing it! She waited; His arms were sort of loosely hanging around her waist. She waited: Nothing was happening. She eventually accepted that nothing more seemed to be likely to happen, if left to Gavin. She took one of his hands from round her waist and moved it to her breast to confirm to him that his touch was accepted. Other than feeling to establish where it was now resting, he appeared immobile. Julie's hand went to his thigh and she then knew how he was feeling without any words from him. Her increasing desperation was for Gavin to take an active part in the 'exchanges' that she now desperately wanted. It was what she had learned to take an active part in, from her 'escort' lessons. She moved her hand and firmly unzipped him. She now recognised his desire and that at last he was responding to what she could do to him. She knew that he did fancy her a little bit!

If this was going to go any further Julie had to know! She whispered to him.

"Gavin, have you never been with a woman?" Or is it just a long time?"

Hesitation. She took his hands in hers and faced him.

"Gavin,will you please make love to me!"

And then. "I have never had a proper girlfriend. Not properly, like, but I want to,if you will show me.?"

She whispered quietly "Undress me Gavin. Take my top off."

If he did just that and then made no move to her thighs then maybe he was not as ready and as expectant, as she was.

She now wanted it to be the right time for him as well as for her. But surely at his stage of life he needed the experience. She pulled him down with her to the lounge rug and straddled him. She lifted her skirt, removed the French knickers. She guided him to her . She was fraught with anxiety with what she was doing and his reaction to it. And then at long last he showed some emotion and began to take the leading role. They were finally together moving towards some mutual climax. Julie realised that she was at last to be fulfilled. But what of Gavin? Was there a glimpse of anxiety in his eye? He looked at Julie not knowing what to see? Their eyes met and saw the others pleasure.. Both relaxed and could then feel the exhilaration, knowing that all was well for them both, with a new mutual loving feeling to relax and better enjoy together. They hugged each other as they gradually wound down, not like a first time couple, but unwilling to break the spell. Basking in the glory of what they had experienced.

"That was wonderful Gavin."

Gavin didn't say much as he prepared to leave and so she kissed him again. Maybe he was still in a daze of wonderment. Julie smiled at the thought! Her own feelings were that her tension had been replaced by the feel-good factor of contentment she had not experienced since she lost Danny.

CHAPTER 12

The Morning After

Julie slept in for a while lying in a contented pose thinking about Gavin and their reactions to the events of the evening. But with Gavin gone with his other commitments she wondered about their age difference, life styles .and what people might think of their relationship.

She was eventually wakened from her slumbers thinking of all the work she had to do that day. Marion would have done the early morning feeds and some of the stable work but there was still Pampers and Madame Fatale to exercise. Perhaps she could put Pampers on the horse walker for a while and then she could ride out Madame Fatale later in the day. She heard a loud banging on the kitchen door. Perhaps this was what had awakened her. She slipped on her dressing gown and peeped through the curtains. Oh My God! It was Gavin in policeman's uniform. The last thing she wanted just now was a tale of remorse and embarrassment from him. Words like, "this should never have happened! You took advantage of me."

Julie opened the door a little in expectation of a concerned figure stood there. Gavin stepped inside quickly without invitation, and closed it behind him. The hesitancy and tenseness she expected of him was gone. Instead an unembarrassed laughing face was immediately close to hers. Long arms enfolded round her in a hug as she tried to grasp the surprising events. He was kissing her all over. Lips, neck, shoulders, beneath her now open dressing gown..

"Steady on Gavin! Calm down!"

Finally Gavin seemed to calm himself a little, as he held her hands smilingly, his eyes dancing alive. She was shocked to the core. This was a different person. Then she recalled the 'electricity' that his vigour brought between them at the farm gates, she with her rifle and he leading with the horses and hounds. The intense vitality and assured confidence he showed then, was being repeated.

"I'm supposed to be on duty, but couldn't resist calling to see how you were after last night. You were wonderful, and now you will be irresistible for me. My life has changed from boredom to paradise in one day. Or in one night. Come on Julie let's make love again" He was coxing her to the couch where they had reached their climax last night.

Julie was aghast at his changed behaviour and personality. She was the one who was being cautious! What had she done to him?

"Aren't you on duty? What happens if the force want you and come looking for you?" She was being swept off her feet and needed time to allow both body and mind to acclimatise to his radiance.

"No, no, Gavin, things are not as simple as this."

"Can I come back tonight then? I know we have to talk. And then make love again. I'll be better next time Julie!"

She had to calm him.

"No you can't Gavin. We can't carry on like this!"

He was completely shattered by her words and brusque manner..

He shouted at her " So you've had better men than me. Better times and many of them, I was just a convenience for you". He calmed.

"But Julie, can't you see that for me the earth moved. I know that you have been married before. Now I need you. I'll not be deterred you know. As long as I know that you want me."

Julie was concerned. She had obviously made Gavin happy, but now he was making her start to realise that this had embroiled her into his life. She was being drawn into his life and the events that he involved himself in. Where does the love come into this? Did she become involved, for kindness to him? Now she was already concerned for his welfare. They had really been 'worlds apart' in some ways, before she had orchestrated last night's event.

Was it desire? Can desire turn to love? What decisions and reactions are to follow? Would either of them be an eventual 'let down' to the other? Would others think of the words 'cradle snatching'?

Julie spoke angrily to him. "Do you know that you are supposed to be on duty?"

"Yes I am going to join the search for the missing girls, but I had to see you first, after last night. Now I wish that I hadn't called." He headed straight for the door.

"Gavin, please be sensible! Come back!" It was to no avail.

Being the local policeman, Gavin was having to play a leading role in the search for the two missing girls. This was a far cry from his routine duties overseeing village life. Gavin was under pressure to plan the police and volunteers search parties to cover a certain four square mile area of fields, and woodland and premises. It was his first real assignment involving police from headquarters and forces from other areas.

Julie now knew that she was distracting him from his task. And should she be forcing herself into his young life?

The search for the missing girls had to be implemented quickly. Gavin again appeared unsure and nervous in the police work ahead. The force was being brought in from the nearby town and they expected Gavin to know all that went on in the village and nearby. The searches of the fields and lanes had found signs of a small camp set up just where a small stream entered the edge of the deeper forest. Some shelters made from branches and foliage remained, near to where a fire had burned. Among the general litter were food bags, empty beer bottles, dirty clothing, cigarette butts and two empty beer kegs which they recognised were from the village pub yard. Closer searching of the surrounding undergrowth exposed a used drug needle. Julie had previously told Gavin about seeing wisps of smoke on the edge of the forest. The searchers had found nothing more as the forest deepened. Julie put on her coat, went outside and told Gavin that she knew the way through the labyrinth of pathways; through the copse and through the thick undergrowth to a part of the forest where she had once been walking with her husband Danny. It was near where the stream widened entering the dense forest. Julie vaguely recalled that the stream deepened as it entered the thicker undergrowth, seeping into a deep crevice, the remains of a disused mining quarry. For some reason they had never wanted to go any further.

After another day of searches Gavin called on Julie again. Now he was depressed at the lack of success in locating the girls and under pressure from his superiors to come up with results. He was seeking reassurance, physical and mental inspiration from Julie.

And then Julie's phone rang . " Was Gavin there?" It was Kathleen from the village where she had heard that one of the 'missing girls', the one called Audrey,had just been found and was returning to her home. The girl seemed distressed and was not saying where she had been nor about the other girl Vera. The police instructions were to continue the search tomorrow, the inference being that Vera was still vulnerable,with the two men, and afraid and in danger.

Dusk was approaching, the searches had been called off for the day. A depressed Gavin told Julie of the situation. Julie seemed agitated. All day she had been unable to stop thinking about the forest. Her psychic was at work. "Have you looked in the forest where the stream drops down into the crevice and the old quarry?"

"Well not intensively. Its such a big dense area to search properly"

"No! Come on we have just got time if we drive the Land Rover to the edge of the spinney and go on foot from there. Bring the police torch and I've got the rifle. I'll show you!"

What's the rifle for? Its not official equipment!"

"Well you never know!" Julie said as she rushed out. Her psychic instinct was driving her. Gavin followed with some reluctance. By the time they got to where the stream became a deep pond it was nearly dark, but Julie pressed on with torch in hand. Her instincts took her forward along a thick hedging. A strange feeling inside driving her on with some urgency. And then she stumbled near the bank and was slipping into the water on her side. She felt the ice cold slimy water round her knees, her boots sticking in the mud .As she scrambled out, with sleeves and skirt wet through, and Gavin pulling her arms, she momentarily saw what she thought was a human hand under the murky water. A shocked Julie shouted out.

"There's something there Gavin. Under the water and those, overhanging branches."

All Gavin wanted was to get away. Darkness was closing in. He was thinking that he had no right to be down here with Julie, without police orders.

"I can't see anything! You're imagining things. Come on it's too dark to try to get down there again. We must go back."

Julie started thinking that perhaps her imagination was playing tricks. But she knew that she could not rest until tomorrow and she found out what it could have been under the surface of the water..

By the time that they got back to Julie's home, a text had been received for Gavin to report to the Super on the areas covered today and about instructions for tomorrow.

Gavin had one extra constable brought in to reinforce the search effort in the forest area. The remaining task forces were concentrating in the opposite direction where the girl Audrey, when interviewed, claimed she had been with the other three. She said that she had left Vera with the two men. They had all been agitated and in some state of drunkenness, and she knew of the two men's intentions,if the girl was willing, or rape if she was not willing!

Audrey had claimed 'natures need 'as an excuse to creep away from them and then she had run as fast as she could and hid from them in a ditch near the edge of the copse, as the two men and Vera moved on, seeking shelter for the night.

Gavin, with Julie's motivation, had suggested to the Super that the search included following the stream deep into the forest. The 'Super's reply was "Right, well you can do that area then."

Despite Gavin's reluctance, Julie again insisted that she accompanied them. She was more than ever convinced that she had seen the fingers of a hand under the murky water when she slipped down the bank. She was leading the way back to the same spot. She' instructed' the two constables, as if she was in charge .They reluctantly waded into the murky water, holding on to overhanging branches with one hand to stop them slipping.

There! Sure enough Gavin grasped what he thought was a thick branch and found it was an arm under the water and he began to try to pull and drag a body to the surface.

"Oh my lord! It must be the missing girl!" The policemen slipped again in trying to reach the body under the water. Julie determinedly joined them waste deep in mud and water to pull the corpse out.

They had a shock! It was a man. It took the combined strength of the three of them to drag the body out of the mud and water and on to the bank.. The hydrated body was icy cold .Yellow and purplish bruises showed on the corpse identified by Gavin. It was that of Mansy.

While Julie felt sick and moved away, policeman Gavin's voice was full of triumph as he reported their findings on his mobile phone. Kudo's for him in successfully finding the body and exhilaration with success. Julie was saddened by events and in a state of shock that she somehow just knew where to look. It was like a 'sixth sense' had guided her to the site of the body.

Police, ambulance, forensics, took over the site. Press anxious for the story, and for a hero, chose Gavin, for his intuition. No mention of Julie, of course! Gavin had reports to write, interviews with superiors who were thankful that progress could be recorded to show their competence. The search for the remaining couple had now widened beyond the local area, and was continuing with concerns that further fatalities might be discovered.

Now Julie really wanted to resume her normal role and distance herself from all that was going on around her.

She was upset by the events and the strange psychic. The search would obviously continue but she needed to return to 'normal' and her work routine with her racehorses.

She had plenty to do preparing Pampers for her first visit to a racecourse. The horse and the preparation work for the race helped her to put the turmoil and the searches aside. Pamper's obvious development and growing fitness excited her. Her excitement was the greater by her remembering the development of Highlight her mother and her magical success in France.

CHAPTER **13**

Pampers's First Race

Some days ago Pampers had been entered for her first race. It was to be over five furlongs at Thirsk Racecourse and was for two year old novices. Julie was feeling in a positive mood as she drove the horsebox the one hours journey to the racecourse. It was a pleasant sunny day and she was enjoying the Yorkshire countryside views. Stunning moorland and heather; then green parkland, darker green forests and lighter coloured small copses as the road skirted the edge of valleys and rocky escarpments. As she drove she tried to forget the traumas around her and she had plenty of time to appreciate life and think about her situation as an 'independent' woman and a good horse trainer. She had been schooling the filly hard and training her in the starting gates. Pampers was a most impetuous filly and it was showing. Julie could read her like a book .What's more, the filly knew what Julie was thinking most of the time as well. An 'understanding relationship' was developing between them and the horse looked fit, able and relaxed in Julie's presence.

When Julie looked at the list of entrants for the race she found that the prestigious Jacob's yard had an entrant, in a well bred filly named Lady Goldie. She was of first class pedigree and recently bought from France by Mark Forshaw for the Jacobs family. Julie started to worry that perhaps Pampers was not ready for such a high class field, and that Julie could have found an alternative 'beginners race'? Her mobile rang. It was Mark Forshaw.

"Just phoning you to wish you luck with Pampers at Thirsk. We have Lady Goldie in the race and I think she'll take some beating. She's high class you know. I think yours may be out of her depth!" Julie had defiantly let her entry stand and determined to declare Pampers to run.

Julie was excited at the thought of this first run for the filly. The trouble was that Pampers was of an excitable temperament as well, and at the racecourse the new experience of the crowds at Thirsk, the babble of noise, the anxiety of many of the other horses, came through to her. Pampers had some 'feeling' from the morning gallops at home when other horses were just quietly exercising, but she was a clever filly and, she naturally wanted a race with them.

The starting stalls were somewhat new to her and incidental compared to the main chase. Her jockey had been instructed to try to get her into the gates last if possible .Pampers entered the stalls alright but then impatiently reared up and forward, just before the starting gates opened and this badly shook her such that the race was on while she was still hurting from the bump. She finally got away but was some twenty lengths behind and disoriented as well. .Her chances were really already over, but when she saw the others well ahead her natural instinct came in and her chase began. The five furlong race was much too short for her to catch up, though she made some good progress when allowed to run freely, before her jockey tightened the reins to ease her down to a trot by the finishing line. Julie was disappointed not because of the result but that her filly had not had a good first experience of a proper race.

Lady Goldie had finished second beaten by a head. Julie checked her horse over for any effects from the stalls upset. Thankfully Pampers seemed OK .When Julie looked her in the eye and held her face to hers she swore that the horse showed some sorrow or at least an apologetic 'sheepishness.' She stroked her face and talked to her as she might to a child.

The relationship between the lady and the horse had seemingly developed with the set back. Perhaps they both had a lot to learn without Danny to help them. The absence of any phone call from Mr Mark Forshaw was as significant as one saying, "I told you so."

Pampers did not eat up that evening! Julie spent the evening with her in sympathy. She had no appetite herself as they shared the mutual feeling.

CHAPTER 14

The Search

The newscast was of one person found alive, one found dead. Two still not accounted for! The discovery of the body of Mansy, brought up many more questions and a concentration of the police search efforts in the area. While awaiting further news, the local press were quizzing how the successful ' search and find' team of the two constables had included Julie Ross. Julie was desperate to avoid any publicity, especially about the friendship between the widow and the young constable .She repeatedly said that she knew the particular countryside and woodland area from an early age and had wanted to help. She avoided any questions that suggested any friendship with the local PC.

The search continued for the two persons still missing. Local transport was being monitored. A car was reported stolen from the edge of the village and was later found abandoned some four miles away, near the railway station. It could have been used by the couple. The search was widening. Bones was identified as having a police record for petty theft. The girl Vera was only 17 years old and obviously her associating with this man was putting her in danger.

Gavin was obliged to report all latest developments to Julie in confidence. She still had 'psychic' instincts that the couple were not far away. While exercising the horses she was still searching the countryside for any presence of the man and the girl. She again told Gavin that "something is telling me that they are near", but the police force thought differently from their computer forecasts of 'possible whereabouts'.

When the couple were eventually apprehended, they had, as Julie said, returned to the near vicinity of the village. A routine search of out buildings attached to a nearby farm showed signs of habitation and on police presence they were found sheltering together in a hay barn, that had been previously searched, and they were arrested. They had stolen the car and then abandoned it near the railway as a decoy. On their arrest, Vera was distraught and claimed that she had persuaded Bones that they should give themselves up.

Under separate police questioning they both admitted that the two men had argued when Bones started to dispute the bigger man's orders.

CHAPTER 15

The Trial

Bones was appearing before judge and jury accused of the murder of his mate Mansy.

Eighteen year old Vera was also accused of aiding and abetting him.

Prosecution and defence lawyers had witnesses to call upon in evidence. Among the witnesses were the Police, Constable Gavin Grossman, and important Forensic experts who were to present their detailed report. Marion and Kathleen were also to appear for some prior knowledge and information about the various characters involved.

The police and Gavin related details of their search and findings.

The actual facts relating to the death and the finding of Mansy's body submerged in the waters of the deep pit, were not being disputed. The two men, previously mates, had fought using thick, heavy clubs of wood. Mansy had gone down from Bones's heavy blow. Out cold,either concussed or dead. Bones had panicked and with Vera's help they had dragged Mansy to the bushes near the pit and he had slid under the water and overhanging tree branches, They had left him, exiting the scene as fast as they could. Vera confirmed that Mansy had struck the first heavy blow, but Bones delivered the last blow. Fatal or not?? The forensic evidence was going to be critical for Vera. Both the deceased and the defendant were found to have heavy bruising to shoulders and head. If the blows immediately caused the victims death, then Vera's role was just of ' assisting the concealment of a body'. If the blows only concussed him, then both Bones and Vera were both possibly guilty of murder by the drowning of the unconscious victim.

The forensic expert's findings were to be critical and would take some time to report on.

And so, before the first adjournment Marion and Kathleen were summoned to the stand to comment on the behaviour and character of the accused prior to the event., and their lawyer had assured them that their own 'lesbian' relationship was irrelevant and need not be divulged.

But then 'out of the blue' the prosecuting lawyer asked "What is the relationship between the two of you? They looked aghast at each other but did not answer. He again questioned them. "Are you in a Lesbian relationship?" Now the press reporters were sitting up! In those days this was something new to the community,. The hall was silent awaiting the answer. The defence lawyer quickly stepped in with "Is this relevant your honour?" There was a quiet expectancy. But thankfully for the two women the judge accepted it as irrelevant and was moving on.

And then Kathleen opened the front of the heavy coat she was wearing. She revealed quite clearly a 'Baby Bump'. She was obviously pregnant!

She spoke loudly.as she pointed at her form." Can you see this! Surely my pregnancy speaks for itself! And surely it answers your question."

The person most surprised was Marion!

There were no further enquiries from the lawyers in this particular direction. The questions were then relating to the characters of the accused and the deceased.

According to Marion and Kathleen.Yes they had all drunk heavily before being told to leave. Of the four of them it was Mansy who seemed to be the one to take the lead that the others followed, on leaving the pub.

After the break the Forensics long winded report said that the state of the water in his lungs suggested that Mansy was already dead when he was submerged and there was therefore sufficient evidence to suggest that Vera had witnessed, but not contributed, to the actual death. Only by assisting Bones in hiding the body had she committed a crime.

Bones's case was committed to trial with Vera liable to be tried seperately for a lesser punishment for her part in the event.

this man was very complimentary in saying ." You've got a good young horse there Mrs Ross. She showed some signs of having great potential. The winning difference was probably in my jockey."

"Please call me Julie."

"Oh thank you, I am William"

Julie asked." How did you manage to employ Desmond Gibson, the Champion Jockey, for the race?"

William smiled. " I know Desmond Gibson pretty well. It takes a lot of time and friendly persuasion." That was all he would say.

CHAPTER 17

Julie's Suitors

B ack home again, and Julie was finding that Gavin was a different person, with not only his fame from his policing success, but also because of his first sexual achievement. He was calling on her regularly and when with her, he made no secret of his primary obsession. Julie was worried that the implications of their relationship was bringing her into his much younger life. Into his whole welfare in fact. Like a mother would advise of the best actions on many challenges and experiences of her offspring. Julie recalled that her own mother's over indulgence in her young life caused her to miss out on learning opportunities. She also thought that one or other of them might tire of the relationship, but for the moment, the sexual intimacy both felt, was obscuring all other implications.

With both of them relaxed by a glass of wine,. this time she was not the teacher but more the partner in a gradual lead up to culmination, with the climax leaving them both exhausted. They both slept for a while but then Julie awoke, and started worrying about their relationship was it right, and what if it became known to all the village; if Gavin was seen leaving her home in the early morning.

She had to swear him to secrecy, when what he wanted was to shout from the roof tops. She had trouble wakening him from deep sleep and when finally awake he wanted to make love to her again. The exuberance of youth against the concerns of the experienced! For her it was like "Don't spend it all at once. Save some for another day". Not for Gavin .He could not really understand being bundled out of the house in the secrecy of the darkness.

It was almost like 'Sods Law' that with Julie hardly dressed, mid morning,after lying in bed worrying about her life, she saw Roberto approaching her front door. It was the last thing she needed at this particular time. She rushed around the kitchen and lounge looking to remove any evidence of last night's visitor. Finally she opened the door to Roberto trying to convey a welcoming smile.

"Hello Roberto. I was just tidying the bedroom, when you knocked. Come on in. I'll put the kettle on."

"Hello Julie, I've been longing to see you again but I've been so busy." Can I use your bathroom, before we have a drink?"

Roberto went upstairs to the bathroom but then, nosey man that he was, could not resist a quick peek into Julie's bedroom.

He noted the unmade bed, passed a thought of how good it would be with Julie in it. He couldn't delay returning to the downstairs lounge any longer and as he went down his imagination was running wild . And then, in his brief glimpse, he recollected seeing two empty wine glasses. One on each side of the bed!

Julie was brewing the tea and talking to him asking how he was keeping so busy. Roberto asked her if her friends were popping in to see her! Julie hesitated a little in answering the general question with a general answer. "Yes they were!" No further comment!

"What's going on here?" Roberto was thinking. He was wanting, even more, to be her partner at the next Dance and Social run by the Hunt committee.

Julie accepted Roberto's company for the coming evening,she was glad to have a dance partner but now she was thinking about how she could keep him 'at bay' afterwards.

The phone rang. Julie picked it up automatically and was immediately shocked that at this inopportune moment

sad memories for Julie. With this reminder of Danny and her past, Julie did not respond. They drank the tea she had made without talking but Roberto was again thinking about the unmade bed and the two wine glasses in Julie's bedroom.

"I am sorry Roberto, but I'm not in a talking mood today. Perhaps you would excuse me. Please call again won't you."

Roberto's imagination was working overtime. The 'brush off'! Had someone been in Julie's bedroom with her! Were they still hiding upstairs somewhere? There was something going on here! He was obsessed with the thought that If someone had been in Julie's bed, Who could the lucky man be that had achieved what he dreamt about!?

CHAPTER **18**

Decisions

Æter her husband's death Julie had imagined a quiet and perhaps lonely existence. Now with three 'suitors' paying her so much attention, her mind and her body were 'all mixed up'. What if each one found out about her 'friendship 'with the other two? They were all pressuring her in one way or another, for a closer relationship. And what were their ambitions as far as she was concerned? And what should her reactions be?

Julie's mother had always said, "If in doubt about someone, look that person directly in the eyes, look long and steadily, hold your gaze. If this puts them off their guard, watch and you will learn something about them from their reaction."

With Gavin, she had just enjoyed bringing sexual experience and pleasure into his young life. But could they have a lasting relationship with their age differences? As he matured, and widened his life's experiences they may 'blend', but to her mind the 'rapture' might wear off. In her gaze to his eyes, she thought Gavin's just showed, ' immature happiness.'

Mark Forshaw probably had the stature and career in the racing field to look after her in comfort, as well as her horses. But were his racing ambitions feeding his intense interest in her? How sincere and 'real' was he? To Julie, his eyes met hers he only showed "self -indulgence."

The third man, Roberto the escort, had previous close relations with her, and was still similarly involved with other women, but he was ardently attracted to her. But could she really trust him, and where would their relationship be if she had not lost her husband?

The prolonged look of his eyes revealed "self indulgence and righteousness."

And how long before one of them found her diversity out? It didn't seem possible for any of them to provide just friendship and companionship.. They all wanted a physical relationship and exclusivity with her. Whatever should she do!

CHAPTER 19

William Stroll

The telephone rang. It was the commanding voice of Mr William Stroll.

"Julie. I have been talking to Desmond Gibson about a future ride for my horse. He's top of the winning jockeys table at the moment. I took the liberty of mentioning Pampers and your good self to him as a prospective winning ride for him. So when your horse is out again you could give him a ring. He owes me a favour anyway, but I'm sure he would be impressed with Pampers."

Julie took the telephone number that William gave her. She was surprised because she had been making a few discreet enquiries about Mr Stroll and his successes and renown in the racing field. Behind his renown he appeared to Julie to be a man of confidence and poise. She had been told that his wife had died recently, after a short illness. She

is now similarly the only horse in my yard that is top class future potential."

"Oh, I'm sorry. It was just me trying to plan a racing future for Pampers. I'm sorry to have bothered you." There was a pause and then William said. "Let me think about things a bit. I will ring you back."

The return call came about an hour later." I would like to help you Julie but there would be obstacles to be overcome. Let me explain."

The gist of it was, that for it to work, the two fillies, Mangel and Pamperlight would have to' get on' together, there being few other horses for their company. Both William and Julie knew that all horses, when together, did not always get on; this showed by 'bared teeth' and selfish aggression, and other typical symptoms. Also, the stress and tension in their life could ruin the horse's fitness and performance. Mangel was a sensitive horse that was used to getting all the care and attention. Julie knew that Pampers was quite unpredictable herself, although Madame Fatale, her 'mother' always calmed her.

Julie took a deep breathe at his suggestipn. "If you would like to bring Pampers over to my yard in the horse box sometime soon, we could at least introduce the horses to one another in adjacent paddocks. If they both settle down in one another's company we could consider the future possibilities.

The following week Julie, put on her own best 'bib and tucker', loaded Pampers and drove the horse box the two hour journey to Mr Stroll 's stables. Pampers was offloaded and placed in the next paddock to Mangel, each with their own haylage feeder placed close together but on either side of the adjoining fence. William and Julie both petted and fed their own horses. Both fillies showed that they were aware of the presence of another, but the feed was the attraction. So far so good. Now to leave them alone for a bit.

"I'll make us a cup of tea and a sandwich while we wait to see how things go?"

"Yes please that would be nice". He seemed such a dynamic personality but friendly enough . Julie felt that maybe he wanted to explain his diminishing presence in the racing world.

"When Jill was diagnosed and then when she died, I just had no head for anything without her .My lifestyle has changed and I have been gradually running the stables down since then. Mangel's potential ability helped me to maintain a little interest. But it is not the same without Jill. I am not yet clear what the future can hold"

It became clear to Julie that William also recognised her sensitivity about many things in her life since she lost her husband .They were gradually learning about each other, particularly after Julie's admission of embarrassment with suitors of the opposite sex. William had probably shunned off many women, but Julie could not quite say the same, and so she was careful what she said.

After a little while they brought the two horses together on the rein, each petting their own. No problems, so far, so good, next time they would try to leave them together in the same paddock.

A few days later Julie and Pampers again visited the Stroll home. Julie arrived in the morning and with the horses getting on together she realised that lunch was being prepared for her. William poured Julie a glass of sherry before the meal. He showed her to her seat at a large dining table before sitting himself. Wine was on the table and a young lady of eastern looks and beauty, appeared from the kitchen bringing tureens of hot food that she had obviously prepared. She was introduced as Gede, and then she stood back in waiting. Was this how William normally lived or was he trying to impress her? Julie felt a little 'out of her league' at the formality and polite correctness of the conversation that William was pursuing, and also because he seemed to be following such formalities. For Julie, the sherry had gone down well ; now followed by the table wine. She was feeling relaxed now as the food was being served.

Yes, Julie thought that another glass of wine might help to lighten William's mood. William was out of his chair to serve her the wine; but Gede was there before him. He laughed at the mutual desire to fill Julie's glass and then Gede, maybe distracted accidently, or nervous, stumbled and the bottle slipped from her grasp. It bounced into Julie's lap, the wine still 'gurgling' out and spilling all over her blouse, dress and legs before hitting the floor. Julie was shrieking as she jumped about as the wine soaked through to her skin. But then the shriek turned to laughter as she quickly shrugged off any embarrassment because she saw how funny the 'formal situation' had now become. She was then hilarious and, bent double with laughter almost ending up on the floor. Next she saw William's face. Formality gradually disappeared as he saw her and he was now bursting out with laughter as he made attempts to wipe her down with the table napkins. They both ended up on the floor unable to stop laughing. A mutual ability to see the funny side of the incident, but was it at her expense?

Gede, presumably in fear of her guilt, had disappeared.

Between the constant bursts of laughter Julie cried out." What am I going to do? Look! I'm wet through to the skin!"

William shouted." Come on upstairs. I'll find you some of Jill's clothes. She was about your size! I have been wondering what to do with them!" He was laughing again following Julie up the stairs. Still laughing as he was throwing blouses, skirts, bras and knickers in her direction. The incident had certainly broken any reserve between them, as she said "I'll try these for size". William did not retire completely while she tried them on but remained just outside of view waiting for her comments.

Any polite reservations between them were gone with Julie's laughter at the situation. Their reactions had pulled them together now as friends, not just acquaintances. The meal eventually continued as a joy for them both with Julie dressed in the clothes from Jill's wardrobe! They were now better able to confide their feelings. They were able to talk smilingly about their changed life since the loss of their partners. And then admit to wondering what each of their deceased partners would think of it all.

Did the two horses get on? For the moment the horses would have to make the best of it! It had dawned on the two of them that Mr Stroll and Mrs Ross were getting on fine! They now were at ease, Julie walking shoulder to shoulder with him rather than leaving personal space between them.

With the happy mood continuing Julie asked William about Gede, the young lady who had prepared the meal for them. William hesitated. The mood seemed to change. Julie imagined that he was thinking about what he should say.

"The young lady is just an acquaintance, ever anxious to help me through the awkward times I have had."

He had spoken more seriously and with great deliberation. Not a real answer, but food for Julie's thoughts! She really did not want to go home. But go home she must and Pampers too. Back to reality. And plenty to think about!

CHAPTER 20

Pampers Eyes Victory

The next morning Julie went to the stalls, to have a 'talk' to Pampers, as she often did when racing matters were to be decided upon; . She stroked her mane and looked her in the eye. She always felt that when alone with Pampers she was as near to her bereaved husband Danny and his beloved Highlight, as she could get to them. The psychic influences on Danny and Highlight in the past were known only to Julie now and maybe she was amenable to them. But what did Pampers feel?

"Well Pampers,did you enjoy your day out? What did you think about sharing things with Mangel. She seemed a bit nervous with you there, but remember she has been on her own and not used to having company. Come on then, I'm looking you in the eyes now. What are you telling me? And by the way, what do you think about William!"

She got a slow relaxed blink of the eye from Pampers-.

"Yes, Pampers, you were happy with the company weren't you. I think you are relaxed and ready for a race entry. Well I was more at ease with William too. The spilt bottle of wine certainly loosened us up."

More training gallops for Pampers and a build up to her next race. Another trip for Pampers and her mare Madame Fatale this time, to meet Mangel. More 'togetherness' for the two fillies who now were getting on well, even thriving and looking fit and happy from their companionship.

Despite a strengthening friendship, William was still very careful and 'proper' with Julie. After a day with the horses at 'Julie's place' and an evening meal and too many drinks to safely drive, he chose to call a taxi for the journey home rather than accept her invite to stay, even in the second bedroom! No, he did not like to impose on her! Or were they both afraid of what the night might lead to? Julie felt that he was not picking up on her 'approaches' and something was holding him back.

Pamperlight was entered in the " Enterprise Stakes" a five furling race for Two Year Olds, run at Doncaster racecourse. She had been given a racing handicap rating of 76, and the nine runners in the race again included the Jacobs filly Lady Goldie, with Mark Forshaw present to supervise the horses run..

When the jockeys were declared and leading jockey Desmond Gibson was shown to be riding Pampers, the racing world were asking how Julie had managed to commission the services of the year's most successful jockey. The betting odds on Pampers shortened to three to one.

They were off! With a good early gallop, Pampers was held back in the middle of the field by Gibson until the right moment two furlongs out, the champion jockey anticipated an opening ahead and his legs squeezed the horses girth .Pampers had been relaxed and running well within herself. When released, she quickened and lengthened her stride. Her undoubted class began to show as she left the rest, including Lady Goldie, trailing in her wake, finishing some four lengths ahead at the winning post. It was a breath taking performance. In the winners enclosure Julie saw Mark Forshaw. She looked him straight in the eye, but did not say a word. What she saw was a mixture of anger and jealousy. He was having to gnash his teeth together in order to mutter congratulations! His horse had finished down the field.

The press were impressed and one news reporter, wanting to interview winning owner Julie Ross, had seen William Stroll and Julie celebrating together near the winning post. William's arm around Julie in celebration. It made Julie feel reassured about all that was happening to her. For a moment his arm around her revealed his desire to be with her. It was good for him as well.

The reporters message was: Watch out for this filly; and also any signs of a William Stroll and Julie Ross relationship! Julie could not understand why William was a little cautious about the inference and publicity that was likely to follow.

Julie. "Thank you for your help in asking Desmond Gibson to take the ride.

William "Get Pampers loaded and away before the press can pin us down."

As they left William said to Julie. "I can tell you Julie,that your filly would have taken some catching no matter who was on board. I think we need to talk about her future; and ours too! Can I ring you later?". Julie just gasped.

CHAPTER 21

Julie and William

When Pampers had won the "Enterprise Stakes" in a comfortable fashion, some of the press had spotted the celebration hug between Julie and William, it left William trying to avoid further publicity. When Julie had thrown her arms around him in celebration, his automatic reaction surprised him. It was the first time since he lost his wife that he genuinely shared this sort of an emotional pleasure with someone else. Julie's excitement at winning was also uninhibited and when she absorbed the fact that she was comfortably in his arms, she too was surprised how natural it had come about and then they both looked at each other seeking the other's reaction to the impulsive celebration in the public domain. Julie was pleased and happy but William seemed a bit quiet as he wanted away and drove them to his home.

a status. Now she wants more from me, as a partner despite our differing ages and situations."

"I don't understand" said Julie.

"Well, it's partly her Indonesian upbringing and its familiarity within. A Balinese home always has a common bathing compound for all of the parents and children together. So Jill and I observed their customs by us all bathing together. It was fine while Gede was young but, now, even with a real daughter of eighteen years one would opt for discretion, but now she acts as if it was her obligation to be there for me! Now she even thinks I owe her marriage. She can get quite angry at times and is obviously acting like a woman with a grudge. I struggle to deal with the pressure she applies to my life. After Jill died I let her take charge of a lot of things that Jill did for me. Now she wants more than everything Jill had. Including being my wife. She found out that, in this country, there are no marriage restrictions between a man and an adopted daughter. It is not the same as a father being restricted from marrying his true daughter."

William realised that his outburst would shock Julie. He was obviously getting hi s words off his chest. He was not finished yet! He took a deep breath before adding to her shock.

"I don't think the spilled wine was an accident. She is jealous of your presence here."

"Oh my God!" Julie was in a trance. Astonished at William 's outburst and this situation. William had seemed such an ideal, genuine, uncomplicated man. In control of events all around him, such that his influence bred confidence in people, particularly in Julie. Moreover, she had begun to realise that she was becoming accustomed to his authority and his consideration of her. In fact perhaps she was falling for him.

Suddenly,in shock, she was realising that his life was rather more vulnerable and complex than she thought

Something made her try to treat the situation lightly.

"William, I don't want to be between any daughter or wife relationship that you have with Gede, but If she did deliberately drop the wine in my lap she would not have expected that I, and then you, would laugh it all off. Nor would she have expected me to be wearing your wife's underclothes to complete our meal!" She giggled as she spoke to make it jocular. From William justa wan smile.

With Julie's comments normality prevailed with their horses to talk about.

Julie left the dining room for a toilet break. Suddenly, as she walked down the corridor something made her glance over her shoulder. Gede was there! She was walking about ten yards behind her with a carving knife in her hand and an anguished look on her face. She lifted her arm with the knife pointing directly at Julie, then there were animated movements and facial expressions. It looked to Julie that she was being stalked. Upon Julie's 'over the shoulder' stare their eyes locked and then Gede abruptly turned into an adjoining room, now swinging the knife casually in her hand. Julie shuddered involuntarily as she entered the toilet. Was that a menacing message to her? Surely it could have been. Was it some kind of Balinese spell with the knife? But what if Julie had not turned her head? Julie decided that it was time for her and Pampers to go back home.

CHAPTER 22

Mark Desperate Forshaw

With Julie back home with Pampers and Madame Fatale and back in her routines, she remembered that she had neglected to follow up on Mark Forshaw's invite to another hotel 'all-nighter'. She did not fancy being lavishly entertained again, when she suspected that he still coveted both the horse and the owner. She texed him to decline the outing, suggesting that if he wanted to talk he called for a chat at her home. She felt safer and in control in her own home and with her own timing while she tried to fathom out whether his motives were genuine, or what he was up to with the horses.

When Mark Forshaw arrived in his white jaguar he was being driven by his chauffer who dropped him off. Mark said that this enabled him to have a drink with Julie. The chauffeur would wait for him and drive him home when he was ready. Of course Mark wanted to have a look at 'Pampers ' the wonder horse, before they went indoors. Even in the relative safety of her own home Julie could not shake off a feeling that he was trying to be familiar with her and she gave him no encouragement. His whole conversation was then about the Jacobs Racing Stables. How he was primary mover in their successes and ambitions, and what their two stables could achieve together. He was filling his own glass up now from the whisky bottle and the more he drank the faster and more suggestive he talked. Eventually Julie had heard enough and was ready to 'call it a day'. She reminded him that his chauffer was outside waiting for him.

"I will be back in the morning to see how Johnny is progressing with the sale and transfer of the Ross horses to the Jacobs Yard" He forced a kiss on leaving. She was glad to close the door behind him. She was falling asleep now and managed to make the bedroom where she flopped on the bed, fully clothed.

The next morning she awoke with a start and a hangover but she had to get on with the stable work and exercising of Pamperlight. Once outside she was immediately apprehensive when she found that the stable doors had not been locked overnight as they should have been. Nor was Pampers her usual 'perky' self. She seemed twitchy, nervous and her muscles seemed tighter than normal. Only Julie who knew Pampers so well could tell that she was not comfortable. She carefully entered the horse's stall and slowly started cleaning out. She gradually moved around the stall talking to Pampers all the time. At this point, son Johnny came in looking for her and behind him, back again, was Mark Forshaw, now standing hind side of the horse. Julie was just about to comment on Mark's early arrival when suddenly Pampers lashed out with both hind legs with a kick that the horse had only been seen to do when turned out in the fields. The vicious blows hit Mark Forshaw in the 'midriff' sending him flying down on the floor in some pain. The horse was then backing up, hooves stamping towards him, in a concerted attack as they had never seen before, particularly from a young horse and it seemed to have been directed solely at Forshaw. It was over in a moment. Johnny braved a return to the horse in her stalls and Pampers gradually settled down so that they were then able to approach and examine her for anything to account for her tense and unusual behaviour.

On close inspection Julie found nothing except that she noticed there was a small scar on the horse's muzzle, which they could not account for. Had she been stung or startled by something? .For once Forshaw was speechless, breathless and hurting. He had been standing behind Pampers unsuspecting of the kicks.

For some strange reason Julie's first thoughts were of Danny, her bereaved husband. He was the only person she had ever known who would react so unexpectedly but so viciously and so decisively when under pressure or danger. Now she was feeling a ' strange' atmosphere and an intuition about the horse . She looked at Pamperlight and wondered about the cause of the' happening'.

Forshaw just wanted to be on his way! They had him sat with head between his legs. Then he was limping and clutching his groin as he went. In his pain and anger he made the mistake of deliberately aiming a kick at the horse's legs. The action showed a lot to Johnny about the Forshaw character and lack of control and suitability for an important coaching role on the Jacobs training staff.

It looked as though the horse had picked Forshaw out for the 'attack'. The question was why?

Julie recalled reading recently about a type of Taser gun being used on dangerous animals. She phoned her vet about it, he had suggested that while they may not stun a horse, they could deliver a 'sting' to startle and unnerve them, and could leave a small scar. He had heard of them being used to 'persuade' a horse in an extreme situation. Julie thought about Pampers nervy disposition that morning. And the stable door she found to be unlocked overnight. She also thought about the new scar on Pamper's muzzle, and Forshaw's reappearance so early that morning. Her mind was in a whirl but perhaps she had some sort of 'inner knowledge'. She could not sort her thoughts out, but she decided that she would withdraw her horse from her next race declaration and she minded to be watching Forshaw closely in the future! She thought about talking to her son Johnny who had Darrell Jacobs, Forshaw's boss's ear.

William Stroll had seen that Pampers had not been declared for the race she had to explained to him what had happened and why Pampers had been withdrawn. He looked quizzically at her as if he couldn't believe what she was inferring. William had heard about Taser guns being used to restrain various animals. William's thoughts were that things always seemed to happen in Julie's court. But now Julie had arrived on his horizon!.

Mark Forshaw was under a lot of pressure. Lady Goldie, the horse that he had staked his reputation on, was losing out to Julie Ross's Pamperlight. He had persuaded Mr Darrell Jacobs to pay 'through the nose' for the well bred Lady Goldie, but as yet she had not shown anything but average talent in her two races. By contrast, Pamperlight had already, in only her second race, collected the prizes with the Pot,the Cash, and the glowing reports for her future. Her owner Julie Ross was singularly training her to future glories. Forshaw was desperate because he had talked himself into a good job with Mr Jacobs. He had to justify his bragging predictions and also his derogatory remarks about the Ross stables and their policies.

Forshaw was beginning to realise that he had taken a big risk by creeping into Pamper's box in the early hours of the morning and using a Taser Gun on the horse. He had learned that it could temporarily shock the animal, so upsetting her equilibrium, her confidence and manner. It was aimed at ruining her relaxed racing progress, with little or no visible evidence left after the shot. The taser should not have gone to the horses head.

In the morning when Forshaw returned to the box to meet Julie and Johnny Ross it was really to ascertain the after effects that the taser had on the horse. He could immediately tell that the horse was disturbed and Julie was just alongside trying to relax and quieten her. His mistake was to stand directly behind the horse who unexpectedly lashed out with both hind legs with some vicious force into his 'guts'.

It could be his last act as an employee of the Jacobs stables. When accosted and reprimanded by Mr Darrell Jacobs, he lost his sense and reason, grabbed the taser gun from the boot of his car and tried to point it at Johnny who quickly hit him with the horse's feed bucket and grabbed the gun from him. His notice terminating his employment and barring him from all further contact was delivered to him shortly afterwards. In his eyes, Julie Ross and her horse were jointly to blame! As for Julie she was not unhappy to see him go!

CHAPTER 23

Roberto's Temptations

When Roberto had visited Julie last, his prime reason was to be sure that she would have him accompany her to the Hunt Social. He liked to think that his own 'prestige' was being raised within the local community because she was an important member of the hunting crowd and he would be her first partner for the evening, since the loss of her husband. He was suspicious of Julie's other liaisons and anxious because he was pretty sure that the two empty wine glasses meant that someone had been sharing Julie's bed. He was also desperate to show off his escorting skills to the community because his escorting business was going through a bad time. The number of Social functions and his 'regular customers' were diminishing, as was their 'class' and ability to pay him. More of his sexual contracts were fraught with financial difficulties. Offers of 'payment in kind 'rather than cash did not always do much for him, and did not help his bank account. He was desperately short

too much. However when he dropped her off she was sober enough to not having him come in tonight. His intent was to call on her very soon to 'return ' the card, or see if she had missed it. She had enjoyed a good time and she had shown no suspicion of his intent, but Roberto knew that he was taking a dangerous gamble. But there was no turning back now.Julie was gullible!

Early the next morning Roberto travelled to various cash points in Leeds city centre, and with face hooded, and armed with the pin number, withdrew a total sum of 200 pounds from Julie's account. When he saw her balance on the account he thought she might not miss this amount immediately .He would risk taking another 200 pounds from another cash point on the other side of the city centre.

His next move was to go and see her this morning. She had been 'well oiled' last night, He needed an opportunity to return the card to her handbag.

"Hello love, I just thought I would call to see if you were OK after last night, because you were' well oiled' weren't you."

For Julie, it was ' The morning after'.She had a real hangover!

"Hello Roberto. Come in. Yes I am still trying to shake off the 'Hang Over'. Would you like a coffee? I am just going to make one."

His golden opportunity was presented straight away. Julie's handbag was open on the couch where she had thrown it last night. Quickly done, and then he sat down in the chair on the other side of the lounge before she brought in the coffees. His ears pricked when he heard Julie say "Do I owe you for drinks last night?"

"No its OK. Mr Hutton bought most of the drinks. I think he likes dancing with you!"

Roberto was still puzzling over who was the man who was successful in having Julie's affections? Possibly that Mark Forshaw from the Jacobs stables where Johnny's rich girl friend came from? He could not help thinking that if could get Julie in bed he knew who could 'entertain' her the best. Money doesn't win all the time!

Then he thought to himself," I've done what I wanted to do today in replacing the cash card,Now I should leave. to avoid any suspicion."

He drank his coffee then bade Julie goodbye and opened the door to leave; and was faced with a uniformed policeman who seemed to just stand there staring at him. His heart sank. He was thinking that, surely Julie couldn't have found out what he had done, and contacted the police so soon! He started to stammer. " I'm just leaving. I haven't been here long. I'll get Julie for you."

"Julie! A policeman here to see you."

Julie seemed surprised and perhaps embarrassed as she waited for Roberto to leave. The policeman had not spoken to him as he went. In fact he was waiting for Roberto to go before speaking. Roberto was quickly on his way!

When Roberto had gone Julie gasped. " Gavin! What are you doing here at this time?"

Gavin replied." Julie, I can't keep away. . I knew you were being escorted by him last night, and I could not rest. He's not been here all night has he?"

"No he hasn't! But he'll wonder what you are here for."

"You know what I'am here for Julie. I want you again!"

"Gavin, this has got to stop! You are supposed to be on duty."

The chance confrontation of the two suitors on her doorstep made Julie, despite her hangover, realise that she had to do something to stop this. What with these two and then the Mark Forshaw incident .Between them they would make her ill.

She sent Gavin on his way back to his work disappointed. It was just as well because shortly afterwards Gavin's mobile rang and it was his Superintendent, with information. The village police station was to be extended and the village force expanded. He was coming over with the new recruit. Gavin was to meet them at the station in one hour. Gavin 's first thoughts were that it was to restrict his freedom to plan his own day. In fact to' clip his wings' when on the beat.

He hastened back to the station. The 'Super' was waiting for him with the new recruit .It was a WPC ! A woman police constable! And a good looking one at that! Gavin's second thoughts were that she appeared so vulnerable that instead of her protecting the public she was going to need protecting herself. His interest in the female form was growing thanks to Julie's 'input'. He would make it his responsibility to look after her! Who knows where it would lead to?

were on police duty. Catherine sometimes had to ask him to instruct her again, because she had not absorbed his words due to the closeness of his presence.

Julie was at first 'miffed' by what she saw between them, for they were clearly enamoured; but when she had time to think, she was pleased with the thought that her' tuition' may stand young Gavin in good stead in due course within his new relationship! She recognised however that she herself now yearned for a settled, mature 'partnership'; and William's situation with Gede was bewildering her.

It was a few days before Julie needed some cash and when she had cause to use her cash card the end of the expiry month had passed, and her new card was valid. This did remind her to check her bank balance, however and only then, did she start to think that her account balance was somewhat lower than she might have expected. Even then, a few days elapsed before she went online to her transaction histories when appreciating her late husband Danny's past financial instructions.. She wracked her brains to try to remember several withdrawals amidst her various regular monthly expenditures for horses, personal household payments, monthly outgoings and cash. When she finally started to question certain withdrawals her first thoughts were of banking errors that had somehow mixed up her account. When she mentioned it at the bank they wanted to 'freeze' her account while they investigated.

She was shocked and then upset when it finally started to dawn on her that her account might have been robbed in some way. It wasn't a fortune but she really didn't know what to do, and that was when she confided in policeman Gavin, turned detective. Gavin took up the cudgels. He had Julie mark off a few of the transactions and traced the whereabouts of one of the cash machines. His policing 'know how' involved finding which machines had a CCTV camera in use.

When the film was played back, the figure using the cash machine had a hood pulled down over his head. For Julie it was some hooded stranger. A man that she could not see or recognize.

And then Gavin spoke. "Let me have another look at the film!"

He watched the figure walking hurriedly away,

"I know who that is!"

"Gavin, how can you know?"

.When I called to see you that early morning after the night of the Social, I wondered about the man just leaving your house in a hurry as I arrived. He did a little' skip' to take him on his way" " This man did the same little 'skip' as he hurried away.

"No! you're mistaken., That was Roberto". Said Julie.

"He's your man. I'm in no doubt." Said Gavin.

Julie's hand went to her mouth as she gasped at the implications. It can't be. Gavin must be mistaken. Her mind was racing. And then she was in shock as she realised that Gavin's words would not go away. Roberto! What has he done? And then. How has he done it?

Gavin was not only so sure that he could identify the theft, but also, with Julie's help he could confront him with the allegations such that he would probably admit to what he had done.

On Julie's conscience however was the thought that Roberto could have managed to 'borrow' the card and return it to her belongings such that she did not know what he had done. She had been careless with her handbag. Gavin had said that crimes against elderly or vulnerable persons were penalised more heavily by the law.. Her careless attitude with her possessions could put her in the 'helpless' category of victims. It did not show Julie in a good light! And she knew it!

However she was now looking at what had happened in the light of her not trusting Roberto. Her handbag had not been with her all of the time when she was dancing. Also when Roberto visited her she had left him in her lounge while she made some coffee in the kitchen. Chances for the card to be stolen and later replaced! He could have done; but she couldn't believe that he would have done. But Roberto had not visited her recently, as he previously had done.

This was upsetting to Julie and making her believe the worst of him but also fearful of a confrontation if he did call. She still hoped for some explanation, and at the back of her mind she wondered whether, if Roberto was so desperate and had good cause for his predicament, she might have leant him money anyway if it could have been a solution for him.

Gavin suggested that Julie invited Roberto to visit her .He and Catherine would be there when he arrived and be prepared to charge him and arrest him on suspicion of theft; but she would have to reveal all the circumstances and they would have to be proven. Gavin could not understand Julie's reluctance to agree to this plan.

Julie's confidence was noticeably deteriorating with all this. She could not face a showdown with Roberto, let alone an official robbery investigation. She was afraid to do anything at all relating to the incident and Gavin could see that this was going nowhere, as time passed by.

Gavin finally decided that if Julie was not prepared to go to see Roberto,then he would.He traced his address from his Escort adverts. It was a dark and gloomy evening when he knocked on Roberto's door. When it opened slightly he quickly barged in and pushed Roberto against the wall. He had expected some physical resistance from him." I'am charging you for robbery of property belonging to Mrs

Julie Ross. Anything you say may be used in evidence against you."

And then he looked at Roberto in the dark hallway. He could barely recognise him. He had been transformed into a fragile, broken man, who was shaking and barely able to stand. He looked like he needed emergency medical attention!.

"I'm sorry. I'm sorry was the cry". Gavin realised that the man was not only guilty, but his crime, and the guilt and fear from what he had done, had likely made him so ill. He was slumping against the wall trembling as if he could hardly stand.

Gavin sat Roberto down on a soft chair where he slumped lifeless and crying. Gavin was not sure of the best thing for him to do. And then he thought. What would Julie, the victim, do if she was here?

He eased the pressure, made the man a hot drink and tried to settle him so that he could talk sensibly to him .When faced with the question the man admitted what he had done and his regret. It looked as though the fear, the shame, and the likely consequences had ruined his health and his life completely. He swore he would somehow pay Julie the money back if he could. It was clear that his guilt and the state of his current health would make it very difficult for him to do this. This would be further shame on him, such that he could not face anyone let alone Julie.

Gavin had decided! "Who is your Doctor? Get that hot drink and then some rest. I will get a doctor to call on you with medication. You must take it. I will talk to Mrs Ross and come back to you later. Don't leave the house."

Julie was shocked at Gavin's news and thought that all she wanted was for the whole business to end. She did not want any money back from Roberto, especially with his condition, as Gavin had described it. But mostly, she did not want to see him ever again! Her relations with Roberto over several years, had come back to bite her. He had used her trust and friendship against her and was now obviously suffering for it. It was his punishment for him and his conscience to suffer remorse at his crimes.

As Policeman Gavin pointed out to her, she had to take action or move on; while she was aware of Gavin's diplomatic handling of the theft.

CHAPTER 25

William, Gede and Julie

Julie had things to learn, about relationships, and took some time to settle down, by immersing herself in 'hard labour' at the stables. The horse's welfare and fitness had to be considered. She arrived at Stroll Stables early one morning .She saw no one about the yard. She had left Pampers in the small paddock overnight together with Mangel . The horses had access to the boxes if the weather was bad. The two horses seemed to be getting on well together. They were relaxed, which was important during their training, this, Julie knew well. Pamper's training and her transfer to William's training environment was uppermost in her thought at present,because the flat seasons big races were coming up and her filly was relaxed and being 'freshened up' ready for her first race entry of the season. Julie wished that her relationship with William could be similarly relaxed. William, however, had seemed to be distracted lately, with other things on his mind. His plans for his horse's racing career were vague. He was reluctant to confide anything, but Julie's concerns persisted. His earlier image had been as an influential, confident, successful businessman. Affluent,honest,decisive and respected for his racing successes with his horses in Grade 1 and 2 listed races. Now he seemed to want to keep everyone, including herself, at arm's length. Julie still remembered her previous marriage style with Danny when, among her many roles, she had become a domesticated wife. She loved to cook a special meal for him, and afterwards she would put her arms round his neck and pull him down to her. She longed to do the same for William but she never felt that he was relaxed and loving enough for her to do this. When she found out that Gede was Williams adopted daughter she would have hoped to befriend her but now she was at a loss to know how to do this.

Gede was still a problem. She was repeatedly throwing her Balinese family customs and traditions at William when it suited her. With his wife's death and William now 'unmarried', she hoped to have him fulfil Balinese traditions, giving her senior family status and opportunity to raise a family. Her Balinese family traditions were also of 'ngurek' marriages which involved, as part of the ceremony, 'puncturing holes' in the surface of their skin. Julie was beginning to realise that the relationship between Gede and William was fraught with problems. She was physically awkward and aggressively obstructive. He was trying to ignore her manner when Julie was around. It eventually came out with some embarrassment when Julie told him that she would not stay any longer in the 'atmosphere' created by Gede. William took a long breath and tried to explain what was behind it all.

"When Jill and I first saw Gede at seven years old she had already learned some of her families customs,practises, and way of relating to the various situations. She had difficulty with the different life we were trying to give to her, She was a seven year old who, had bouts of sadness with disturbances and nightmares, crying out in fear. Jill would bring her into our bed to cuddle her and try to settle her down. I would cuddle her too, in a father and young daughter relationship. . And when she settled we eventually got some sleep. As Gede got older and started to develop I tried to gradually move from a father and little child relationship, on to a father and growing daughter relationship. For the good of us both I started to distance myself from her close presence, conscious that she was no longer a child but was developing into a strong, beautiful young woman. Her Balinese experiences made it difficult for her to understand as I became less demonstrative with her, At the same time Jill's health was now not good. Gede finally realised that she was not my real daughter at all. She was dismayed at what adoption was. Her life changed. She was further unsettled by Jill's demise and our knowledge that she was dying. Then, as she could not have me as her father she would try to have me as the man in her life, and by Balinese ways, her future husband. She was shocked that I would not do that, when she wanted me unreservedly.

Some time after Jill had passed away, Gede entered my bedroom one night and my bed with me asleep and dreaming.. Gede took Jill's role in the bed, before I awoke and realised what was happening and what she wanted of me. I was very angry with her.

Julie; you have to understand that Gede has become panic stricken about your emergence into my life and this has caused her desperation."

William's flow of words of explanation had come to a stop. He was out of breath, devoid now of words or energy and wondering what Julie would think now, about all that..

Julie however, knew of William's strong will and beliefs that were still important to him and had helped him to get through Jill's traumatic illness and death, with dignity and personal reserve. She did need time to think about his revelations however and without speaking went outside to the stables.

Once outside she saddled Pampers and went out to exercise her on the gallops and also to get some fresh air.

William's part time stable hand took Mangel out with her. They were out some two hours giving their horses a full workout including starting at speed from the stalls, and leisurely cantering before walking them back to the yard, followed by a wash over and brush down. Time for Julie to think!

Julie saw that the two horses were relaxed and fed but, there was no other sign of activity at the house or round the yard.

After William's outburst, Julie was beginning to understand his dilemma. She wanted to say that she understood better his difficulties, and was prepared to keep things to a friendship level for a time. She went looking for him. Gede, who she was wary of confronting; could not be seen.

She knocked on the door, and with no response from inside, she opened the door and entered the lounge and then the kitchen and dining room. No sign of anyone but some muffled noise from the bath and shower room. She remembered quite distinctly William 's tale of the Balinese customs of communal family bathing, so she did not proceed with her search for William. She would be embarrassed if she found them together particularly after Gede's gestures the last time she had seen her, and what William had told her.

She sat down to wait in the lounge, although she could hear banging, splashing and shouting noises. Eventually she started to sense that something was wrong. She listened at the door and heard Gede shouting.She heard it clearly

: "Now you don't want me. I will not let you go. Now you have got me, and you will have no one else but me! I will die first."

Julie hastened forward, cracked the door open and peeped into the mini bathing pool.

What she saw was enough to make her scream out, aghast.

She saw William, fully clothed in the pool up to his waist in blood red water. And then she realised that with his hands under her arms he was trying to drag a naked Gede out of the pool .She seemed barely conscious and unwilling to help William's efforts to drag her out of the water.

Julie could now clearly see that the blood was from cuts to Gede's side and on her arms with one wrist bleeding profusely. The instincts that Julie had developed over her full life of shocks and crisis, sprung her into action. Without hesitation she jumped into the bloodied water. She took William's hold under the girls arms and shouted to him. " Lift her legs while I lift and pull ".Between them they managed to lift and pull the naked body to the side and on to the bathroom floor.. As she lay there still, Julie immediately saw the severed wrist; snatched a towel, folded it into a roll and tied it very tightly round the arm, then gripped it tightly and held it high to stem the blood flow.

William had recovered a knife from the water, climbed out of the pool and was barely on his feet before Julie shouted.

"Quick,ring 999 for an ambulance. She's losing blood, I will have to keep my grip round her wrist until they come." They had laid the girl flat on the floor and Julie was holding the severed wrist up in the air as high as she could. No sign of breathing! No sign of life!

"What do we tell them?" William shouted as he rushed out of the room.

Julie shouted back" Nothing!"

He mobiled 999 and returned with an emergency fibrillator. He knew how to quickly set it up and apply it. Gede eventually recovered, coughed, and was gulping for breath. Now conscious but still naked, she would not lay still but was almost fighting to break away but Julie's strength and her vice like grip stayed firm. Julie recognised William's embarrassment and sent him to find a blanket from the bedroom to cover her over and keep her warm. All the time she kept a firm grip on her raised arm to stem the flow of blood. Other cuts to Gede's body were apparent The cuts to her wrist had been exuding blood and was definitely life threatening. She became still and quiet, weak but breathing.

Julie looked at William. Between them they had probably saved the girl's life, providing that an ambulance arrived quickly. Now she saw that William was distraught. While still supressing the blood flow, Julie put her other hand round his neck. It was at this moment that she felt that she loved him. She pulled him closer to the floor and kissed him. She knew, even in this situation, and vulnerable as he was, that she wanted him, if he would reciprocate. He responded to her kiss while Julie's vice like grip still held the tourniquet tight on the rolled up towel!

-What a situation! They were a good couple together and this crisis was showing that. Julie did not move or release her tight grip until the ambulance arrived. It seemed an age before the medics came, but they quickly assessed what to do to stem any further blood loss from the wrist and, were soon ready to stretcher Gede, weak as she was, to their vehicle.

The medic spoke to William." Could you make your wife a hot drink." He indicated to Julie." She has been on the cold bathroom floor for so long. She saved the girls life."

Julie had looked at Gede as she was wheeled out. Thoughts flashed through her mind. She was thankful that the girl should survive, but could not but wonder what had happened to result in her life threatening injuries. It was clear that Julie and William had saved her life, but had she really stabbed herself?

William confirmed that Gede had confronted him with the knife to be used in 'ngurek' wedding ceremonies which involved partners cutting each other and exchanging drawn blood. When he would not participate she had 'gone crazy' with the knife.

William was obviously anxious that the medics did not reveal what they had seen to any newsmen, so that their privacy was maintained. However their report on the incident had to be made.

Julie's feelings for William had been exposed by her arm around him amidst the crisis. But also he had responded to the comforting kiss, despite the distraction of the circumstances and her desperate hold on the girl's wrist. And now William still held her tightly against him. The other thought that Julie could not dismiss was that by the very Balinese traditions that Gede followed, the girl should recognise that she was now indebted to Julie!

Julie stayed at William's until the day that Gede was strong enough to leave hospital. During the time that they had together they were both able to develop their feelings for each other, and their unmarried relationship. Sleeping in separate bedrooms was not what Julie hoped, for she secretly knew that she wanted him, but William did not respond to her subtle invitations .Perhaps he saw too many obstacles still to be overcome.

The training of their two horses took up a lot of their time. Pampers and Mangel were happy working together, just as Julie was with William.

On Gede's release from hospital she still needed some assistance. It was then that she quickly saw that a closer relationship had been developing between William and Julie. And Julie wanted Gede to see that to. William spelled it out to her:-

"Balinese customs were, that a family member's status could be enhanced by contributions to the whole family's welfare. Gede should,with time, change her attitude to Julie's presence and input. She was now indebted to Julie and her contribution such that Julie's primary rights to partnership with William should be recognised by Gede's beliefs. She should have to act as a daughter would, even in a Balinese family."

But William and Julie were not yet a family! The crisis had brought them together and it had made them both realise this. Would the future allow them to prosper towards marriage and then fulfilment, with both of them still encumbered with previous memories of their past lives?

Julie had never really considered being married again with all that it entailed. She still missed Danny. But for the first time she recognised that, with him gone, the future was always going to be different. And it could be with this man. William was a strong person of means and authority, and yet very human.

For William, it was the first time since his wife died, that he had really ever thought about his future. And maybe he wanted that his future be a different one, and not the same life again. He could stay with this vibrant woman and both move at the pace that Julie lived her life.

Since her unsuccessful suicide attempt, Gede had seemed to be respectful to Julie. But while William tried to forget, Julie kept an open mind on Gede., She could not forget that Gede had shared William's bed,because he could not stand listening to her night mares, caused by the upheaval of her young life in Bali.. He had tried to insist that she always slept in her own room. And then it was that Jill with her illness needed to sleep alone undisturbed. William had slept alone listening always for his wife wakening .And all the time Gede was growing up and forming frustrations that her instincts decreed.

Alongside the human family turmoil, the training and the welfare and of racehorses was a further challenge. William, and Julie together could influence many things to the good.! That applied to both relationships and also to their Horses.

CHAPTER 26

At The Races

The 'one to one' training of the two well -bred filly's was a full time job. Pampers was re-stabled, housed and trained with Mangel at the Stroll 's facilities, but Julie still wanted to train her in the ' one to one' way that her deceased husband had done and this presented Julie with a reason for living part time at William's and spending much of her time with Pamperlight's fitness and welfare . She had entered Pampers for The Juvenile Stakes at Thirsk racecourse, a six furlong flat race and the first race on the card, to get the meeting underway.

It was Pamper's race date. It was a very wet morning, heavy overnight rain continued making their journey unpleasant and even putting the meeting in doubt, but a steward's inspection called the meeting on, maybe because of a large field of runners and a big attendance likely.

At the start of the first race, Pampers was drawn No 1 on the inside position against the rails .Julie was at the start to see if her training to exit the gates had been successful. And suddenly the wind and the rain intensified soaking everyone to the skin. Lightening flashed. Thunder rolled as the horses were all loaded in the starting gates. Too late to stop the race!.

They're off! The roar of the crowd at the off, quickly descended to a great hush! As the gates opened, some part of the end Starting Gate bracket had become loose and had fallen down on the No1 Stall hitting both rider and horse. Jockey Gibson was knocked sideways from Pamper's saddle,but his left foot was stuck in the stirrups. Pampers lurched forward, crumbling to the floor as her knees buckled, hit the rails, and slid forward on the wet grass. The screaming crowd saw her head lolling down, and then she was still. The red flag was waved to now abandon and bring the racing horses to a halt. Julie had been specifically watching Pampers . She rushed forward in a panic to the fallen horse and its rider. Her heart in her mouth. Pampers lay there flat out and still. Gibson 's twisted foot was freed. He had been dragged a few yards but Pampers had hit the rails, gone down and lay there still, as if dead.

Tarpaulins were being rigged up to shield the public's view of the horse as Julie got there. The Course Vet arrived and kneeled over Pampers who was lying prone and not moving, on the grass under the enclosure rails.

After a cursory examination, the vet stood up and with a shake of his head he went towards Julie who he knew as the horse's owner, thinking of words of commiseration.

Then suddenly Pampers opened her eyes, jerked her head, rolled her neck, lurched to her feet and struggled to equilibrium. It was like pure magic! Now the vet staggered in shock at the horse's recovery. The jockey who had regathered his senses, managed to grab the reins and keep the horse against the rails to prevent her from moving. Back from the dead! Unreal! It was like a miracle had occurred.

Julie again, in her shock, was convinced that this horse had something magic and special about her as if influenced from another world and by some other psychic. She looked Pampers in the eye, the horse herself was tense and shaken, as if she knew that she was part of a miracle. The whole episode was frightening to Julie. Why Pampers, she wondered? She sat in the horse box in silence with Pampers as William eventually drove them to his home. It was as if both horse and owner felt that somehow the happening was not under their own control but directed by external influences. She had never before felt so upset and out of control. Both would need time to regain normality in relaxation.

Shocked as he was, William could see that Julie had been upset and was still on edge. She was quiet, as if her thoughts were running away with her. As soon as they were indoors he poured them both a large sherry, joined her on the couch, put his arm round her and hugged her. It was a natural approach and a sign of intimacy. Just his concern for the way she was feeling so tense. With this closeness and protective gesture Julie gradually started to relax and feel safe within his arms. Different thoughts started to flash before her. It might be the first time that she had any feelings of being comforted like this, since her husband Danny was taken from her.

Strangely, Julie's thoughts were racing. It was about how. She had acceded to Gavin. Was it because of his innocence and his virginity? Or was it because of her desire for some of the sensuality of her marriage that she had lost?

Julie also wondered about William's feelings for her and her imagination of what a future life style would be like with him.. He had been a dominant and successful horse trainer. With his wife Jill they had hit the winning enclosures, collected Racing awards, and also hit the high life style. Until Jill's illness gradually changed everything for them.

And now William was holding Julie quietly on the sofa watching a weak play on television. And both of them were wondering!

Julie was feeling safe within casual but protective arms. Her response to his kiss was such that it became passionate and prolonged. Both of them were flushed in anticipation and knew that it was not only the ambient temperature that was rising!

Experience told them both that they were on common ground, but that here and now should not be the time and the place! And what Gede think if she was around! Gede's presence and belligerence was a 'thorn in the side.' William, was desperately important to her.

For Julie, the budding relationship with William was producing a desire to know him better and be involved in all he did and even to move into his bed if he showed that it was what he wanted. However Gede's presence cast a shadow over her enthusiasm for day to day household intimacy with natural exchanges, and personal confessions, about themselves. They were sometimes held back. Simply being in the same room with Gede had become stressfull. Why? She thought, who was the one with the problems?

To William she said "Do you think that anyone can ever take Jill's place in your life.?" What are your plans for Gede?

Williams reply was just another question. "Can someone love more than once; and each loving have its own way"?

Her memories were secure with her, but on thinking, maybe she was at last casting off the feelings of insecurity that had come after her own husband's demise. She had at last begun to appreciate, even cherish, the pleasures she now had. William was a bit older than her. But was that partly what attracted her? She tried to analyse her feeling towards him. They had not gone to bed together when, often, all was revealed in a relationship. Some 'familiarity' had begun to boost their desire for something closer and deeper between them. For the first time, during some intimate moments, natural modesty was disappearing, his body hard and sleek with exercise. Her yearning for him had risen uncontrollably when he kissed her, his hand behind her neck gently,then with growing urgency..

"William " she had uttered, her fingers threading his hair. She held him tight. They both were wondering whether this should happen right now. And then hesitation made way with William's doubt apparent.

Was she disappointed at not being able to find the natural physicality she had with Danny?

Can anyone love completely, when it's second time round. Each in his and her own way? They both felt that they could; but each of them questioned the others ability to do likewise; while Gede was still around.

CHAPTER **27**

Gede's Dissapearance

After a few days break at home, Julie next visited William to sort out her horses training programme. However, she could tell straight away that he was obviously in a state of panic.

"Gede has disappeared. She went off somewhere and has not come home for the last three days. She has never been away more than overnight before."

Julie tried to calm him. " Teenagers have 'stay overs' nowadays. It's a new fashion". She'll show up soon I'm sure". Do you know where she usually goes and who with?

Williams reply." I know that she has to make friends;But some of her apparent friends seemed to me, to be somewhat out of control, so anything could have happened. She tells me nothing and has been awkwardness itself lately."

William's recent calmer authority had disappeared and been replaced by a worried mind ."Gede's very vulnerable at present as you well know. The trauma of her past life means, even now that Its difficult to talk sense to her when she is in such a state .I had been busy on other things and then she was gone!"

Do you know where she's been going when she has been out? and who with? Where might she go?"

"No, I just can't keep up with her awkward moods and threats to self harm again".She won't tell me anything."

After his words Julie could not speak. Was he holding something back? Her thoughts were running awry. She thought that Gede had left because of her presence. Later, when she was able to think about it she began to fear that maybe something could have happened between Gede and William. Gede was a beautiful young woman . Sleek hair, lithesome limbs, fit and sexual figure. No modesty or inhibitions, completely unrestrained desire for William.She was not his real daughter. And now, her imagination was running away with her. Open thighs enticing him? Inviting him? Forcing him to respond?. Awake or dreaming? Would or could William resist? Had something happened that he was not revealing?

Julie shook her head to try to banish such thoughts. She knew of William's character. Surely that could never have happened. It could not be true; but then,It might be linked to an explanation for her disappearance.

Only the girl and William knew.

She had disappeared. And if found, she might not even want to tell the truth!

William was disappointed with Julies mode, but it made him more determined to find Gede, bring her home, and find out what she was doing that kept her away. At eighteen and a vulnerable young woman he should have been a better father to her in the recent past and should have realised that while she had grown up in body, she was still immature in mind. It was he who should have seen that she was not led into trouble.

William had only a vague idea of where she might be and what she might be involved in. She had always been inquisitive about her young life in Bali. Jill and William had always been reluctant to say much about it.

William knew that Bali was a wonderful holiday resort, but also, under the surface he remembered that, unpublished and supressed violent crimes were taking place. It seemed that Gangs ruled all family groups by extortion, violence, and child abuse. Illegal marriages of young girls. Everything illegal had a price!

It was what they saw, that had encouraged Jill to pay the supposed head of a family to let them adopt Gede as a young child, take her out of there and bring her home to give her the opportunity of a good life.

Ten years on William reflected on Gede's growing up and recent behaviour, His wife's illness and untimely death, recent traumatic events and Julie's presence and companionship,had obviously affected Gede. And now he was facing her disappearance, more seriously by the day.

He searched for clues in her room. Had she planned to leave and taken any clothes ? No mobile! He rang her mobile number again and again before, it rang, but then the receiver stopped his call by cutting off.

He found some books in her cupboard and CD's on Indonesian languages They were hidden behind a drawer in an envelope that had an old address in Birmingham crossed out. However it was stamp marked with a Leeds post code. He could find out just where that postcode area was.

Had she met someone from the country of her birth, and started some relationship?. He hoped not because he had read of the past influx of foreign immigrants into northern cities .Publicity that rumoured of Indonesian immigrants forming the same sort of crime gangs over here. Certainly the numbers of crimes, in the city center areas had risen, and fingers had been pointed at some of the immigrants.

William knew that Gede had been less communicative since the incident in the bathing pool; She had been less approachable, constantly annoyed,and been going out more. Occasionally overnight and coming in later at night. He had always waited to see her back home and had asked about her evening and where she had been.

"Leeds!" She only ever answered his question briefly without advancing any details, but she would still flaunt herself to him. Now she was missing into the third day. He had called the police "missing persons" line.. They did not class his call as justifying a missing person category until at least five days missing, and then, if it was reported, she became one of many, many missing persons that the police had on file, without the time to investigate them . William needed action. He was realising that he could not answer a lot of the questions about her regular habits, friends and movement. He was now searching her room looking for something in particular. It was the Indonesion ¬ marriage¬ Knife. He thoroughly searched the rooms which Gede used. No sign of the knife anywhere. He was certainly worried.

Julie was having some regrets.. She had been so phased by Gede's behaviour when the two were alone in the house .She feared a William and Gede relationship and now there was the news about her disappearance. She began to appreciate what a difficult task that William, a man on his own, had in seeing Gede safely from being an innocent teenager, but with ingrown traditions, to a mature and sensible young woman in England.

CHAPTER **28**

Gavin's Role

Police Constable Gavin Grossman was just thinking how lucky he was. In the city areas, the overworked Yorkshire police force were overwhelmed by increases in crimes of every order. However, Gavin had earned respect, even praise, from fellow police force, for his part in the search for the two girls who went missing. The Roberto' ' stealing' incident had not been reported, but Julie expressed her appreciation, and when Roberto had started to recover his health and came to apologise and ask forgiveness, he thanked Gavin for what he had done.

The area Gavin had to police had been extended, he had now been provided with a police car, a nice Ford Escort, And now he was linked in with a computer, housed in the refurbished village police station. No traipsing round the village on foot now. Also, country people were more law abiding anyway; or more careful!

But most important to Gavin; his junior colleague was still Catherine Marsh, a beautiful young woman who depended on him for police training and frankly every other sort of training you could imagine. They got along well together. In fact, for efficient police working assignments they were beyond criticism, so keeping their jealous probing superiors at bay. In actual fact he was falling in love with her, or else was very desirous of intimacy with her. He never forgot his sexual initiations with Julie, but now he wanted to make love to Catherine. He guessed at her innocence, but she seemed to be more than attracted to him, in fact on his tentative advances she had not rebuffed him. Her only worry seemed to be that everyone; colleagues, associates in the force, and in village life, took a relationship between them for granted; with a nod and a wink.

But they were not yet a 'mating pair'.

Gavin was surprised to receive a phone call from a worried Julie. He knew that Julie was now training her horses at the William Gross stables. He had read from police files about the 'confidential self harm' incident with Gede and the bathing pool. Julie explained that Gede was again a problem. Now she had gone missing, over two weeks ago and nobody at the police missing persons unit had time to listen. Gavin made time to call Leeds city colleagues and see if anything could be gleened about Gede 's presence in the area. Teenaged Gede's desire to find Indonesian friends was all they had in trying to find her.

The Force were tracking ruthless Leeds city gangs who were extending their drug running operations by violently forcing teenagers to carry and deliver drugs to drug addicts, and pressurise and then exploit them. Some of these gangs were known to be made up of illegal immigrants. With this'County Lines' threat and with Gede's interest in Balinese immigrants and her disappearance, she just might now be in danger of violence, sexual abuse, rape, and torture from both gang leaders and drug addicts.

Discreet enquiries about criminal gangs, through Gavin's contacts in the Leeds police force, brought to light an Indonesian gang of illegal immigrants who were clearly involved in violent crime in that area of Leeds..

When his thoughts were passed to him, William had recalled that when they had been in Bali, Gede had an elder brother, who was desperate to emigrate .His name,of Wayam Komang, had now cropped up from Central Leeds police activities and research teams.

Gavin,on his first break from duty was going into Leeds to see if he could identify whether Gede might have been in touch with her brother in the area . Maybe staying voluntarily; or even be imprisoned . A photo of her was Emailed to Leeds Crime squad. Julie had the mobile numbers from her note book and was not going to let Gavin go to Leeds without her, despite the potential dangers. The thoughts she had about Gede's mode were bringing on the tingling in her shoulders which intuition usually meant trouble ahead.

Julie had now become involved with William and his crisis.. She knew that together they now had things to deal with, and that she needed to support him. Her 'psychic intuition' was racing at overtime. And she hoped that it could guide her actions again!.

The threesome came out from the Leeds Police headquarters having been given details about the efforts to trace Gede and information about crime gang culture and habits in Leeds. The bad news was that the name Wayam Komang had cropped up on police files, as a ruthless criminal of Balinese origin.. He had appeared in the Leeds city area where the ruthless methods he had learned in Bali had enabled him to viciously impact the drugs scene and the 'County Lines' distribution.

It was a hazy night after a hot day.. Not a good evening to be wandering around without some plan. Only Julie's intuitions were guiding them. She just wanted to 'feel' the atmosphere of the areas around the city and promote her intuitions. She guessed that there was very little police presence or deterrent in the area after dark.' Gavin's feet were aching and he was not keen on wandering about in the closing light. But, after the experience of Julie's psychic with the missing girls in the village, he was beginning to feel that her ideas were not to be easily ignored. William was asking her what the point of this was, when they could be having an evening in a hotel or heading for home.

In was starting to rain as the day was closing in and they were crossing an overnight cinema car park. No one was about, except that Julie saw the shape of a young woman carefully picking her way through the cars, walking presumably to her own car. She watched her as she tried a car door but then walked on to another. Suddenly she realised that she was systematically walking aisles trying car door handles to see if any were unlocked. Now her path was deviating to take in more rows of the parked cars. Julie drew back towards Gavin and held him still, indicating the woman she had seen. Her routine of trying car doors to see if any were not locked was halted. She looked around her and then opened the back door of a car, quickly pulled out a small brief case and she was quickly on her way. It could have been her own car, but Julie saw that if it was, then she had now left it unlocked. They watched her as she started again to quickly try for other cars left unlocked by any careless drivers. Julie had decided that she knew what she was up to! Without a thought she ran out to try to grab hold of her. The girl was too sharp and quick for Julie to keep hold and she twisted away, turning to run for it but ran straight into Gavin's grasp. He twisted her arm up her back to stop her struggle. It was not Gede, but startlingly another Indonesian looking girl of similar age, build and features. .When she realised that she could not escape, the girl started to shout out and tried to say that she was collecting something for a friend. She was under some pressure from the way Gavin was gripping her and threatening to physically hurt her arm and from Julie's demands for answers to her questions. Julie was shouting at her. "Do you know a girl your age and Asian like you, called Gede!"

She responded to the shouting..

"Komang will have you if you don't let me go. " On hearing the name Komang, Gavin produced his police badge. This was getting serious and was not for amateur sleuths. The girl stopped struggling on eventually recognising her predicament.

Julie said to her,"We'll let you go if you can tell us anything about her. Her name is Gede."

"Komang has her. He took her to work in the gang. He makes us try to get more young women to work for him. He's the boss and he ties your hands behind your back. Gede is being controlled like I was and he'll force her to supply the druggies and collect or get young recruits. You can't stop him.. And he'll beat her if he has to make her. He's vicious."

hidden under floorboards, cash, and a gun,and a knife. They were all arrested, and had been interviewed . The two men were both illegal immigrants. They would be held for questioning about Komang.'s whereabouts. 'The women were clearly showing the effects of their imprisonment at night and could show cord marks and body bruises where they had been tied up and punched around in 'persuading' them to do the drug running. Gede's search for her brother from Bali had turned into the terror that his mental and physical treatment of her had become.

After police questioning, the two male immigrants were held in custody on drugs and other criminal charges, and the whereabouts of Komang. Gede and Maria would be released on bail. Assistance would be provided to secure, search and then clean and return the flat for Maria. William, with Julie's assistance, would assure the judge that Gede would not abscond from their home again. They were warned that custody would be inevitable and her present misdemeanours would be taken into account if she were later found guilty of other offences.

The whole business had been an immense shock to Gede and had dinted her confidence and independence .She was in relief when she knew that she would be able to go home. A first gesture of her appreciation? Julie was still wary. It had taken Julie to save her from not one, but two, life endangering situations as if Julie was her real mother.

Back at William's home, life resumed with William appearing' distant' from both women as he struggled to maintain control of events and of his emotions. Julie was still wary of Gede, who often distanced herself by locking herself in her bedroom. Gede was acting in a temperamental way. Sometimes she tried to act as though she was William's wife. Sometimes she would make food for just William and herself, completely ignoring Julie's presence . On one occasion she had appeared in an undressed state before William and for Julie's embarrassment. When William admonished her she insisted that she was only doing what she was entitled to do with her status of William's wife. Relationships had not changed very much.

The necessary running of the stables and the horse's welfare and fitness were the only factors to keep Julie at the Stroll household and keep her active and busy. Pamperlight and Mangel were both near to the levels of fitness required for racing starts. When out on the gallops, Julie felt that that was the only time she could relax, and cast out the domestic turmoil being created by the Wiliam/Gede troubled relationship.

Julie had Pampers entered in a five furlong race at Haydock Park's evening meeting. Julie made a midday start, on a warm sunny day, just glad to be on their journey over the Penine moors. Pampers was quickly registered and stabled, exercised and readied for the 7.35 race. A quiet meal for Julie, before having the horse saddled and in the parade ring, with brief instructions to the apprentice jockey. "Let her get into her rhythm and stride length early on in the knowledge that once underway, a gradual easing of the 'accelerator' by squeezing with his thighs and the speed and class would show through, probably without the use of the whip as a reminder."

Julie decided that she would watch the race from the elevation of the stands above the grounds enclosure. Pampers was quoted at 3 to 1. From the stands above she watched how a good crowd were placing bets with the bookies before some of them would rush to the rails to see the last furlong to the finishing line. She was enjoying the sight and feel of the atmosphere. And then suddenly her general view from above seemed to be focused to one man placing a bet and then standing alone as the race commenced. A shiver went down Julie's spine as she stared at the man from above. No! She could not possibly know him, but yet, from police video, the far eastern look and certain mannerisms.! She was imagining that it was Komang, the crooked and vicious brother to Gede, who the police were still searching for.

They're off, the crowd watched the horses via the TV screen and listened to the commentator in anticipation. Julie had forgotten about the race. All she could do in her shock was to watch the man! In the last furlong Pampers had shown her class, winning by some two lengths.. From the stands above she saw the man rip up his betting slip in disgust and throw it aside and disappear among the racegoers. Julie tried to dismiss the thoughts from her mind, but she still rushed down to the stables, to Pampers, and then to the prize presentation. She just had an uneasy premonition making her feeling desperate to leave and get on her journey back. She did not relax until she was well on her way home, when the class of Pampers winning performance sunk in!

CHAPTER 29

Catastrophy

The hot summer weather continued and the horses were just as uncomfortable as anyone else. Cold showers and cold drinks for all. On the moors the ground had become hard and dry, unsuitable for horses and riders alike. Shady places and Mist Sprays were required. Julie felt uncomfortably hot and tired when tending to the horses welfare and also a bit annoyed at William's absence when jobs were required to be done in the yard.. Staying at William's stables always meant that she was busy. An early night was in her thoughts so avoiding recent tensions between them.

The green grass and moist vegetation of the Yorkshire Moors had parched so that even the heathers were gradually changing, to brown, dry and flammable ground cover. For visitors, walkers and the like, the starting of fires was strictly prohibited.

Fires had occasionally occurred on the moors in the past. They were usually slow spreading and were easily contained and doused when rain came . However if the fires crept through dry heathers, reaching shrubs and brushwood and then trees, if fuelled by strong dry winds, they became a real uncontrollable danger, especially to the game birds,the grouse and pheasants,and then to hedges, wooden barns buildings and all property in their path.

When she stayed overnight at the Gross household,Julie's bedroom was on the back of the house and away from the other two bedrooms occupied by William and by Gede.

It was early morning when Julie awoke from a deep sleep; but not a relaxed one..

In her sleep she was having a 'psychic experience'; a dream that was frighteningly real and difficult for her memory to ignore. Her dreams were often' sparked' by a fear of something worrying her.

This time the ' experience' was so much more intense than the dreams she used to have as a frightened young girl and the 'psychic' intuitions she experienced. She was dreaming of riding bareback on Pampers with hands round her withers and travelling like the wind! Pampers was relishing the freedom of no saddle and girth. Her breathing from flared Nostrils. Suddenly danger was in front of them. Both horse and rider were shrouded by bellowing smoke and frightening flames which the winds were blowing towards them and the stables. A panicky nightmare, the barns and the house were in danger. She rushed to William's bedroom to warn him!

And immediately she gasped at what she saw from Gede's open bedroom door. It was Gede's form in bed, her body partially covered by a male form. Julie turned in horror and slammed the door shut and then she stumbled and fell. She was falling,falling like in a deep quarry.

Out of bed! She had hit the floor with a bump. It made her waken from her 'nightmare' with a jolt!

Thank goodness! She had been having a nightmare; not real, but so frightening that she was still disoriented as she lay on the floor. She gradually recovered her senses. She lay there in recovery. She knew that a psychic message had been impressed upon her. Not like a dream that she could brush aside when awake and thinking rationally. No ! This intuition was clearly such that she must not ignore the thoughts of fire, and more.

It was still dark outside but she rose trying to find some memorable sense out of what she had been submitted to. She felt hot sweats and automatically went to open the bedroom window, and then something jerked her memory of the first dream she had just come out of. Not an illusion about William and Gede. It was Fire! The smell of smoke and burning!!

She opened her bedroom window and could actually see smoke that was coming from somewhere .It probably had triggered her nightmare!

But she had been warned of danger!

Try a she might she had difficulty now recalling the mode of the dream only that it was some frightening happenings in her troubled sleep. She now lay there in bed in the darkness of this half asleep mode.

Some sixth sense was disturbing Julie as she lay there. She had not heard a thing, but yet she knew that someone was now hovering over her. She felt someone's breath over her in the dark room. Was she dreaming? Was it a nightmare?

NO! This was reality!

She felt strong hands grasping at her throat. And tightening on her windpipe. The weight of a body on top of her. Julie desperately clawed up with her hands, her finger nails digging into the flesh of the hands but the grip on her throat remained. The weight of the body on her remained. She was gradually going under. She was losing consciousness. Panic gave her strength, as she jerked her head up, felt flesh and bit as hard as she could. The grip loosened. She shouted and screamed as loud as she could. She rolled off the bed on to the floor with a thump. The body landed again on top of her. The hands were back at her throat. Julie swung out with the full force of her fist and she made contact. She felt something sharp cut her arm .

The knife clattered to the floor beside her. She was just too late to grasp it as it was swatted away from her and then all was still. She was unable to move for some time. Her body and mind, in fear, would not seem to function. Just for how long she knew not. In fact reality came from a pain on her arm which was bleeding.

It seemed to be the early hours of the morning. She could smell smoke again but now sensed flames and the heat and crackling of fire. She staggered down the landing towards the other bedrooms. William's door was unlocked and she opened it to an empty unmade bed. She rushed further down the landing to Gede's bedroom. The door was locked . She crashed against it and could not budge it, but she could tell from the heat and the noisy crackle of flames that the room was burning! The bedroom was being gutted, by fire!

Julie realised that as she could do nothing with the door locked. With fire so close She had to get out herself! She tumbled down the stairs, scrambled to her feet, unsure.

. A fire coming fast on the wind. Her next thoughts were for the horses. They had to be taken to safety.

Julie knew that horses could easily panic in fear. If they tried to bolt from the paddock they might injure themselves. If they got into the fields they would run away from the fire, but the gale force wind, now blustering up, could cause the fire to spread rapidly in any direction . She thought that she knew why William and Gede were slow to absorb the danger!. Did neither of them smell the smoke, see the flames rapidly ever nearer or recognise the danger from the strong winds? They needed to be aware of, and escape the burning bedroom.

Julie's thoughts however were now with the horses. That they would obviously be feeling the imminent fear and danger.

She looked out,at the weather. An increasing wind and a gusty breeze and blowing towards them. In these conditions, the fire was spreading rapidly and had got to the hedgerows .It could ignite the adjacent hay barn; and was spreading. She thought that part of the house itself was also burning. And then what? The wind was suddenly increasing with gale force gusts. Julie s, sight of flames and the smell of smoke, became a panic for her. What was William doing? Julie still could not separate reality from psychic experience; but she had to do something about the horses!.

What should she do first?

Call the fire brigade! She grasped her mobile phone and dialled 999.

"There's a fire on the edge of the Moors, and at the Gross Stables and it is spreading rapidly to the house."

She thought about her nightmare again and it almost felled her. Was William lying on top of Gede? Somehow she could not try to warn them of the fire again, and at the same time save the horses!.

Her priority was to save the horses! Where could she take them? She opened the paddock gates to let them loose. Only Pampers was in the paddock. The other two were in the stables. She ran straight to Pampers; grabbed her mane and tried to pull her away towards the horse box parked in the yard. Pampers resisted. Julie ran and dropped the ramp. With the ramp down Pampers trotted in readily as though she now knew that Julie's action was to get them away from the danger of the onrushing fire.

Julie stumbled in her panic, she rushed to the vehicles cab door. But she could not leave the other horses in the stables. She ran towards the stables, again feeling the 'whosh' of heat and smoke coming nearer, she grabbed the reins of Madame Fatale and ran with her to the vehicle. Mangel had no reins on. She had to hope that the filly would follow them towards the horse wagon. As she pulled Madame Fatale forward, Mangel ran straight up the ramp into the box next to Pampers. It was as if all the horses knew what she was doing for them as they seemed to 'make room' in the van for the three of them . Julie threw up the loading ramp. It closed with a bang. She ran to the cab again, jumped in and turned the ignition key. The engine did not start! The shock was almost too much for her. She was feeling faint. Her hands were trembling. Please, please! She turned the key to try again; and begged at the same time. Third time and the engine spluttered to life! She crashed into gear and headed for the gates at speed and barely under control. Then she saw that a fire engine was racing towards the gates from the opposite direction. Neither driver was stopping to let the other through. They both swerved at the last moment just scraping vehicles as they rushed through the gates and on, in opposite directions, Julie just anywhere away from the fire and hoping that the loose horses in the van were not injured with the haphazard movement.

The fire engine driver headed straight into the yard. The flames were licking up the walls nearer to the farmyard but he was concentrating on a burning upstairs room.

Julie just drove fast away from the scenes for perhaps a few hundred yards and then in recalling all she had seen and all she had done, she stopped, fell out of the cab and was sick and trembling all in one. She just could not move for a short time. Every time she tried to settle her nerves she recalled not just the fire but the nightmare of the bedroom scenes she had 'witnessed', and it made her relapse and tremble again. Eventually fear gave her strength and she started to think rationally again, and wonder what to do. What was real, and what was in her nightmare?

But then as her mind cleared she started to recall:

Firstly, her nightmare of smoke and flames. It must have been in her dreams; but on awakening she remembered the smell of the smoke was real! The fire was real!.

And then the episode in her nightmare- the vision of Gede together with William. Was this nightmare real or just apparitions with no reality? But her dream of the smoke had later been seen to becoming true. Then perhaps her psychic apparition of William and Gede was also a pointer to coming reality?

Julie's real life was being influenced.by her psychic experiences. Were they just dreams? Or was there something more to her intuitions? She couldn't accept that William was unable to resist Gede's uninhibited desire and the temptations she put before him. But, what took them so long to react to Julie shouting and the danger of the fire.?

In desperation she left the horse box and the horses and started running back to the farmhouse. She realised the dangers of the house being engulfed by the fire. Her panic somehow gave her energy to keep running. As she ran something told her that the fire would likely destroy the house. She collapsed to the ground again in exhaustion. She could run no further and was unable to get up immediately. Again,after some time, she eventually recovered her sense, got to her feet and stumbled forward until the farmhouse was in her sight . The annex, which was where William's bedroom was and adjacent to that of Gede's, was gutted in flames. Immediately she remembered her nightmare. If they were together they would likely be burned to death together whatever they might have been doing.Or they would have had to make a hasty exit from the annexe. She staggered on towards the firemen fighting the fire. "There's two people in there she shouted" again and again. And then she fainted and collapsed again.

It was a little while before she again recovered to her senses and she gradually opened her eyes. William was there looking at her. He had a look of pain and anguish on his face. But he was alive and safe!

"Where's Gede ?"

"She was in there!" Was William's croaked reply.

He staggered towards Julie, arms uplifted. He pulled her to him and they clung together starting to realise the implications of what had happened."

"Gede's dead. The firemen got to her in her room,but they could not bring her round."

Why did she not get out? Was she asleep? Could she not smell the fire,or see and hear it coming?"

Julie could not absorb what William had said.

"Gede has died of smoke inhalation inside the bedroom,her body against the locked door. The door was charred and damaged.. Her underwear charred on her body! The bedroom door was locked . She had been inside!"

But Julie 'knew' that someone was inside with her!

An ambulance had been called and both Julie and William were taken to the local hospital. The drinks they were given included sedation. They both slept for several hours . Julie woke, was offered light refreshment which she could not stomach as her mind was churning over the horrific disaster that she had become embroiled with.

After a hot cup of tea and a bit of time to think she was quickly asked if Superintendent Roberts could see her with a few questions about the incident of the fire and the girl's death.

D S Roberts had been waiting until she was considered well enough to speak to him and answer his questions'. He sat down at her bedside obviously ready for a fair session of questioning Julie.

"Hello Julie. You have been living at Stroll Stables for some months now, I believe". Julie nodded.

"OK Julie, lets go through the events . I need to know your movements. When you went into the house, when you climbed the stairs, When you were in the back bedroom .The one that you use when you are at the house. When you first saw the fire and last saw Gede. I want a non –fiction version. The truth from you."

Julie's already anxious state of mind, was shaken further by his demanding and unsympathetic manner. She realised that he was serious about this. He must suspect that she might have had some part in the shocking events leading to

Gede's death. He had already got some background to the case; and he had her as one of the leading suspects!

The police D S knew from experience that two women living as a family with one man could bring about friction . The Inspector also had information of a previous police attendance at the house involving the two women and one man, when Gede was found bleeding from stab wounds requiring hospital attendance. And now Gede had been trapped in a fire leading to her death..

Julie hesitated in answering his words. The truth was that her mind was such that she did not clearly know which of the incidents prior to the final event, were real or were any part of the psychic influences, and omens she remembered.

She was silent.

She needed the Inspector to be aware of her previous psychic experiences, and intuitions that had started for her shortly after her husband Danny had been killed. Over the years since then, many times she had experiences in the form of dreams or psychic, sometimes nightmares, foretelling the immediate future. They were often something more than intuitions.

How she reacted to them was the crux. Her sleep on that night had been interrupted. She dreamed that she could smell smoke. The dream awoke her but it was not until a little later when she opened the window that she knew that the smoke was real and was representing a danger. Her dream could have been a warning to her in her sleep.!

But her next recollection was at the door to Gede's room . Was this reality, and was Gede with William real or was she sleep walking or imagining thoughts that were brought on by William's earlier confessions about Gede?

Her next memories were of her struggle with someone on her bedroom floor.

Again She burst out to DS Roberts.

"I was wakened by someone on top of me trying to strangle the life from me."

"Are you sure?"

The Police Inspector was undoubtedly thinking that she might have locked Gede in the bedroom with the fire coming. He had been waiting and watching Julie and could see that she was weighing up her options about what to say to him. Was she trying to create a "Red Herring" to confuse things?

Were the events real or just part of Julie's dreams that were foretelling her what was going to happen?

Julie's mind was completely in shreds,

With a hopeless shrug she started trying to explain what she recalled, but she started badly.

"I was asleep in bed. Suddenly a body was on top of me with hands tight round my throat. Someone was trying to strangle me. I fought them. I bit their face. We rolled off the bed but they were still on top of me trying to strangle me. They had a knife. I swung out and fisted them and heard it drop on to the floor."

The struggle, the fight. That was certainly real. She had the marks to show it. She had then rushed to Gede's room again and found the door shut.

"I was angry and then I must have passed out. As I came round I just knew the house was on fire. I crossed the landing. There was no sign of Mr Stroll. Gede's bedroom door was locked but I could hear the burning and crackling of the fire in her room. And I felt the heat of it. I could not open the door and I did not know where Gede was. I then realised that the horses were in danger from the fire. I had to get out of the house to move the horses!

Inspector Roberts was suspicious of the story so far. He wanted to go through it bit by bit. A bit sarcastically he said! " And what were you first dreaming about in bed?"

Julie couldn't hold her answer back."Williams body on top of Gede. She was desperate to have William's children and be his wife by Balinese customs."

"Whoa. Stop there!" " What Balinese customs?. We are trying to establish the cause of this young woman's death here!

Interview suspended!"

D S Roberts was taken aback at this new aspect. He had still to interview William Stroll! He was now interested in William's version of the relationships that had developed from the three of them living together. Julie's psychic and Gede's unpredictability were unique situations for him to explore.

As was the N'guri knife.

And he still had not divulged to them, the finding of a second body in the burnt out bedroom!!

Hours later Julie was again asked to the interview room. D S Roberts had obviously established, in a long interview with William, that Gede was susceptible to irrational behaviour in her part of the life style being led by the three people. She had become 'out of control' and desperate to live by Her Balinese customs and carry on her belief in the traditions of their family lifestyle. That was almost any deed that would have William the family head, and father of her child.

With a clearer mind, Julie was now also able to enlighten him of Gede's atitude. and also of the many psychic influences that she herself lived with when circumstances brought them about. She told him of instances in the past when she was prewarned of potentialy disasterous events or some sense or knowledge of what the future held and even what she could do to pre emp a situation. She told him about how she recently knew the whereabouts of the two missing girls. And now a pre warning about the smoke and the fire.

He went away to think! No nearer to establishing the true facts. but still wondering about Julie's influence on events. And the second body found in the burnt out bedroom.

Gede had clearly been in the bedroom which had gone up in flames. But under what circumstances? Locked in by Julie? By William? Or by herself to the avoid someone else entering? But he was still taking into account the relationship conflicts between the two determined women and one man.

DS Roberts was holding back divulgence of another suffocated body found in the burnt out bedroom!

Finally on searching the charred contents inside Gede's bedroom, a further bedroom door key was found on the body of the second victim of the fire in the locked room. Also his possession of the n'guri knife.

The Superintendent had no way of telling whether Gede might have locked herself in and by doing that, accidently or purposely taken her own life! Or an intruder had locked the door! And his only means of escape.

He had now seen the report on the previous 'bathing incident' when police and ambulance services were in attendance and the girls life was endangered. Apparently her knife wounds had been self inflicted and maybe showed the state of Gede's mind.

During further separate interrogation of Julie and William. DS Roberts's felt unable at this stage to lay guilt, or eliminate Gede taking her own life by design or misfortune. And were did the other body come from? There was much work for him to do . Eventually it was Gavin the PC who again held many clues . He knew all about the Leeds 'Drug gang Bust ' the drug running and the crimes. The family relationship between Gede and Komang brought a breakthrough for D S Roberts. The other body in the room was eventually identified as Komang; who having escaped jail confinement, had obviously come looking for Gede and Julie with revenge in mind. His actions and those of Gede, inside the locked door and the burning bedroom could only be speculated on. But both bodies showed signs of cuts and bruising suggesting a vicious fight between them

Maybe the psychic of the form that Julie saw on top of Gede might have been that of Komang!! Bruises and stab wounds on the bodies indicated a fight. How would Julie know!

The full facts were slowly being revealed from their complexity and a clearer and likely story of events emerged.

CHAPTER 30

Realism

Life must go on and Julie was on a cleft stick. After the drama and the tragedy, She was dubious about remaining and living at William's. She really wanted to live her life her way, and not in the confines currently being set by William's mode. However,the two horses in training together needed her presence. And she was following a fitness programme whereby she could get them both in peak condition for declaration at the next Doncaster meeting. William expressed surprise when she mentioned that she might return home, but he had been somewhat withdrawn and seemed unable to put the past behind him. Mangel was really his horse and he needed to face up to that and not leave Julie to deal with her wellbeing.

As far as any relationships went, Julie knew that he cared for her but she needed him to show some sign and want some limited intimacy at least. It was as if they both feared rejection. A confident and decisive William of old,was who she admired and needed now. The horse racing was what had brought them together initially, and the 'togetherness' of the two racehorses was now their example to be followed. Gradually the effects of the trauma started to wear off and clearer thoughts,clearer desires, began to emerge. Encouraged by Julie's undoubted regard for him a closer understanding relationship was developing with Julie's encouragement. Could marriage cement things together?

William was encouraged to enter Magnel for her first race. A five furlong dash at Goodwood meant William and Julie staying overnight in a nearby five star hotel.

Julie expected that she, and not William, would have to book hotel rooms and she was surprised when the hotel replied that a room had been already booked by William.

"One room "? she asked.

"Its taken care of" was William's response. Almost as an afterthought he said "Can we become a couple intending to marry soon."

What a way to propose;! but typical of William's way! A loving embrace followed.

The hotel booking was extended to a further night when Magnel was successful, performing brilliantly to win on her first race appearance; and the' room and double bed share' also worked out very successfully. .A good meal and more than a few drinks ensured that at last, true desires and mutual feelings had naturally come together as one.

Julie's children, Johnny and Marion eventually heard the news of the relationship they were always hoping for, as they knew that some intimacy was gradually developing at home. As though William was feeling his way forward in to loving gestures that Julie was initiating.

More practical developments were afoot; by closing down the famous Ross stables, combining the two stables as one.

The coming marriage was being planned, low key in respect to both the partners previous marriage, but it would cement them together as one. Julie's future was clearer and assured. She forsaw just happiness everafter !

Practically,by William finally getting rid of all of Jill's clothes. And lovingly as the couple relaxed together on the couch as they watched TV at home.!

Julie's son Johnny and Samantha Jacobs were themselves planning an engagement celebration in a few weeks time, with her fathers approval. Julie wondered wether Johnny had been' interviewd' by Samantha's parents!

Marions extensive knowledge of the horse training business had landed her a post on the management of Public Relations for a top northern racing venue. A job with vaste potential for her,right up to TV appearances!

Kathleen was back behind the bar at the Pub.

Julie hoped that all her friends and family were now as happy as she was!

For a time Julie had became overwhelmed .William was not for her? She was widowed, struggling to compete in the racing scene, but also socially, with not many real friends among village people locals. William had been a successful,affluent winning trainer. But the way the two racehorses had struck up a friendship brought Julie closer to William by need and companionship for both horses and humans.

Julie blessed her Good Fortune!

The End